"You betrayed me."

Lulu blurted it out, and then was sorry. Neil should've known without her spelling it out. She felt diminished for having had to do so.

"That was undoubtedly the way you perceived it—"

"Am I going to hear a treatise on betrayal now? Come on, Neil, just say what you mean."

"We were in love."

"We were *twelve!*"

"We were still in love."

"It was just a kids' thing. You make it sound like Romeo and Juliet." She started to laugh at the whole idea.

Neil didn't even smile. "Lulu, we had something perfect, and your acting like you don't remember doesn't change that."

"I can't believe I'm hearing this. Are you telling me you've been hung up for twenty years on some crush you had when you were a kid?"

"Be honest, Lulu. Are you telling me you haven't?"

D0752723

ABOUT THE AUTHOR

Beverly Sommers says that she is living a "hermit's existence" in her New York City apartment, which "desperately needs painting."

Books by Beverly Sommers

HARLEQUIN AMERICAN ROMANCE

HARLEQUIN INTRIGUE

Don't miss any of our special offers. Write to us at the following address for information on our newest releases.

Harlequin Reader Service
901 Fuhrmann Blvd., P.O. Box 1397, Buffalo, NY 14240
Canadian address: P.O. Box 603,
Fort Erie, Ont. L2A 5X3

A Little Rebellion
Beverly Sommers

Harlequin Books

TORONTO • NEW YORK • LONDON
AMSTERDAM • PARIS • SYDNEY • HAMBURG
STOCKHOLM • ATHENS • TOKYO • MILAN

"A little rebellion, now and then, is a good thing: as necessary in the political world as storms are in the physical."

—Thomas Jefferson

Published June 1989

First printing April 1989

ISBN 0-373-16298-7

Prologue

Lulu was back.

Kevin had heard the noise coming from the apartment next door that morning and had known right away. The only one Mrs. Lenahan screamed at in that screeching way was Lulu, who was the only one in the family smaller than Mrs. Lenahan.

"You sure?" Andy asked him. The three of them were huddled in the clubhouse, exchanging information. Neil wasn't saying anything, which should have tipped Kevin off. Neil not saying anything was like an ocean drying up.

"I'm sure," said Kevin. He had gotten out of bed and put his ear up against the wall. The wall separated the bedroom he shared with his brother from the living room of the Lenahan apartment. Something smashed against the wall, jarring him. He figured it was Lulu. Lulu was always getting smacked around by her mother.

"Knock off the noise," his brother had said. Kevin ignored him and stood by the wall, listening to see if he would hear Lulu's voice. He finally heard her say something to her mother that was sure to get her bashed again. Lulu had guts. If he said that to his mother he'd probably get thrown out the window.

"I heard her this morning," said Kevin.

Andy made a low, whistling sound, which was the best he could do. He practiced whistling all the time when he was alone, putting two fingers in his mouth the way Lulu had taught him, but he could never make the piercing noise that she was now able to make without even having to use her fingers.

"I didn't figure she'd get caught," said Andy.

Kevin shook his head. "Me, neither. Lulu's too smart to get caught."

"I wonder if they got Bobby," Andy said.

"Who cares?" said Kevin.

Neil was silent, engrossed in a beetle that was making its way across the floor. So far it was the longest period of time since Kevin had known him that Neil had ever sat with his mouth shut.

Kevin picked up the gallon jug, took off the top and drank a long swallow of water. Only nine in the morning and the water had already heated up. He put the jug down on top of the beetle and waited to see if it would crawl out from under it. It didn't.

"I hope she can get out," said Andy.

"She'll get out," said Kevin. "I wouldn't be surprised if she's already on her way here."

That thought made Andy feel good. He was always happiest when Lulu was around. "I'm glad she's back," said Andy.

"You better not let Lulu hear you say that," Kevin told him. "She'll kick your butt for sure if she hears that."

"I missed her," said Andy, looking at the floor in case he started to cry. He didn't really think he'd cry. He hadn't cried in a long time. But something about the fact that Lulu was back was making him feel as though he might.

"She's only been gone a day, stupid," said Kevin, punching Andy in the arm.

"Hey, that hurts."

Kevin punched him again, softer this time. Just to let him know he didn't really mean it.

"I wonder how far they got," said Andy.

"I don't even know how long it takes to get to Canada," said Kevin. "You know how long it takes, Neil?"

Neil shook his head. "I guess it would depend on how many stops the train made."

"Oh, yeah. I hadn't thought of that," said Kevin. He wished he was as good at figuring things out as Neil was. Neil practically always knew the answers to stuff, and he didn't even go to a parochial school. And everyone knew that kids at public schools didn't get a good education. Maybe it was because Neil sometimes read books even when he wasn't in school. It was the only thing about Neil he didn't like.

Andy heard it first, cocking his head a little bit and squeezing his face in concentration.

"What?" asked Kevin.

"Shut up, I hear something," said Andy. He got up off the floor and walked over to the door. "Someone's coming. I think it's Lulu."

Andy already had the bar off the door by the time the other guys scrambled to their feet. They pushed their way through the door, getting in one another's way, and they were all standing outside on the roof when Lulu's head came over the top of the fire escape.

Kevin saw Andy's hand disappear inside the front of his pants. It was a sure sign that Andy was nervous. "Hey," said Kevin, poking Andy in the side. "Relax, okay?"

Andy's hand snaked back out as he watched Lulu negotiate the roof. "Should we cheer her?" asked Andy.

"I think we better just shut up," said Kevin, seeing even at a distance that Lulu was in a black mood. He wondered what else Mrs. Lenahan had done besides throw Lulu against the wall. Not that he'd ask. Not that he'd ever confess to Lulu that he could hear everything that went on in her apartment.

The three of them were standing in a line, trying to look cool, but then Andy broke away from them and went running across the roof to Lulu.

He stopped just short of her and tried to assess her mood. She didn't look happy, and he tried to get rid of the smile on his face, but he was so happy to see her he couldn't. It was as though the muscles in his face wouldn't listen to him.

"Hey, Lulu," he said.

"Hey, Andy."

"You okay?"

She nodded once, then looked down at the roof, scuffing the toe of her shoe in the tar that had not yet started melting in the sun.

Lulu started toward the others, and Andy followed along, one step behind. Lulu was wearing a yellow T-shirt that had a picture of a green four-leaf clover on the back and black letters that said Murphy's Bar & Grill. In smaller letters it said Est. 1895. He wondered what "Est." meant.

Lulu walked up to the others. Kevin said, "Hey, Lulu," and Lulu said, "Hey, Kev, hey, Neil." Then she walked past them into the clubhouse. Kevin and Neil followed, and Andy brought up the rear, closing the door behind them and putting the bar up.

Lulu sat down on the milk crate and reached for the bottle of water. When she lifted it up, Kevin could see the beetle squashed flat on the bottom of it.

"Tough luck," said Kevin, squatting down in front of her.

Lulu shrugged.

"How far did you get?" asked Andy, coming up behind Kevin and leaning against his back.

"Not far enough," said Lulu.

"Hey," said Kevin, "you want to try to sneak in Fenway this afternoon? There's a day game."

"Maybe," said Lulu, but the thought didn't appear to cheer her up.

"Hey, have you heard the one about the people camping in Yellowstone Park and these bears attacked their tent?" asked Andy. He had no idea where exactly Yellowstone Park was, but it was a real funny joke. If he didn't screw the end of it up like he usually did.

"Can it," said Kevin, turning around and glaring up at him.

Neil was leaning against the wall, his thumbs hooked into the Indian-bead belt he wore in his jeans. It had a white background and pictures of arrowheads in red and black. He'd offered it to Andy once, who much admired it, but Andy refused, knowing his dad would think he shoplifted it and probably use it to whip him.

It was only when Neil spoke that Andy realized he hadn't said anything before. He knew, because he always listened to Neil. Neil knew a lot of stuff the rest of them didn't know.

"I'm sorry, Lulu," said Neil, and Andy immediately realized that was the proper thing to say.

"I'm sorry, too," said Andy.

"Me, too," said Kevin.

Lulu shrugged. The corners of her mouth were turned down, and her eyes looked as though they'd seen bad things while she had been away. Andy wanted to hug her, the way he sometimes hugged his mom, but he was afraid to. Lulu didn't go for stuff like that.

Neil was looking at Lulu and ignoring the others. "They have no reason to be sorry," he told her. "I was the one who told your parents."

Three pairs of eyes flashed to Neil, who was still looking at Lulu.

"You *what*?" said Lulu, and Andy could sense something coming to life inside of her. He wasn't sure he wanted to be around when whatever it was got out.

"I told your parents where you were," said Neil.

Kevin knew that if he was the one saying those words, he'd now be halfway across the roof and running for his life. Neil had guts, he'd give him that.

Andy held his breath as Lulu slowly got to her feet, her lower lip jutting out, even her small boobies, which she usually tried to hide, jutting out.

"You better be joking, Neil," said Lulu. Her voice sounded deadly.

Andy started backing away from them, although there really wasn't enough room in the clubhouse to back very far. He saw Kevin's eyes going from Neil to Lulu, back and forth, like he was watching a Ping-Pong game or something.

"I thought it was the right thing to do," said Neil, "and I'm not sorry I did."

Andy couldn't believe Neil's bravery. If he had been the one to rat on Lulu, right now he'd be at her feet begging her to forgive him.

"Hot damn," whispered Kevin.

Lulu sucked in her breath and then let it explode. "Why, you rotten, sniveling, mealy-mouthed snitch," she said in a low, scary voice, shoving Neil in the chest with her hands and throwing him back against the door. "You dirty, lousy, tattletale Protestant. Is that what they do in public schools?"

She shoved him again, so hard this time that the jury-rigged door came apart from the frame and Neil was propelled out onto the roof, where he fell down in a heap on top of the door.

Lulu was after him like a shot, with Kevin and Andy huddled in the doorway.

"Stop her," said Andy, but Kevin just shook his head.

Neil was already getting to his feet when Lulu said, "Get up and fight like a man, you scum!"

Neil held his hands out in a gesture probably meant to pacify her but which only infuriated her further. "I'm not fighting you, Lulu. I'm not apologizing, either."

Lulu lit into him like a fury. Fists clenched, she pounded him around the head and chest, driving him back as he didn't even try to protect his face. Andy saw Neil's lip start to bleed, and then his nose. Lulu's fists were getting slippery with blood as she relentlessly pounded him farther and farther in the direction of the edge of the roof.

"She's going to kill him," breathed Andy. "She's going to shove him off the roof."

Neil never even looked behind to see how close he was to the edge. He just faced Lulu, taking the blows, not even near tears.

Just as it looked as though Neil was close to falling to his death, Kevin shot out of the doorway, raced across the roof and tackled Lulu to the ground. Andy ran into the clubhouse and emerged with a jug of water.

"Let me up, you traitor," Lulu screamed, and that's when Andy poured the gallon of water over her head. A still snarling, quite drenched Lulu looked up at him for a moment, then her fury seemed to subside.

Lulu wrenched her arms out of Kevin's grasp, where he had been holding them behind her. She shoved Kevin aside and got to her feet. Neil was still standing there about an inch from the edge.

"You're out of the gang," Lulu told him.

Andy and Kevin kept very quiet. Kevin's eyes kept going from Lulu's face down to her chest, where her shirt was so soaked it was practically transparent. Andy looked there once, too, but it made him nervous, and he had to swallow hard.

"You ever show your face in this neighborhood again, I'll kill you," Lulu said to Neil, and Andy and Kevin had no doubt she meant it.

Neil, showing more dignity than a twelve-year-old should possess, walked slowly across the roof to the fire escape. He didn't hunch over, he didn't wipe the blood from his face; he just walked away from them without a backward glance. He was like some guy in a Western. He was like Clint Eastwood.

Lulu walked over to the clubhouse. She stood looking at it for a moment, and then slowly and methodically she began to kick it to pieces. It was made of old pieces of wood and held together with a few rusty nails, and it fell apart in minutes.

Then Andy did feel tears coming to his eyes, and he turned away from the sight of the demolished clubhouse and tried to concentrate on one fat cloud that seemed to be hanging directly over the building across the street.

"Holy Mary," he could hear Kevin say behind him.

When Andy finally turned back around, Lulu was standing in the middle of the wreckage, her arms folded across her chest.

"What'd you want to do that for, Lulu?" Andy asked her.

"The Rooftop Gang is dead," said Lulu, and then she stepped over the boards and headed for the fire escape.

The boys, in silence, watched her go.

Chapter One

It was November and already cold. A chill wind was blowing down from Canada, causing people in Boston to turn up the collars of their coats. Lulu Lenahan headed into the wind, her eyes tearing and her hair blown straight out behind her. She'd been singing a little song to herself as she walked: *Three more blocks and I'll be inside and warm; two more blocks and I'll be inside and warm; one more block and I'll be inside and warm.*

She could almost hear her mother's voice saying, "A good night to stay at home." It was something her mother had said often when Lulu was a child, usually when Lulu's father was heading out the door on his way to the corner tavern or when Lulu or one of her older brothers, just as eager to escape the house as their father, was trying to sneak out without being seen by their mother.

Lulu turned a corner, and the wind died down. She pushed the straight bangs back over her forehead with a mittened hand, then pushed open the door to Flanagan's and stepped into its familiar warmth. It was like coming home: as warm and as comforting and every bit as familiar as her own bed.

"I've got a surprise for you, Lulu," Kevin had said to her on the phone an hour earlier. It was Kevin's annoying tone of voice, the one that said he had a secret that she didn't know. He'd used that tone of voice on her as a child and had gotten his head pushed in the dirt as a result. Now, from the safety of an office across the city, he seemed to be exulting in the fact she couldn't retaliate.

"Don't tell me something like that and then make me wait," said Lulu. "You know that makes me nervous." Although *furious* was more like it.

Kevin chuckled. "If I told you, you'd be even more nervous." And that was all he would say on the subject, despite the fact that Lulu threatened him with everything, including bodily harm.

Lulu didn't want a surprise. Friday nights were perfect just the way they were. All week she looked forward to Friday night, and now she was sure Kevin, somehow, was going to mess with a good thing. Kevin never thought first. Kevin always plodded in and regretted it later. He'd done it at school, mystifying the sisters by some of his outrageous answers; he'd done it in football, often losing games for his high-school team as a result; and he'd done it with marriage, only finding out after the honeymoon that there was more to marriage than just sex. Kevin never learned from his mistakes.

Lulu hung up her jacket on one of the wooden pegs by the door, then pushed through the crowd of after-work drinkers who stood four deep along the length of the bar. It was a young crowd, not quite blue-collar but not yuppie yet, either. If ever, considering that most of them looked like civil servants. Lulu was a civil servant herself and knew the look: off-the-rack suits for the men, and don't bother with the alterations; trendy outfits for the women that would disintegrate the first time they were laundered. Thanks be to those in charge who had designated she was to dress down for the job, meaning she could get away with jeans and a soft flannel shirt.

She avoided the glances of some of the men at the bar who'd give any female still alive the once-over and looked for carrot-colored hair in the crowd. She spotted it, and joined Andy Keely at the end of the bar.

"Going to be a cold winter," said Andy, giving her a hug and a kiss on the cheek. He was wearing a wooly crew-neck sweater, and she warmed her cheek against it for a moment, trying not to look like she was deliberately wiping off his kiss.

She was, though. She didn't like that kiss-on-the-cheek business and couldn't figure out where Andy had picked it up. The only people she knew of who kissed like that, instead of a plain handshake, were New York types, and she seldom came into contact with them. With Andy it seemed an affectation, and she wished he'd drop it from his act. She didn't even allow her mother to kiss her on the cheek, not that her mother often tried.

Lulu said, "First cold day we get, someone always says that."

"And don't we always have a cold winter?"

"If you ever move your business out to the Silicon Valley, you'll have to think up something new to say."

"We're in a good mood tonight, aren't we?"

Lulu called out to Patrick, who was tending bar, ordering herself a beer. "What's this surprise Kevin has up his sleeve?" she asked Andy.

"I don't know about any surprise."

"I thought maybe you two were plotting something." She looked closely at Andy, whose face always gave him away, but there was no blush that made his freckles stand out, no nervous hand pushing back thinning hair. Andy had always been incapable of deceiving anyone.

Her beer arrived, along with a refill for Andy. They were thick mugs with an inch of foam on the top. Andy held his up. "To Friday nights," he said, but Lulu was already drinking hers.

This was the time to drink, to unwind from a week of work. Later, after Kevin arrived, after they'd all had one of Flanagan's hot roast beef platters, they would argue. They always argued. Half the fun of being together was the arguments. And half the fun of arguing was that she always won. Andy would give up in the interests of peace, and Kevin would give up when he'd had so much beer he couldn't think clearly any longer. Lulu never gave up.

The six o'clock news was on the color TV over the bar. It was a new addition, the old black-and-white one having come to a dire end when an overzealous Red Sox fan had thrown a bottle at the screen during the crucial moment in a game with the damn Yankees. The sound had been turned low, but now Lulu saw Patrick Flanagan turn the knob, and the conversations at the bar died down as all eyes turned to see what was happening that had caught Patrick's attention.

It was no surprise to Lulu to see that it was news from Northern Ireland. It was an Irish bar in an Irish neighborhood and, among the older patrons, at least, support for the IRA ran high.

"Another bombing," said Andy. "I heard about it in the car on the way over." He was shaking his head, his brown eyes looking disappointed, the way they sometimes looked when Lulu argued beyond the bounds of friendship.

There was a picture of the remains of a car after a bomb had exploded inside of it. There was a picture of a bomb going off at a funeral, for which the car bombing was in retaliation. There was a picture of the Iron Lady, Margaret Thatcher, which drew hisses from some of the patrons at the bar. Then the news switched to the latest evidence of *glasnost* in Russia, and the sound was turned down and the customers went back to their drinking.

Lulu was about to move the time for arguing ahead by a couple of hours, and challenge Andy, who fancied himself a pacifist. She already had her mouth open as she turned to him, the words dancing the length of her tongue, when she saw him looking past her toward the entrance.

"I think your surprise just walked in," said Andy, looking as though he wanted to smile but not entirely sure that he should.

"Don't tell me Kevin brought his wife with him."

"That'll be the day," said Andy.

Lulu turned around but couldn't see above the heads of the men crowding the bar. Then Kevin McCrory came in sight, a royal-blue muffler wrapped around his head, setting off his black-Irish good looks. Damned if he didn't look like a movie star with his curly black hair, his eyes as bright a blue as his scarf and that cleft in his chin. There'd be plenty of civil-service women giving her dirty looks the rest of the evening when they saw who he was headed for.

He was already smiling at her, and she was starting to smile back, when she saw who was behind him. She hadn't seen him since Kevin's wedding a good ten years ago. She broke off her smile and tried to settle her face into a look of indifference. What she wanted to do was walk out. If she couldn't do that—and she couldn't, not really, not to her two best friends—then the next best thing would be to down her beer. Quickly.

She started to reach out for it, but Kevin was at her side by then, giving her a one-armed hug that pulled her away from the bar, and saying, "Guess who the cat dragged in?"

Andy was already grinning and shaking hands with Neil. It seemed strange to Lulu, this grown-up way they had of shaking hands. Twenty years ago they would have punched each other in the arm, now they were all handshakes and smiles, models of civilized adult behavior. Sometimes she really hated civilized adult behavior.

Neil Blessing turned to her and, as always, his cool gray eyes masked his feelings. "Hello, Lulu."

The same words, the same inflection, the sense that it was nine years ago or nineteen years ago and he still didn't have the slightest understanding that things had changed.

"Well, look who's slumming," said Lulu, hearing the scorn in her voice and not caring. And he did look like he was slumming in his leather coat and cashmere scarf and the flash of gold that showed at his left cuff where his hand rested on the bar. The outlay for this one outfit alone would no doubt feed and clothe a homeless family for an entire year.

Kevin's gaze was going from her to Neil. "Hell, Lulu, we're all slumming," he said. "Except maybe for you." He turned to Neil, saying, "Lulu still lives in the neighborhood. You can take South Boston out of Lulu, but you can't seem to take Lulu out of South Boston."

"Ha, ha," said Lulu, having heard this a hundred times. Kevin had the misguided notion that the more times you said something, the wittier it became.

Andy, the pacifist, the peacemaker, the one who demanded that everything be well-ordered on the outside, as though that could control what was lurking just beneath the surface, the one who didn't have a fraction of Kevin's looks or Kevin's charm but possessed three times the sensibility when it came to human behavior, threw one arm around Kevin's shoulder and the other around Neil's and pulled them up to the bar and away from Lulu. "A couple of drafts for my friends," he called out to Patrick Flanagan.

"Make that three," said Lulu from behind him, downing her beer in two hurried gulps. The sooner she got some beer in her system, the easier it was going to be to stomach Kevin's unfortunate choice of surprises. And to think she had been afraid he'd be bringing Caroline along. In comparison, she would've welcomed his wife with open arms. She would even have kissed her on the cheek without vomiting. But Neil? That was tantamount to treachery.

"Let's get that table now," said Kevin. "We've got some catching up to do. God, what's it been, ten years since we've all been together? And then it wasn't really together. I mean, I was half out of it at my wedding."

"Good idea," said Andy. "You want to find us a table, Lulu?" He was giving her a warning look, as though reading her mind. But, as Andy always told her, he didn't need to read her mind; her feelings were written on her face for all to see.

What Lulu wanted to do was sneak out through the crowd and avoid the rest of the evening altogether. Friday nights were a tradition. Kevin wouldn't bring his wife along any more than Andy or Lulu would bring a date. Hell, Friday nights were practically sacred. Hadn't Kevin changed his wedding from a Friday to a Saturday because it would have interfered with them getting together that week? Hadn't two of Lulu's relationships come to an end over her boyfriends' feeling excluded from her circle of friends? And the one time they hadn't met on a Friday night because Andy had been in the hospital, hadn't she and Kevin stopped by the bar and gotten food and beer and then taken Flanagan's to Andy? And kicked everyone else out of the hospital room? What made Neil Blessing an exception?

No, she wouldn't leave. She'd be damned if she'd let Neil waltz in and take over. He'd done that once; she'd be damned if she'd let him do it a second time.

She found a table in a corner far from the bar. It was an older crowd at the tables. Mostly old men from the neighborhood, the same faces year after year with the occasional one dying off and his place being taken by a newcomer. The talk all around was of the latest bombing, but if they were looking for an argument, they weren't going to get it here. The IRA had a long tradition in this neighborhood, and most of these men still had relatives in the old country. The men reminded her of her father when he was half-drunk, which was most of the time. The rest of the time he had been dead drunk. But while he could still talk, he'd be railing against the English, except for the few exceptions when he'd be railing against his wife.

Lulu sat down in one of the wooden chairs and rolled up her shirtsleeves so that they were above her elbows. The red-and-white checked plastic tablecloth would soon be a disaster area of spilled beer and catsup, and if she didn't drag her sleeves in it, she'd be able to wear the shirt another day. The less laundry she had to cart three blocks every Saturday, the happier she was.

There was a wooden napkin holder in the shape of a duck, its paint peeling off, a bottle of Heinz catsup, and half-filled salt and pepper shakers. She aligned them in the middle of the table so as to be out of everyone's way. The smoke, which had been hanging near the ceiling only a moment ago, was already drifting downward. She looked over at the bar and saw only one or two of the younger people smoking. But back here, where the old men were, she couldn't count a mouth that didn't have an unfiltered cigarette hanging from a lip. Smoking was becoming an anachronism in her own time. Smokers were being preached to and harassed at every turn. It was almost enough to make her take it up. She'd always been partial to underdogs.

Neil. Neil Blessing. She'd thought if she led a good life she'd never have to meet up with him again. Obviously she had sinned in some way she wasn't even aware of, else why was she being subjected to this? No wonder Kevin hadn't revealed his secret. He knew damn well if he had, she never would have shown up. And blast Kevin and Andy for never really understanding. Andy, she could forgive. Andy wasn't capable of holding a grudge against anyone, although he never had quite forgiven her for turning down his marriage proposal, halfhearted though it may have been.

The men finally showed up at the table, setting pitchers of beer in the center. At first Lulu was relieved to see that her two friends flanked her at the table. Then she realized this left her open to Neil's watchful eyes from directly opposite her. Well, she'd just have to look past him to the painting on the wall of the wolf going for the stag's throat. Not the most soothing subject matter for her eyes, but a great deal more calming than looking at Neil.

Andy was pouring the beer, being careful at this early stage of the evening not to spill it all over the table. He still hadn't learned how to pour it without the mugs ending up half-filled with foam, though.

"Here's to the old Rooftop Gang," said Kevin, lifting his mug and blowing off the top two inches of foam, his eyes smiling as he looked around the table.

"I'll drink to that," said Andy, shifting his eyes to Lulu and all but holding his breath.

Neil seemed to hesitate before lifting his mug, as though waiting for Lulu.

You're acting like a child, she told herself, but the child in her reacted with stubbornness. She had to will her hand to grasp the handle of the mug and lift it with the others. "To the Rooftop Gang," she said aloud, begrudging every syllable. *And to betrayal,* she added to herself.

NEIL STILL FELT LIKE an outsider, and it wasn't just because of Lulu's cool-to-nonexistent welcome. He still felt like the odd one out, the rich boy hanging out in South Boston with the poor kids.

He had kept in touch with Kevin, and knew he was doing well at his job with the Celtics. He had read numerous articles in newspapers and magazines regarding Andy's computer company. They were as well educated, as successful in their fields as he was, and yet there was still an imparity, and he'd be damned if he knew why that was. And yet that imparity didn't seem to be there with Lulu and hadn't been from the start.

He thought the difference was that the guys had always treated him a little differently. They'd shown a deference toward him even at age ten, when they'd taken one look at his expensive clothes and ten-speed bike, listened to the way he talked and then elected him coleader with Lulu without a word being spoken. They were still treating him with regard, and he didn't know how to break through it. It seemed as impossible to break through as it was to demolish the wall that Lulu had constructed between them, although with her the reason for the wall was known to him and had been for twenty years.

Where, from the start, the boys had treated him with deference, Lulu had reacted with scorn. To her he was the enemy, even at age ten. She had sized him up that first day, hazel eyes narrowed beneath crooked eyebrows and straight bangs, lower lip thrust out in defiance, thumbs hooked into the waistband of her jeans, the toe of one dirty, torn sneaker kicking at the curb. She had been itching for a fight, but he wouldn't give it to her. He had two rules for fighting in those days: he didn't fight anyone smaller than himself, and he didn't fight girls. Lulu was both.

The boys had been alternately eyeing his ten-speed and Lulu with awe. He could tell that they were waiting to see what her reaction would be to him before making any moves on their own. Neil knew a leader when he saw one. Finally he had shoved the bike in Kevin's direction, saying, "You want to try it?"

"Yeah," said Kevin, his eyes almost popping out of his head. Avoiding Lulu's gaze, he swung his leg over the bike and took off at high-speed.

Andy stood for a moment watching Lulu and then, at an almost imperceptible nod of her head, he took off at a run after Kevin, yelling, "Hey, wait a minute, wait up for me!" Neil had watched as Kevin slowed down and Andy jumped on the handlebars for a ride.

As soon as they were out of sight, Lulu said, "Get lost." They were as nasty a two words as he had ever heard. She had a low voice for a girl, lower than any of the boys he knew.

Something in Neil always blossomed at the sound of a challenge. So she thought those two little words were going to scare him off, did she? Poor girl, she didn't know who she'd run up against.

"Get lost? Is that what you're telling me, kid? As a matter of fact, I already am lost. What is this crummy neighborhood, anyway? Do people actually live here? Is this part of Boston? Is it even part of the planet Earth?"

Having imparted what he considered a prime insult, he turned his back on her, wondering if she'd attack him with teeth and fingernails. In his experience that was the only way girls ever fought. That and maybe kicking.

She surprised him. She grabbed his arm and swung him around and then pulled back her arm and let loose with a strong punch to his jaw. It didn't knock him down, but it hurt. It hurt like hell. But he wasn't going to give her the satisfaction of knowing that. He didn't turn his back on her again, though.

Instead, he spread out his arms. "Is that it? Is that the best you can do? I got a three-year-old sister can land a better punch that that. I got a baby cousin six months old has more force in his fist. Practice, kid, that's what you need."

In a contemptuous move, she spat on the sidewalk, just missing his shoe. "So you're tough, is that it? You a tough guy? Kid, you don't even know tough. You don't fast-talk your way out of things in this part of town. I'd advise you to go back to your own neighborhood where it's safe." It was said in a disinterested tone, as though imparting information and nothing else.

"Well, the way I see it is like this, kid. It's a free country. I can ride my bike into any neighborhood I feel like riding it, and no snot-nosed kid like you is going to tell me otherwise. So if you don't like it, I suggest you start taking a walk."

She looked totally unimpressed. Her mouth curled down sarcastically, and her eyes bore into his.

Neil tried to stare her down, but she didn't even blink. Then he played a wild card and brought out his smile. The one with his lips closed that a couple of girls in his class found devastating. Not that he liked girls much, but this girl wasn't even acting like a girl, and he wanted to test out its effectiveness with her.

Her lip curled further in contempt.

Okay, so he'd struck out twice. This time he'd let loose with a screwball. "Maybe I'm a spy sent in to find out about you."

Her eyes widened for a second before narrowing again. She started walking toward him, inspecting him from all sides. She shook her head a little at his clothes, at his Red Sox cap worn backward on his head. He was wearing the clothes he always played in, but next to hers his looked brand-new. The clothes she was wearing looked like something his mother would throw directly in the trash and not even bother calling the Salvation Army to pick up. Either that or have their cleaning lady, Emmaline, tear them up for dust rags.

And yet there was something about the girl that intrigued him from the start. He wouldn't have stuck around for the boys. The boys weren't that different from the ones in his neighborhood. But the girl was unlike any he had ever met.

"What grade you in?" she asked him, stopping right in front of him, her face just inches from his. She was so close he could smell the bubble gum on her breath.

"Going into fifth. What about you?"

"I'm asking the questions," she said. She scanned the streets as though hoping her friends would come back and rescue her from having to make conversation with someone she obviously considered an alien.

With some trepidation—a slight amount, but still there—Neil casually walked over to the curb and sat down. He put his arms around his knees and rested his chin on top of them. "You guys play baseball?" he asked her, knowing instinctively that he better include her as one of the guys.

She stepped into the gutter and reached down to pick up a stone. Then, side-arm and with amazing speed, she sent the stone flying up onto the rooftop of the building across the street. She was a lefty with a lot of style.

"We have better things to do," she said, and the words were offhand and a bit grudging.

"Like what? If there's something better than baseball, I'd sure like to hear about it. Not that I believe there is. As far as I'm concerned, baseball's the greatest thing ever invented, and that includes *Star Trek*."

She stood looking down at him, one hand scratching the inside of her thigh. "Take my advice, kid, go back to your friends and play your games with them. We'll let you out of the neighborhood in one piece this time, but don't come back."

That brought a smile to his face but he quickly got rid of it. "So what do you guys do for fun?"

"Look, kid, we don't have tennis courts in this neighborhood, and we don't have pony rides. There was a public pool but it got closed because of knifings. What we have is gangs. It's not a healthy neighborhood for a rich kid."

He was impressed despite himself. "You're in a gang?"

"I *have* a gang. You just met them."

"It's *your* gang?"

"That's what I said."

"Has it got a name?"

"Yeah. And it's a secret. And what's more, I'm getting real sick of all your questions."

As though dismissing him, she strolled across the street and sat on the curb directly opposite from him. Nothing more was said between them until the boys came back and he politely asked Lulu if she wanted a turn on his bike. She gave him a scornful look and turned away. And even after they were close buddies, she had never ridden his bike. It was as though to do so would be giving in to him. As though it were some point of honor for her not to want anything that belonged to him.

And now here she was seated across the table from him, looking not much different from the girl of ten. The same small triangular face; the same straight bangs across her forehead, only the shoulder-length brown hair was pushed back behind her ears instead of in two pigtails; the same snub nose with the sprinkling of freckles across it; the same stubborn mouth with the full lower lip; the body still small and boyish; the fingernails bitten to the quick. Even her attitude was the same, saying to him, *You're an interloper here. Why don't you get out of our neighborhood?*

But he was just as intrigued by her now as he had been twenty years ago, and this time he wasn't going to be so easily driven off. This time he was prepared to stay and fight.

"AND LULU?" NEIL ASKED, then looked at her. "What are you up to these days? Married? Any kids?"

Lulu snorted, her eyes going to the picture of the threatened stag.

"It's funny when you think about it," said Kevin. "I'm the only one of the gang who got married."

"You didn't exactly set a very good example for the rest of us," said Lulu. She thought Kevin should have left Caroline years ago.

"You never got married?" Andy asked Neil.

Lulu found herself holding her breath waiting for the answer, then expelled it in a rush when she realized what she was doing. She couldn't care less if Neil had an entire harem of wives.

"Still waiting for the right woman," said Neil, catching Lulu's eye and making her squirm.

Andy nodded in commiseration. "My partners are married, and I envy them."

This is the first Lulu had heard of it. "Then why don't you find yourself a wife?" she asked him.

"Because he's a workaholic," said Kevin. "The only time Andy's not at work is when he's sleeping, and I'm not even sure he sleeps."

"Except Friday nights," said Andy.

"You have women working for you," said Lulu. "Don't you ever get interested in any of them?"

"They're all computer geniuses," he responded.

"So are you," said Lulu.

"Two workaholics in the family wouldn't work out," said Andy. "I'd like someone who'd stay home, fix up the place. I'd like kids."

Kevin turned to Neil. "Andy has a great loft, and the only piece of furniture—if you could call it that—is a mattress on the floor."

"You're getting rich," Lulu said to Andy. "Who don't you get an interior decorator?"

"I don't need furniture," he said. "I'm never home."

"What're you doing these days," Neil asked Lulu. "Come on, let me in on it, I'm curious." He knew she didn't even have to answer because one of her friends would do it for her.

Right on cue, Andy said, "She runs one of those city shelters for the homeless."

"Homeless *women*," Lulu corrected him, still managing to avoid all eye contact with Neil.

"Our Lulu's ever the do-gooder," said Kevin, but his smile was loving as it rested on her.

"It's a problem," said Neil.

"Doing good?" asked Andy.

"The homeless. You don't see much of it in my neighborhood, but coming down here I couldn't believe how many there are this year."

"In your neighborhood I'm surprised you'd see any," said Kevin.

"Oh, they wander in now and then. Just to remind us that nothing is permanent."

Lulu almost barfed. It was so easy for the rich to sound the right note of disquiet.

"Tell him your theory, Lulu," said Andy. "Lulu's got this plan to solve the homeless problem."

"Forget it, Andy," she said.

"Well, I'm not surprised," said Neil. "Knowing Lulu, I'd be surprised if she didn't have one. If ever anyone was a born organizer and a maker of plans, it was our Lulu."

The "our Lulu" made her furious, and she stared straight at him, not even trying to hide her anger.

"Hey, I'm not making fun of you," said Neil. Then he looked from Andy to Kevin, his face the picture of innocence. "I mean it. It's a compliment, sincerely meant. And I assure you from the bottom of my heart that I'm sitting here waiting in breathless anticipation to hear about this plan. I know the federal government hasn't come up with any solution, the state sure hasn't done a thing, and the mayor acts like he can't see what's right in front of his eyes. But I have every confidence that you know how so solve the problem."

She could've killed him. Glancing at Kevin and Andy, she was also ready to kill them. Kevin was openly laughing, and Andy was almost choking in an effort not to.

"You sure haven't changed," she said to Neil.

He smiled at her. "Wouldn't you have been disappointed if I had?"

"If you ever kept your big mouth shut for ten consecutive seconds, I'd know you were dead," she retorted.

"Are you listening to her, guys?" asked Neil. "And this from Miss All-Time Big Mouth of South Boston. Didn't you win that title three years in a row, Lulu?"

Lulu turned to Kevin. "You brought him here, you get him out of here."

"Don't blame Kevin, it was my idea," said Neil. "I could sense from what he says about you, Lulu, that something important was missing from your life. So I decided that the humane thing to do was to come and fill that void. I mean, come on, these guys are too nice. These guys don't have it in them to give you a hard time."

Lulu was steaming. "If you don't shut up, Neil—"

"What're you going to do, punch me out? You still settling arguments that way, Lulu?" His lips slid into a grin. "Hey, can't you take it anymore? Listen, I really would like to hear about your plan for the homeless. Despite the fact that you're not going to believe this, I really do care."

After two seconds of silence, Andy rushed in to fill the empty space. "I think maybe we could use some food, he suggested.

"Not yet," said Lulu, and Andy fell silent.

"If she's not going to tell you, I will," said Kevin. "Lulu thinks that every family in Boston with an apartment should take in another family without an apartment. Share and share alike."

"Rather like communism," said Andy.

"You don't see homeless in Russia," said Lulu.

"Lulu, of course, is the leading authority on Russia," said Kevin, "having been out of Massachusetts once in her life."

What was going on, were they all going to gang up on her now? Well, she could handle all three with her hands tied behind her back.

"Have you taken in a family?" Neil asked her.

"I live in one room," said Lulu, in much the same way she would have said, "Go to hell."

"You'd be surprised how many people can manage to live in one room," said Neil.

"I've told her she can take me in, but she's having none of it," Andy said.

"Actually, I've given it some thought myself," said Neil.

Kevin laughed. "Moving in with Lulu?"

The camaraderie wasn't there tonight. Partly it was because of Neil's presence, Lulu thought, forcing a wedge into the group. Partly it was because of her feeling of late that her best friends were turning into yuppies with no regard for those less fortunate. They had all been dirt poor as kids. They knew what it felt like to be one step away from homeless. They should be able to imagine what lay beyond that step. "Let's order the food," she said finally.

"It's too early," said Kevin. "We never eat this early. Let's order another round instead."

"We care about the homeless," said Andy, putting his hand on Lulu's arm as though to prevent her from leaving the table.

"Oh, sure," she said, sounding a little bitter even to herself. "You talk a good story. For five minutes or so. And then it's back to the Celtics' chances."

"You like the Celtics just as much," said Andy.

"That's not the point," said Lulu.

"What *are* the Celtics' chances?" Neil asked Kevin, who was public-relations director for the team.

"Great. As usual," said Kevin.

"We sympathize, Lulu," said Andy. "But if the federal government and the state and the city can't solve the problem, we're not going to solve it over a few beers."

"That's what everyone says," said Lulu, segueing into her argumentative mode. "Any problem can be solved if you care enough about solving it."

"Okay," said Neil, looking at his watch, which appeared, to Lulu's eyes, to be made of solid gold. "Let's give it a good thirty minutes. Let's discuss it in depth and see if we can come up with a solution."

"And in the meantime," said Andy, "let's order another round."

Three pairs of eyes focused on Lulu. The ball was in her court. Thirty minutes to solve the homeless problem? Well, at least they were listening. And at least, for once in his life, Neil's mouth wasn't open.

"A place of their own," said Lulu. "Is that too much to ask? A rich country like this shouldn't even have homeless."

"Tell us something we don't know," said Kevin.

"I'm not talking about the ones who choose to be homeless," said Lulu. "There have always been people who want to live that way, who feel confined within four walls. Okay, we live in a free country, and they should be able to live where they want. But the ones who are forced into homelessness by circumstances, they should be helped. Look at the kids. How do you send a kid to school when you're living in the streets? How do you go out and look for a job when you're living in the streets? How do you even survive if you're not equipped for it?"

She saw Kevin sneak a look at his watch, and she exploded. "Damn it, Kevin, why don't you just get drunk and forget the situation even exists? Or better yet, go home to your four-bedroom, three-bath house on two acres of property and feel sorry for yourself because your wife doesn't give you enough space."

"What're you yelling at me for?" asked Kevin, innocence shining through his blue eyes.

"Take it easy, Lulu," said Andy, putting his hand over hers. "I have a pretty large loft all to myself, and maybe that makes me a greedy capitalist, but what do you want me to do? Get a woman to move in with me? Would that help the homeless situation?"

"Sorry," Lulu apologized, but she pulled her hand away from Andy. It was Neil's fault. He just sat there, listening, totally unnerving her. She didn't trust Neil when he was silent. He was all control, and she was a series of explosions.

"You're doing what you can, Lulu," said Kevin. "You work with the homeless."

"Yes, but some don't get helped. Do you know how many will freeze to death this winter?"

"How many?" asked Kevin.

"I don't know," she admitted, "but there's always some. If everyone in Boston just bought an extra blanket and handed it out to a homeless person, it would be a start. Just a blanket. It wouldn't even have to be an expensive one. A Woolworth's blanket would help keep someone alive."

"Hell, I'll donate a blanket," said Kevin. "We've got a whole linen closet full of that stuff."

"I'll do better than that," said Andy. "I'll donate a comforter. I'll donate a dozen of them if that will make you happy, Lulu."

"Remember when we were kids," said Lulu, and then she shut her mouth. Right now, with Neil across the table, she didn't want to remember when they were kids.

"What about it?" asked Andy.

"Forget it," said Lulu.

"No, go on—you were going to say something," said Andy.

Lulu sighed and avoided looking at Neil. "Remember our clubhouse?"

"Yeah," said Kevin. "We built it ourselves."

"Sometimes I remember it and get nostalgic," said Andy, "although at the time I couldn't wait to grow up."

"How long did it take us to build it?" asked Lulu.

"Not long," said Kevin. "I think we put it together in one day, didn't we?"

"A very long day," said Andy. "I remember getting hell that night from my mother because I missed dinner."

"What did it cost us to build?" said Lulu.

"Nothing," said Andy. "We found most of the materials and stole the rest."

"Picture it," said Lulu. "It wasn't bad as clubhouses go. It had a roof and a door and even a floor of sorts. But best of all, it was private. It was ours, and no one else could come in."

"I wonder if the materials are still there," said Andy.

"Maybe some other kids rebuilt it," said Kevin.

"They tore down the building," said Lulu. "Half the neighborhood's been condemned and torn down. Don't you guys ever drive back to the old neighborhood? Anyway, forget it. I'm not trying to lead you down memory lane. All I'm saying is, if we could build a clubhouse when we were nine, we could sure build a shelter for some homeless person now."

There was silence for a moment, and then Neil said, "Are you talking about public housing?"

"Nothing that elaborate." Then Lulu totally ignored him while she said to the others, "I'm saying that the three of us could put up a little home for some homeless person."

"Look," said Kevin, "they might've let us get away with it as kids, but there's no way the owner of some building is going to let us build something on the roof. They'd throw us in jail."

"It doesn't have to be on a roof," said Lulu.

"Well, I don't know about you," said Andy, "but I don't happen to own any land. And in order to put up a structure, you need land."

"The problem is," said Lulu, "you're thinking in terms of doing it legally. I say, do it illegally and it'll have more of an effect."

"Explain that," said Andy.

"This is Boston, right?" asked Lulu. "We have parks. We have historic monuments. I say put houses up where everyone can see them and maybe people will begin to care. Maybe the government will have to do something about it."

She looked at Kevin, who was studiously avoiding her gaze by looking past her at the TV screen over the bar. She looked at Andy, who was unraveling the edge of his sweater. She looked across the table at Neil and saw that he was sketching on a napkin. She had forgotten about his sketching. When they were kids he used to draw pictures of all their favorite comic-book characters for them.

"All right, forget it, let's order another round," said Lulu, feeling as though trying to persuade her friends was as hard as fighting city hall. "It's just good you guys weren't involved when we had the Boston Tea Party, that's all I've got to say."

Neil shoved the napkin across the table to Lulu. She ignored it.

"Take a look," said Neil.

Feeling put-upon, Lulu glanced down. What she saw was a drawing of a simple structure. It was boxlike, with a flat roof, a door and a window. It was like a simple drawing of a house a kid would do, only at the same time it had perspective and looked professional. She looked up and met Neil's eyes. Some of his light brown hair had fallen down over his forehead, and for a moment he looked twelve again. Then something came into his eyes that hadn't been there at twelve, and the moment was shattered.

"Something like that could be done for about thirty bucks," said Neil, his voice suddenly soft so that she had to pay attention.

"How do you know?" she asked him.

He shrugged. "I just know. I'm an architect."

"Prefab?" Lulu asked him.

"Just about."

"How long would it take to put up?"

"With four people doing it? A couple of hours."

Lulu felt the grin spreading across her face. She shoved the napkin over to Andy, who perused it before passing it across to Kevin.

"Well, guys?" asked Lulu, sitting up, prepared to take charge as their commandant again.

"What do you think," said Andy, "the cops are just going to let us put up little houses in parks? They'll haul us to jail before we get the roof on."

"We do it in the middle of the night," said Lulu.

"My wife doesn't let me out in the middle of the night," said Kevin.

"She lets you stay out on Fridays," said Lulu.

"Ah, Lulu," said Andy, "our Friday nights are sacred."

"We need this after a hard week's work," said Kevin.

Neil was looking mildly amused. "What's the matter with you guys, you getting old? You'd rather sit around with the old men, drinking beer and talking politics instead of going out and doing something? Come on, it would be an adventure. Plus I could get us a discount on the materials."

Lulu was silent. She had never intended that Neil be involved.

"You serious about this?" Andy asked Neil.

"Why not? Someone should do something."

"The money wouldn't be the problem," said Kevin. "Hell, we spend more than thirty bucks coming here on Fridays."

"It might be fun," said Andy.

Lulu was getting angry. "How come when I suggest something you laugh, but as soon as Neil says practically the same thing, you take him seriously?"

"Because he's a man," chorused Neil and Andy.

"You think you're joking, but you're not," said Lulu. Maybe she'd been their leader at ten, but by eleven, after Neil had shown up and taken over, she had lost a lot of her authority over them. Now it was happening again. Not that she bossed them around anymore, but Neil seemed to be taking over. And in that same annoying way of his.

"I'd hate to miss out on our Friday nights altogether," said Kevin.

"Who's stopping us from lifting a few when the night's work is over?" asked Neil. "I know you Irish have to have your beer."

Kevin muttered some derogatory comment back, but it was said good-naturedly.

"I already have the tenants to move right in," said Lulu, her mind racing with the possibilities.

"Now wait a minute," said Andy. "I'd say that's discrimination. There are more homeless men than there are women."

"You know what I think?" said Neil. "I think we're going to produce a little economic miracle of our own."

Andy grinned and lifted his mug. "To us," he said. "The Rooftop Gang strikes again!"

"To the Rooftop Gang," echoed Kevin.

Neil was watching Lulu, waiting for her to join in the toast. She could see amusement in his eyes as well as remembrance. She found it ironic that her old nemesis had been the one to come to her aid in persuading Kevin and Andy. She found it doubly ironic that the attraction was still there, alive and well after so many years. Still, was it any different from the attraction for the devil's ways that the nuns had warned them about back in grade school?

It just took some strength of character to resist, that was all. She had free will, didn't she?

She lifted her mug and saw Neil lift his. "The Rooftop Gang, Part II," she said, getting a few chuckles from Andy. Kevin started to whistle the theme from *Rocky*.

Neil seemed to be laughing at her when he said, "I always wanted to recapture my youth," leaving Lulu to wonder just what he meant by that.

Chapter Two

The woman showed up at the Shelter for Homeless Women on her own. Most of the homeless women were sent by various city social-service agencies, although occasionally one would show up at the shelter's door. When this happened, though, the shelter's staff wasn't allowed to give them a bed, but had, instead, to send them to one of the agencies for a referral slip.

It was Wednesday, and Lulu was eager to get out of there on time. She was supposed to meet the gang—at Neil's office and at his request—to approve a scale model he had made of the little house for the homeless. Neil had called her personally, hadn't taken the hint that she didn't want to talk, interrupted her every time she tried to get a word in and had finally had worn her down so that she agreed to go just to get off the phone. By God, he hadn't changed.

When the woman knocked at the open door of Lulu's office, it was only a few minutes before five, and Lulu was attempting to straighten up the papers on her desk prior to leaving. Lulu looked up and saw the woman and didn't immediately recognize her as one of the homeless. Her eyes held none of the despair that Lulu had come to recognize, but more than that, she was absolutely lovely. Lulu didn't see how someone that lovely could survive on the streets.

"Yes?" said Lulu.

"I was told to see you." There was an accent there, the kind of accent Lulu's grandmother had had.

"You're Irish," said Lulu.

"Yes."

"Come on in."

The woman seemed to drift into the office, ending up in the wooden chair facing Lulu's desk. The woman's black curly hair framed the perfect oval face of a Madonna. The eyes were the same blue as Kevin's and as thickly lashed, her luminous skin looked as though it had never been touched by the sun, her small nose was slightly tilted at the tip, and her thin mouth was sweet in repose. She appeared lost in a black nylon jacket two sizes too large for her, her slim legs clad in tight-fitting jeans rolled up twice at the hem, her feet sockless in a pair of raggedy sneakers. She was the most beautiful woman Lulu had ever seen off a movie screen, but this fact caused no jealousy in Lulu; she felt only awe, pure and simple.

"How can I help you?" Lulu asked.

"I need a place to sleep."

"Have you been here long?"

"A few weeks. I'd a place to stay but I was thrown out."

"Are you employed?"

"I was getting room and board at my place of employment."

Lulu knew the city was filled with au pair girls from Ireland, all of them escaping the high cost of living and high unemployment rate of the Republic. Some were dismissed by unfeeling employers who either didn't know or didn't care that they were throwing the women out on the mercy of the city. And many of the women were in the country illegally and could only get jobs in private homes out of reach of the government bureaucracies.

"I'm afraid you have to be sent by one of the city agencies in order to stay here," said Lulu, "and even then it's only for the night."

"I didn't know that. I saw the sign and thought it offered...sanctuary."

"If you want, you could go to one right now. We still have some beds for the night, and they'll probably refer you."

The woman, pride fighting need in her face, seemed to make a decision. She stood up and faced Lulu with dignity. "Thank you, I'll be going then."

"Perhaps you could try one of the churches. St. Anselm's is just around the corner, and Father Andolini is a friend of mine."

"I prefer not, but thank you very much just the same."

"You have some place you can go?"

"I'll find a place."

Lulu thought of her plan to save the homeless, about everyone with an apartment taking in someone without. Was she all talk after all or, for once in her life, would she act on her convictions?

"Would you like me to go to the agency with you?" Lulu asked her, hating herself for her cowardice. What would be the harm in taking in the woman for the night?

"No. Thank you, but I'll manage."

"Do you have money?"

The woman was silent.

Lulu stood up and held out her hand. "I'm Lulu Lenahan."

"You'd not be one of the Lenahans of County Cork, would you?" asked the woman with the beginnings of a smile. Her eyes were wary, though.

"Antrim," said Lucy.

"Ah, then it would be Belfast."

Lulu nodded.

"A sorry place, and you're well out of it."

"My grandparents were from there."

The woman grasped Lulu's hand firmly. "I'm Mary Moore of Dublin."

Mary's eyes seemed to be questioning Lulu in a way she found unnerving. It was as though the woman could see into Lulu's soul and found her wanting.

"You could stay for the free meal if you like," said Lulu, thinking she could at least send her out with something warm in her stomach.

"You are kind, but I will be all right. One hears there are Irish pubs to be found."

Lulu had heard that, too. She had heard there was an entire underground network to help the aliens. Still, Mary was young and beautiful, and one also heard of men who took advantage of the fact that young women were in the country illegally. If Mary was even half as innocent as she looked, Lulu hated the thought of what might happen to her.

"Well, Mary Moore, why don't you come home with me tonight? There's somewhere I have to go this evening, but I can drop you off at my apartment first, and I won't be long."

"You're kind, but I'd not want to be putting you out."

"You won't be," said Lulu. She retrieved her backpack from her file drawer, then put on her heavyweight baseball jacket with the red pile lining. It was then that she noticed Mary wasn't even carrying a handbag.

"Do you have your things with you?" Lulu asked her.

"I'd a knapsack, but it got lost."

Stolen, more likely, Lulu thought. They looked to be about the same size, and Lulu thought she'd be able to find a change of clothes for Mary to take with her. If she'd accept them. Sometimes the homeless were so proud they refused to accept anything.

"It's only a short walk to my flat. We'll stop on the way and get you your own toothbrush."

"I can manage without, thank you."

"Never mind that stubborn Irish pride of yours," said Lulu, having long recognized the same trait in herself. "One toothbrush will not put you everlastingly in my debt, Mary Moore."

The woman grinned, revealing a crooked front tooth, and it changed her face entirely. Then the grin relaxed into a smile, and she turned from gamine back to Madonna once more. "I'll be glad of the chance to wash my teeth," she said.

"Come along, then," said Lulu, turning out the light in her office.

It was seven blocks to Lulu's building along some of the poorest streets of the city. Not even night yet, there were already bodies huddled in doorways and on the stairs leading down from the subway entrance. She knew down below, inside the station, there'd be dozens more already camping out for the night.

"I didn't think it would be like this in America," said Mary.

"You have a warmer climate in Dublin," said Lulu, thinking she was referring to the weather.

"Not the cold. It gets so damp in Ireland, I don't mind the cold here. I mean the homeless. We grew up believing everyone over here was rich."

"It seems to get worse every year. I happen to be working in a business that I wish would go out of business."

"And if it did? What would you do then?"

"Oh, there'll always be problems. If not the homeless, then the poor. Or the children on crack. Or the ones with AIDS."

"It's a fine thing you're doing. It must give you a good feeling."

"More frustration than anything else," said Lulu. She was tempted to tell Mary about the plans of the Rooftop Gang. They had sworn each other to secrecy, though, and the fewer who knew the better.

When they reached her old building, Lulu led the way down the steps to the basement apartment. There were two windows looking out on the street, both duly covered with bars against burglars. There was a small cement patch where she could have sat out in the summer if the building's trash cans weren't housed there, attracting every fly within blocks in nice weather. There was also a little patch of earth. Every spring Lulu planted a sapling there, and every summer the young tree died.

She opened the locks on the door, then swung the door wide and reached inside for the light switch, saying, "Watch out for the steps."

Mary proceeded her down into the apartment, seeming to take in the haphazard furnishings with one glance. Lulu was sure they weren't any better than what Mary was used to at home, most of them being from secondhand stores. Mohammed roused himself from his spot on the windowsill and began to stretch.

"I hope you like cats," said Lulu. She knew the Irish were superstitious, and Mohammed was very black.

"I do not mind them."

"Mohammed showed up last winter in the middle of a snowstorm, howling at my door. Now he won't even go out, although there's a bit of dirt outside that would do him as well as a cat box."

Mary was prowling around, much as Mohammed had done when Lulu had first brought him in. "You make a habit, then, of bringing in strays?"

"You're not a stray, Mary."

She saw the woman looking at the bars, measuring the size of the room with her eyes. She reminded Lulu a little bit of a caged animal.

"This is a darlin' flat. Darlin'. But you don't have room for another person."

"The couch makes into a bed if you don't mind sharing."

"I grew up sharing a bed with two sisters."

"I was lucky," said Lulu. "I only had brothers. The only time I had any privacy growing up was when I was in bed. It was my refuge against the world."

Lulu opened the louvered doors that hid the kitchen from the rest of the room. Mohammed followed her and sat watching with veiled interest as she opened the far right cupboard, chose 9 Lives Savory Stew for him, took the lid off and served it to him out of the can, his bowls all being dirty in the sink. She filled up his water bowl, then watched as he pushed the can around the floor.

She left the cupboard door open. "Help yourself to anything you can find to eat," she said to Mary. "There's plenty of soup and the makings of grilled cheese sandwiches. And tea, of course." She could use a cup herself, she thought, as she filled the teakettle and lit the stove.

Mary was picking up one of the angels and setting it back down before picking up another. "Are these darlin' angels for Christmas, then?"

"No," said Lulu, "I collect them."

"You collect angels?"

"I figure it can't hurt to surround myself with guardian angels."

"No, it cannot hurt," said Mary, and Lulu decided to add an angel to the package of clothes she'd be sending Mary off with. A woman alone on the streets had more need of a guardian angel than she did.

"What kind of work would you be looking for?" asked Lulu, smiling to herself because she was already picking up Mary's manner of lilting speech. It was a talent of hers, matching her speech to anyone she spoke with.

"Oh, anything will suit me. I don't mind cleaning houses or watching the wee ones. I'm a hard worker."

"Waiting tables?"

"If I have to. Any honest work will do."

"I'll ask around. The friends I'm seeing tonight might know of something. Mostly, though, the people I know can't afford to hire help."

"Would you be needing anyone to clean the shelter?"

"You'd have to be a city employee for that." The water was boiling, and Lulu turned off the burner. "A cup of tea before I go?"

"I wouldn't say no."

Lulu fixed the pot of tea and carried a tray over to the table in front of the windows. All she could see from here of the people passing on the sidewalk was their legs, but there was something soothing about watching legs hurrying by to get home to their dinners. And the angle meant that no one could easily look in.

"Help yourself," Lulu said, then she went over to her one closet and opened the door. On the shelf she found a clean flannel nightgown and a pair of wool socks to warm the feet. She set them on the couch and said to Mary, "You can use these tonight, and if you want a hot bath, there're clean towels on the shelf in the bathroom."

"You're making me feel very welcome," said Mary.

"You *are* welcome." Lulu sat down at the table and poured herself tea, spooning in enough sugar to give a dietitian conniption fits. She'd been brought up on tea and had never liked the taste until she learned that with enough sugar, she liked anything.

"You have family in Ireland?" asked Lulu.

"A mother. And numerous aunts and uncles and female cousins."

"You could call your mother if you like. She might be worrying about you."

"My mother'd be more worried about the cost of ringing her."

Lulu smiled. "That sounds like mine. I wonder sometimes why it's the Scots who have the reputation for being thrifty. My mother is still as careful of a penny as she was when a penny was worth something."

The buzzer sounded, and Mary jumped, the tea spilling over the sides of the cup and onto the table.

"That's only Andy," said Lulu.

"You want me out of the way?"

"Of course not. He's a friend, one of my oldest friends. And perfectly harmless, although he wouldn't thank me for the description."

She got up and went to the door and unlocked it. When she opened it, Andy stood there, not making a move to come in.

"Come in," she told him.

"I'm double-parked," he said.

"Just for a moment. I want you to meet a friend of mine."

Andy's eyebrows were lifting, but then he looked past Lulu, and they settled back in place along with a look of amazement.

"This is my friend Mary Moore," said Lulu. "And this good Irish lad is Andy Keely."

TWENTY-FIVE YEARS of being hopelessly in love with Lulu were forgotten in an instant. Lulu had been Andy's protector when they were children, fighting his fights for him when the other boys, the bullies in the class, had ganged up on him, and that had made him adore her. But now he was looking at a woman who was bringing out all of his own protective instincts. It was a new experience for him, and it made him feel powerful.

Poised on the couch with the look of a bird about to fly away was the most beautiful woman he had ever seen. But where beauty alone might have intimidated him, this woman also looked fragile and lost and very much in need of protection. And yet, how he could be sure of all that in one glance, he didn't know.

Andy realized he hadn't said anything and that Lulu and Mary were looking at him expectantly. "A pleasure to meet you," he said to Mary, and caught a spark of something in her eyes before it faded. "Do you work with Lulu?"

"No," said Lulu and Mary at the same moment, and then Lulu added, "Mary's not been in the country long."

"You from Ireland?" asked Andy, which wasn't the most intelligent bit of conversation, but he felt almost tongue-tied with emotion.

"Dublin," said Mary, making the one word sound like music.

"I love Dublin," said Andy.

"I forgot you'd been there," said Lulu. Then turning to Mary, "Andy was over there on business. Setting up a computer program for the university, wasn't it, Andy?"

Andy nodded.

"I'd be knowing nothing of computers," said Mary.

"And I know very little of Dublin," said Andy. "They put us up at the university and kept us working night and day."

"Don't let him fool you," said Lulu. "He works night and day here, too."

"It's a shame you didn't get to know the city," said Mary. "It's a lovely place if only there were work."

"We'd better be going," said Andy, wishing he had spent the extra minutes necessary to find a parking space. "Are you coming with us, Mary?"

"No, she's staying here," said Lulu, "but I promised her I wouldn't be late."

And then Lulu was hustling him out the door, but he didn't mind because, although there were a lot of things he wanted to find out about Mary, it would be easier to ask Lulu, who didn't tie his tongue in knots when he talked to her.

"Lock all the locks when I go out," Lulu said to Mary. When they were outside and climbing the steps she said, "Is that how you act around women, Andy?"

"What do you mean?" He knew exactly what she meant.

Lulu just laughed, getting into the car and settling herself in the seat.

Andy got in and waited for her to put on her seat belt. When she didn't, he tilted back his seat and pretended to be going to sleep.

"All right," said Lulu, fastening the belt, "but I don't know why you're such a fanatic about seat belts."

"I don't know why you're such a fanatic about risking your life every chance you get." Andy took off down the street. "Why haven't I heard about this Mary before?"

"Because I just met her about an hour ago."

"Then you're not friends?"

"I think we could be. She walked into the homeless shelter looking for a place to sleep."

For the first time Andy envied Lulu her job. "And you took her home with you?"

"The street's no place for her."

"You actually did it!"

"Did what?"

Andy turned to her with a grin. "You're sharing your apartment with the homeless. Kevin's not going to believe this."

"I think she's in the country illegally."

Andy wasn't surprised to hear it. "There was a television special about that a few weeks ago. About all the young Irish in the country illegally, most of them in the Boston area." He'd also noted several articles about the situation in the newspapers, although he hadn't bothered to read them. Now he wished he had.

"We let all the Russians in who want to come. Why not the Irish?" Lulu was moving right into her argumentative mode, as usual. Andy wished she'd give it a rest once in a while.

"I'm not responsible for the quota system. Ask your congressman."

"I just may do that," said Lulu.

"Mary Moore," mused Andy. "She's a pretty woman."

"That's like saying Larry Bird is a fair basketball player, my friend."

Andy chuckled. "Okay, so she's astonishingly beautiful. That face should be on an icon."

"The Irish don't have icons."

"You know what I mean."

"All these years I've known you, Andy, and I never suspected you were the kind of shallow guy who would be attracted to a woman for her looks."

"You have to be initially attracted by something, and that's as good a place as any to start."

"On second thought, I don't think that's it at all. There's a lost quality about her that I think appealed to your chivalrous feelings."

"What chivalrous feelings?"

"You're a softie, Andy. You're always for the underdog."

"Which is something we share."

"Ah, but I'm not a softie about it."

It was time to change the subject unless he wanted to be analyzed by Lulu, which he didn't. "So, have you talked to Neil?"

"Don't start in with me. I have no wish whatsoever of discussing Neil."

"You can't hate him forever, Lulu."

"Why not?"

"Because it wastes a lot of positive energy when you use it for negative thoughts, that's why."

"Don't tell me you're into EST or something now."

"I'm just saying it's time to forgive him and move on. We were only kids. What were we, twelve?"

"Twelve or twenty-four, he knew exactly what he was doing."

"I'd hate to be blamed for everything I did as a kid."

Lulu was silent for a moment. "We'll never be as honest, as exactly ourselves, as when we were kids." If Andy wasn't mistaken, she sounded wistful. Lulu, wistful, was something he'd never encountered before.

"I don't believe that."

"Well, it's true.

"Lulu, I was a cowardly wimp when I was a kid. Is that how you see me now?"

"That was at seven, and you were small for your age. You weren't a coward by twelve."

"I was when you weren't around. But the point is, I'm not today. We change. We grow. All right, maybe you haven't changed, but the rest of us have."

"Neil hasn't changed."

Andy sighed. She had a point. There had been something very intimidating about Neil when he was a kid, and it was still there. And it had nothing to do with the fact that he had a big mouth. Lulu had a big mouth, too, but that hadn't stopped him from loving her. Not that Neil wasn't warm and friendly and likable, too, it was just that there was something below the surface, some secret impregnable barrier, some sense of absolute integrity, that made the kind of closeness he felt for Kevin and Lulu impossible to feel for Neil. In some sense he had always seemed too good for them. And it wasn't a class thing; Andy had no problem with that. If at some point, over a drink, Neil had confided in him that he was from outer space, Andy would've thought, "Yes, that's it. That's the difference." And it wouldn't have surprised him.

"I don't think you're being completely honest," he told her.

"When have I not been honest with you?"

"I'm talking about being honest with yourself. If it had been me or Kevin, would you still hold it against us?"

"Neither of you would've done it."

"I think we would've if we hadn't been afraid of you."

"Kevin wasn't afraid of me."

"All right, maybe that's the wrong word. But we were used to doing whatever you wanted."

"It was a matter of loyalty."

"But perhaps misplaced."

"He betrayed me, Andy, and I'm not forgiving him for it."

"But I think the reason you're not forgiving him is because it was him and not one of us. Because he was the outsider."

"That's nonsense."

"And because you were in love with him."

Lulu practically jumped out of her seat, but the seat belt held her back. "Are you crazy, Andy Keely? We were only twelve years old."

"Be that as it may . . ."

"Don't give me that. What do twelve-year-olds know about love?"

"Believe me, I didn't realize it at the time. But later, thinking back, I saw that it was true. And maybe you didn't know it, either, but it was there for everyone to see. Ask Kevin."

"Kevin?"

"Yes. He knew it, too."

"He knew no such thing."

"You're denying something that I thought at the time was really wonderful."

"I don't want to hear any more of this nonsense out of you, Andy Keely, do you understand?"

"You've always had a way of conveniently deflecting reality when it suited your purposes."

"I'll deflect you right off the road if you don't watch it."

They drove the rest of the way in silence.

"WHAT DO YOU THINK? Is that perfect or what? I swear to God, I was really inspired when I designed this little beauty," said Neil. "Go on, don't hold back. I'll take all the compliments I can force out of you."

The office itself was a thing of beauty, but all eyes were on the scale model of the house that was sitting on a glass table next to a model of an elaborate shopping complex. The house was of a simple design, much like the one he had sketched at Flanagan's. He had demonstrated how the walls worked on hinges and how the roof folded over and needed only nails to attach it to the walls. The two windows were already built-in, and the door was the only thing that would take them a little time to hang.

"A few pillows, some hanging plants, and you could call it home," said Andy.

"I was at a sporting-goods store last weekend," said Kevin, "and they had camping cots on sale. I thought maybe we could throw in a camping cot and blanket, maybe a folding table."

"Is there some way the person could lock it so the things wouldn't get stolen?" asked Andy.

Neil nodded. "There'll be a padlock on the outside of the door and a bar on the inside. Come on, guys, let's hear a little enthusiasm. Am I the best architect in the city of Boston, or what?"

"You're the greatest, Neil," conceded Andy.

"Brilliant," agreed Kevin.

"Umm," was all that Lulu would allow.

"What do you think, Lulu?" Kevin asked her. "You haven't said a word."

Lulu, who had been off in a fantasy world where all the homeless were housed in miniature houses, shook her head a little and concentrated on the structure in front of her. "I love it. I could live in it myself." She picked up the house and held it in her hands, then looked at Neil. "Could I have this?" Much as she hated asking a favor of him, she wanted the house more.

"Sure. Keep it as a souvenir."

She opened the door and peered inside. She had scorned dollhouses as a child, but this was different. This was amazing.

"How're we going to transport them?" asked Andy.

"I can borrow my brother's pick-up," said Kevin.

"So we're all set?" asked Neil. "Are we on for Friday night, or has the old gang chickened out?"

"It won't be us who will chicken out," said Lulu, thinking he had a lot of nerve even suggesting it.

"Well, we're not kids now," said Neil. "We could conceivably end up in jail for something like this."

"I'm not worried about it," said Andy.

"I'm not, either," said Kevin. "Anyway, if it should happen, my sister-in-law's a lawyer."

"The police won't do a thing," said Lulu. "With the crime in this city, they're not going to be worried about a few little houses going up. They'll probably pin a medal on us for getting some of the homeless off the streets."

"I'm not so sure about that," said Andy.

"I'm telling you," said Lulu. "I talked to my uncles, two of Boston's finest, and all they said was, 'Good luck.'"

"Actually, I wouldn't mind going to jail for it," said Neil. "It would be good publicity for the homeless."

"If you want to go to jail, there are quicker ways," said Lulu.

"And I'm sure you know them all," Neil shot back.

"Well, let's get a few put up before we start thinking about publicity," said Andy the peacemaker.

Kevin and Andy were halfway out the door when Neil checked Lulu's exit with the soft voice he used when he wanted to get his own way. "Have you had dinner?" he asked her.

Lulu turned, unsure he had actually said that. "Dinner?"

"Yes, as in food. You know, the meal that usually takes place at night after work? Sometimes at home, sometimes in a restaurant, sometimes alfresco at a hot-dog stand. I was wondering if you'd like to get something to eat with me. The two of us. Together. We need to talk."

"If anything, Neil, your sarcasm has improved over the years."

His smile lit up his face. "Thank you. From you that's a real compliment, you being the expert in sarcasm."

She could say she had plans to eat with Andy, but that wouldn't convey what she wanted to convey, which was that she had nothing to talk about with him, that it was much too late for talk. Instead she said, "No, I wouldn't like to eat with you."

"I don't believe you."

"Believe what you want, but the last thing I need is to fight with you over a meal. I get bad enough indigestion just listening to you."

"Another compliment! You're full of them tonight, aren't you?"

"And you're full of blarney," said Lulu, "which is a real talent, considering you're not even Irish."

"I guess we better not eat together, after all," said Neil. "All these compliments of yours would start to go to my head."

"If you're worried about it getting bigger, don't. It couldn't possibly."

Andy came back to the office, looking for Lulu. "What's the holdup?"

"No holdup," said Lulu, "just Neil running off at the mouth again."

"See you soon, Lulu," said Neil, his voice filled with good cheer.

"Just get me out of here," muttered Lulu.

MARY, CURLED UP ON THE COUCH with Mohammed in her lap, opened her eyes when Lulu came in. She looked like an angel in the high-necked, faded gown that had once had a pattern of violets but now had only gray smudges where the flowers had been. Lulu thought it suited her far more than the jeans and black jacket had, although, practically speaking, one couldn't go around all the time in a flannel granny gown.

"What's the wee house in your hands?" Mary asked her.

Lulu set it on the coffee table along with the pizza she had brought for supper. She squatted down in front of it. "It's a secret, but I don't see why I shouldn't tell you. It's not like you're going to run to the police with the information."

"You've stolen it, then?"

Lulu smiled. "No, it's not stolen."

"I cannot see an upstanding citizen like yourself worrying about the police."

"Oh, nothing really criminal, more like trespassing, I suppose." She told Mary about their plan.

"Regular urban terrorists, you and your friends," said Mary, not sounding altogether approving.

"But we're not going to hurt anyone, just help them. You're homeless, you should understand."

"Aye, it's jealous I am."

"Of what?"

Mary picked up the house and pressed the roof against her cheek. "One could be happy in a darlin' house like this."

"I know. That's exactly what I thought. I've always been one to prefer snug, cozy places. I'd feel lost in a large house. We had a clubhouse when we were kids that was just the right size."

"I'd not suppose," began Mary, then set the house back down next to the pizza carton and looked at the box. "What's in there?"

"I got us a pizza, but what were you going to say?"

Mary opened the box and looked inside. "Ah, smell that delicious odor."

"Mary, do you want to live in the house we're going to put up? If you do, just say so. I was going to choose one of the women from the shelter anyway."

"There are probably those more needy."

"It's just that I think ... Well, you're so beautiful ... to be all alone outdoors like that. The house won't offer that much protection."

"It's the elements I need protection from. Humans I can handle."

"Then it's yours. I'll help you fix it up. We're going to put a cot and a blanket in each one, but you'd probably like a lantern and a little camping stove."

"I could help you put it up."

"No. There's always the possibility we could get into trouble over this. You can stay here until the weekend. We'll be putting it up Friday night, and we'll move you in Saturday morning.

"Sure and it was fate that brought me to your door, Lulu Lenahan."

"I've never believed in fate," said Lulu.

"You don't have to believe in it," said Mary Moore. "It's out there waiting for you whether you believe in it or not."

Lulu took the pizza carton to the kitchen and set it on the counter. She took down a plate from the cupboard, lifted the pizza and slid some slices onto the plate. It even looked better than it smelled. She opened the refrigerator and took out the shaker of Parmesan and sprinkled a lot of it on the pizza. Then she salted it, found the powdered garlic in the cabinet over the sink and poured a little of that on. She bent down and sniffed. It was smelling pretty good. Better all the time. She took the crushed red pepper from the spice rack over the stove and shook out some flakes of that. Then she opened the refrigerator again and took out a couple of bottles of beer.

She carried the pizza, some paper napkins and the bottles of beer over to the coffee table and set them down. Only then did she let herself topple back onto the couch.

"Are you ready to feast?" asked Lulu.

"Aye," said Mary, "my mouth is near to waterin'."

LATER, WHEN BOTH OF THEM were in flannel gowns and tucked beneath the down comforter, side by side in the sofa bed, drinking mugs of hot cocoa, Lulu felt the kind of sisterhood she had never felt before. She'd never been to a slumber party as a girl, never had a sister or even a close female friend.

Mary was telling her about the high cost of living in Ireland, the highest in Europe, and also about the high unemployment rate. The words were drifting over Lulu, now and again one sticking in her mind, but most of the time becoming lost as she thought about how nice this was and how it wasn't something she could ever do with her male friends.

Lulu had grown up with boys and had always found girls to be too soft and silly. Nor would she have thought someone like Mary, so sweet and soft-spoken, would be the type of woman to appeal to her as a friend. But there was something soothing about being with someone so different, someone who wasn't rowdy and argumentative. With men she always felt competitive, but with Mary there was none of that one-upmanship at work, and they could talk of their respective families and childhoods without any of that getting in the way.

"Can I ask you something personal?" Lulu asked Mary.

"And what could be more personal than what we've been talking about?"

Lulu hesitated a moment, but she really wanted to know. "If you'd rather not answer, that's okay. I'll understand."

"What is it you'd want to be knowing, Lulu?"

"Are you in the country illegally?"

The expression on Mary's face didn't change. "How did you know?"

"I didn't know, I just guessed. There are a lot of Irish coming in here illegally these days."

"Aye. I told them I was here for a vacation, but that wasn't the truth."

"Things are that bad in Dublin?"

"Just as I told you. If there was work, I would've stayed. I love my country, Lulu. I'd no wish to leave it."

"But it's not easy to get work here without a green card."

"Aye, but Americans like to pay less than minimum wage. There are jobs. I got a live-in job easy enough, but then the wife got jealous because the husband was paying too much attention to me. As though I'd be interested in a man with a great belly and wee piggy eyes."

"Have you thought of getting married?"

"To get citizenship?"

Lulu nodded.

"I'd not be marrying for such a stupid reason."

"The Church?"

"Of course, the Church. And if you're so enthralled with marriage, Lulu, why are you still single?"

"I look for too much in a man, I suppose."

"Aye, and never find it. I know the feeling."

"Still, you could do it as a business arrangement. A civil ceremony just to get citizenship."

"That's not as easy as you think. The government checks up on you. I've talked to others who were considering the idea, and they say it's not that easy anymore. They put you through a long investigation.''

Lulu rolled over to look at her. "I'll bet Andy would marry you to get you citizenship.''

"And why would he want to be doing that?''

"He likes you.''

"You shouldn't be so manipulative with your friends, Lulu. If he likes me, then there'd be no joy for him out of a business arrangement.''

"He's a good person. I don't think he'd be asking any more of you than just to help you.''

"I've not hit bottom yet," said Mary. "I'll find work. And it'll be easier now because it won't have to be live-in now that I'll be having my own wee house.''

Mary asked her how she'd met Andy, and Lulu began to tell her about the day on the playground when they were both in the first grade and some of the bigger boys had Andy trapped in the jungle gym and were tormenting him. She had gotten to the part where she sped to Andy's rescue and pulled the uniform pants off of one of the boys, when she saw that Mary's eyes were closed and her breathing even.

She turned off the lamp and snuggled down under the covers, the bed extrawarm and cozy with two people occupying it. Lulu, who never relaxed with anyone, found that it was relaxing being with another woman.

Another part of her, though, knew that there were more interesting things to do in bed than relax. And most of those interesting things involved having a man in bed with you.

But that wasn't something Lulu felt like thinking about.

Chapter Three

"I thought you were playing bridge with the girls tonight," said Kevin, trying to sound innocent and going on the offensive immediately since he had been caught in the act of returning home when he was supposed to be in the city.

"Don't use that condescending tone of voice on me, Kevin McCrory. As though playing bridge is in any way as juvenile as you and that old gang of yours meeting in a bar every Friday night to get drunk."

Caroline, her arms folded across her chest, her eyes narrowed, her mouth a straight line, was blocking the front door and looking as though he'd have to move her bodily if he was to get out. She still looked gorgeous, in that cool blond way that had first attracted him, but her looks had long since become part of the landscape, and that cute mad look of hers that he used to find adorable failed to move him anymore.

"Caroline, honey, let's not fight about that again."

"And don't 'Caroline honey' me, either. What's your brother's pickup doing in the driveway, and why are you dressed all in black? What happened to Friday nights at Flanagan's?"

He made a move to go past her, but she stood firm. "There's a good explanation for all of this," said Kevin.

"And you're not leaving the house until I hear it."

He could always make a run for the back door, but how childish could he get? And why should he have to be sneaking out of his own house, anyway? "Is that some kind of ultimatum, Caro?"

"No, that's not the ultimatum. The ultimatum is, if you don't tell me where you're going, don't bother to come back."

These were words he'd waited a long time to hear. He'd always assumed that when the day came that they were finally spoken, he'd be out of there like a shot. And yet now, instead of saying, "Fine, if that's what you want," he instead backed off a little. Maybe he wasn't as ready to walk out on his marriage as he thought he was. Maybe he had just gotten used to thinking like that when there was no basis in reality for the thought at all. At least, now that it had finally come, he found he was in no hurry to take advantage of it.

He tried to put a little shock in his voice when he said, "You don't mean that, Caroline."

"I mean it."

So he'd be a little late; it couldn't be helped. They had hours to kill in Flanagan's before they got to work, anyway, and Neil would wait if he was a few minutes late in picking him up.

He took off his wool watch cap and unzipped his parka. As usual, she had the damn thermostat turned up to eighty degrees, and he was already sweating. He walked away from her, down the hall and toward the kitchen. On the way he passed the thermostat and flicked it downward. He was opening the refrigerator and taking out a beer when she appeared in the kitchen door.

"Well?" she said.

"What do you want to know?"

He sat down in the custom-made breakfast nook and set his can of beer on the butcher-block table. He waited for her to yell at him to put a napkin under the can.

Caroline moved into the kitchen and sat on one of the bar stools in front of the counter, one camel-hair pant leg ending in a soft leather boot stretched out in the direction of the back door, as though to block any escape attempt by him. As though at five foot five and one hundred and fifteen pounds she could physically stop him from going anywhere he wanted to go.

"You can start with the mysterious phone calls you've been getting all week and move on to whatever's hidden beneath the tarpaulin in the back of Danny's truck."

"Oh, that. It's just some stuff I'm delivering—"

"Delivering? Since when are you delivering things? And don't bother to lie. I always know when you're lying because you never look me straight in the eye."

Kevin looked her straight in the eye, started to speak and then faltered. "It's a secret," he finally said.

"I gathered that."

"If I tell you, you'll just go blabbing it around."

"How do you know I blab things around if you never tell me anything?"

"I promised Lulu—" He broke off at the look on her face. Lulu. The magic word guaranteed to anger her every time.

"Just tell me this, Kevin. Why didn't you marry that precious Lulu of yours?"

Should he tell her it was because Lulu wouldn't have him, or was that just asking for trouble? Of course, it was asking for trouble, and at certain times he wouldn't have minded throwing the truth at her. But if he wanted to get out of the house tonight, it wasn't the right time to be spouting the truth. And if he wanted to be able to ever return, it definitely wasn't the right time.

"You've got to swear to secrecy if I tell you, Caroline, because we're breaking the law."

"Is that why you're dressed like some robber?"

"I'm not dressed like a robber."

"All in black? I know you better than that. Ordinarily you'd be wearing something blue to bring out the color of your eyes."

That hurt. Could he help it if his favorite color just happened to match his eyes? "Are you looking for an argument, or do you want to swear you'll keep quiet about it?"

"You look like a little kid who's up to no good. But if you think I take you seriously, Kevin, you're very mistaken. You don't have the guts to break the law."

"It's nothing bad. In fact it's a good thing we're doing, but against the law nonetheless."

"Now I'm going to hear about Robin Hood and his merry band of men, only in this case I'm sure that Lulu is playing the role of Robin Hood."

"Well, she's the ringleader, that's for sure. She has some hair up her nose about the homeless in the city."

Caroline gave a snort of derision. "Does she think she's the only one."

"She wants to do something about it."

"Kevin, I think you're leading me down the garden path."

"I'm telling you the truth. We're going to put up some little houses for the homeless."

"Since when is that against the law?"

"We're going to put them on public property. Without permits. In the middle of the night." He knew how ridiculous it sounded as he said it. Like something a bunch of kids would do, not at all how professional people spent their Friday nights.

Caroline got up, and for a minute Kevin thought she might be going to the phone to call the police. Instead, she went to the refrigerator and got herself a can of beer. He hadn't seen Caroline drink a beer since college parties during their Harvard days.

She came over to the table, popped the tab, then took a long drink. He was all set to be blasted by her, but then she said, "I want to go with you."

"*You?* You play bridge on Friday nights."

"I play bridge on Friday nights because you're never around and I'm bored. And I don't bug you take me along with you because I'd find it just as boring to sit around Flanagan's getting drunk and solving the problems of the world." She paused and smiled. "But this sounds exciting."

"It's freezing out, Caroline."

"I've got a warm black parka of my own."

"Look, I appreciate the offer, but we're talking about hard work. We're going to have to assemble the house."

"Excuse me for mentioning it, Kevin, but who is it who puts the storm windows on every fall? And which of us built the bookcases in the den? And who changed the tire when we had the flat coming back from the Cape last summer and you almost had a nervous breakdown?"

"I don't know if the others—"

"To hell with the others! I would think you'd be glad of any help you could get. And as for you, you're totally useless around tools. You couldn't even assemble the vacuum cleaner when we bought it. You had the handle on backward."

She was bluffing; she had to bluffing. You'd never get Caroline outdoors on a cold night when she could be inside, in front of a fire, drinking martinis and playing cards with those old sorority sisters of hers.

He took another swallow of beer, then grinned at her. "Okay, you got five minutes to change."

He thought she would say, "No, never mind, I just wanted you to invite me, that's all." But she fooled him. She returned his grin and ran upstairs to get ready.

"Caroline," he yelled after her, "you better reconsider. We could all end up in jail."

No answer came from Caroline.

And how was he going to explain to the others about bringing his wife along?

NEIL REACHED TO THE VERY END of the rack and pulled his old college peacoat out of the closet. It was the darkest jacket he owned, except for one in black leather, and he wouldn't care if he caught this one on a nail. It seemed like a talisman, a relic of the days when he had still been adventurous.

He located a nylon hood he used for skiing and a pair of worn leather gloves that would offer some protection against slivers in the wood. Then he picked up his clipboard one last time and checked off all the items. Finally satisfied, he reasoned everything had been done that needed to be done.

He had even found the perfect spot for their first foray into anarchy. It was a historical sight, a place honoring the American Revolution, and he thought it fitting that this was where they would erect their first house and perhaps foment a little revolution of their own into the bargain. Bunker Hill was about to be taken over by the resuscitated Rooftop Gang.

He was excited. He found he was more excited about this small structure than he had been about the latest office building he had designed. It might have a little bit to do with the fact that he was actually going to be involved with putting this one up, but he knew that it had mostly to do with the fact that this one was going up unauthorized. There was something about breaking the law that had a perverse appeal to him, and had had it since that day when he was ten and met the rest of the gang. He wondered if Paul Revere had felt the same way.

He couldn't remember feeling so excited since the summer they had hidden the fugitive in their clubhouse. In retrospect, the fugitive had been just a scared boy of sixteen who had escaped from the police, but at the time he had seemed like a dangerous criminal to them.

They had been on the rooftop adjacent to the one where their clubhouse was located, playing one of Lulu's favorite games called Lookout. One would have a notebook and pencil—he thought it had been Andy that day—and the others would be posted on three sides of the roof watching for any activity in the streets.

Entries in the notebook would read something like this:

8:17 a.m.—Mrs. Fogarty comes out of #21 and heads for corner. Blue dress, green shopping bag.

8:32 a.m.—Jiggy Staunton rides by on bike in direction of playground.

8:47 a.m.—Three eighth-graders from public school seen whispering, then disappear into #27. Watch them!!

Neil couldn't remember the entries up until the time the police car cruised down the block, but he could remember that event as clearly as if he'd seen it in a movie last night. They always got excited when a police car entered their block. Half the time they were secretly convinced the police were looking for their clubhouse; some of the time the car would actually stop and the police would get out and enter one of the neighboring buildings. At this point they would abandon the rooftop and go down to the street to see what was happening. Once in a while the police would come out with Lulu's father in tow, dead drunk. At such times the boys would pretend not to see what was happening, although it wasn't unheard of for Lulu to scream down at the cops.

This day the kind of thing happened that they had all been waiting for. As the police car cruised slowly down the street, the back door flew open and a thin kid jumped out, rolled once in the street and then got up and started running for the corner in the opposite direction in which the car had been traveling.

Neil yelled to the others, and they all came running across the roof as Neil tried to watch the kid and the police at the same time. The kid was fast and ran around the corner. Two cops, both of them overweight, got out of the car and took off after him. The way they were running, though, a three-year-old could have evaded them.

Thinking the kid might be heading for the alley behind the building they were on, they raced across the roof and looked over the edge. The kid was already in the alley. He had slowed down and was looking around for some means of escape.

Not even hesitating for a second, Lulu climbed down onto the fire escape and yelled out to the kid, "Up here!"

The kid, out of desperation, Neil supposed, came clambering up the fire escape. When he got to the top and climbed onto the roof, Lulu said, "Let's go," and then stopped a moment and said to Andy, "Stay here in case the cops come up. If they do, you didn't see anything. Just act dumb, Andy."

The rest of them jumped across to the next roof and followed Lulu to the clubhouse, which was hidden behind the structure housing the water tank.

"You can hide in here," said Lulu, pushing open the door.

The kid really looked at them then, and seeing that they were just kids, younger than he, he finally ducked down and entered the clubhouse. The others followed.

"They won't find you here," said Lulu, motioning for the kid to sit on one of the cartons they used as chairs.

"If you're thirsty, there's water in that bottle," said Kevin, pointing to a gallon plastic bottle in the corner.

The kid, sweating and out of breath, reached for the bottle, and they all watched wide-eyed as he drank half its contents. He was dressed in torn jeans and a black T-shirt, and his hair hung down to his shoulders. His running shoes were so worn they had no treads, and the stitching was missing from the left one. He had a thin, rodent face, marginal acne and eyes that kept moving from one of them to another.

"What'd you do?" Neil asked him.

"Don't hassle him," said Lulu.

"I'm not hassling him," said Neil. "I think we have a right to know. I mean, he's hiding out in *our* clubhouse, isn't he?"

"Shoplifting," said the kid.

"The cops won't do anything to you for that," said Neil.

"Yeah, they will," said the kid, "it's my third time. And this time I had a cassette player on me when they caught me."

"You can stay here," said Lulu. "They'll never find you."

They heard running steps outside on the roof, and they all fell silent as Lulu went to the periscope they had devised and looked out. "It's only Andy," she said.

A moment later Andy was knocking on the door with their secret knock, and Lulu took the bar down and let him in. "Where're the cops?" she asked him.

"Gone. They circled the block a couple of times, but then they drove off."

"They'll be back," said Lulu, and they all nodded.

Neil could still remember the way he felt that day, the first day of the fugitive. It was a powerful feeling, the feeling of them against the police, them against adults in general and the even stronger feeling of them against the world. It was a heady feeling of a kind he hadn't had since.

He had also felt a very strong sense of closeness with the others, particularly with Lulu, whose idea it had been. He had felt good just standing with her to protect the fugitive and defy the authorities.

And just maybe, tonight, he'd get those feelings back.

ANDY DOUBLE-PARKED IN FRONT of Lulu's building and left the motor running. Then, like an idiot, he got out and automatically locked the car door. He realized immediately what he had done and cursed himself out loud as he headed down the steps to her door.

"I can't believe I did this, especially tonight," he said when Lulu opened the door.

"What's the matter?"

"I just locked my keys in the car," said Andy. "I'm going to have to call a locksmith, and that means we're going to be late." Belatedly he noticed that Lulu and Mary were both dressed in dark clothes, their hair covered by scarves. He gave Lulu a questioning look.

"Mary's coming along," she said.

"Do you think that's a good idea?"

"No, I don't," said Lulu, "but she talked me into it."

Andy didn't mind; in fact he was pleased. It would give him a chance to get to know Mary better. He had known of Lulu's decision to let Mary have the first house, but he'd rather get to know her before she moved in so it wouldn't look as though he was being somehow charitable if he were to stop by to see her. Someone thrust into homelessness might be shy about visitors.

He turned to say something to Mary, but saw her rummaging in Lulu's closet and then returning to the door with a hanger in her hand. "I can get the auto open," she said, moving past them and out the door.

By the time Lulu had picked up a couple of shopping bags, closed and locked the door and followed him to the car, Mary had the car open and was tossing the bent hanger into the back seat. Then she climbed back with it.

"I didn't think you could do that with this car model," said Andy, having once tried unsuccessfully to open his car using a hanger.

"If you know how, you can open any of them," said Mary.

Lulu slid into the passenger's seat, and Andy pulled out into the Friday-night traffic.

Although he wasn't giving her an argument, Lulu said, "I don't see why Mary shouldn't be included. After all, Kevin dragged Neil into this."

"Thanks to Neil we're as far as we've gotten with it," Andy reminded her.

"That's not the point. Kevin knows how I feel about Neil."

"I don't think any of us exactly knows how you feel about Neil," said Andy, "including yourself. You can hardly keep blaming him for something that happened when we were twelve years old.

Lulu was silent.

"Come on, Lulu," said Andy, "we were just kids then."

"He betrayed me," said Lulu.

"He was worried about you. Kevin and I would've done the same if we weren't so afraid of you."

"You weren't afraid of me."

"Hell yes, we were."

"You were my friends. You wouldn't have betrayed me."

"Don't be so sure, Lulu."

Mary leaned forward in the back seat, and Andy could see her dark eyes in the rearview mirror. "How did he betray you?" she asked.

"It was just something that happened when we were kids," said Andy, who had brought up the subject in the first place hoping that Mary would ask what it was about. He thought maybe Mary's opinion would sway Lulu into dropping the feud with Neil.

"We had this gang," said Lulu. "The Rooftop Gang. We had a clubhouse on top of one of the buildings where we used to hang out, and one summer we hid this kid there whom the police were after. His name was Bobby Fogerty."

"I doubt they were really after him," said Andy. "I mean, I know we thought so then, but he was only wanted for shoplifting. I'm sure they had better things to do."

"Well, at the time we believed they were. Anyway," said Lulu, "we hid him there for the rest of the summer. Then, around the end of August, Bobby decided to try to get out of the country, head for Canada—"

"You gave him the idea to begin with," said Andy.

"It was a good idea."

"And Lulu decided to go with him."

"It wasn't so much with him," said Lulu, "it was more that I wanted to run away from home."

"Why did you want to do that?" asked Mary.

Lulu was silent.

"Her father drank," said Andy.

"And whose father doesn't drink?" asked Mary.

"It wasn't my dad," said Lulu, "it was my mother. Always screaming at me, always telling me I was worthless and just like my father. I looked just like him, and I was his favorite, so when she couldn't get at him, she'd take it out on me. I used to run away regularly. One of my earliest memories is of collecting road maps, the kind you used to be able to get free at gas stations, and then packing up my treasures in a handkerchief and taking off."

"But not with some sixteen-year-old," said Andy.

"Oh, Bobby was harmless," said Lulu.

"He was a normal sixteen-year-old in many respects."

"You're talking about sex," said Lulu. "He didn't see me as a girl. I didn't have any boobs to speak of, and I dressed like a boy. He never once gave me a problem. In fact, I think he probably liked me the least of all of us because I was always ordering him around."

Andy said, "So Lulu got the idea that she and Bobby would ride the trains to Canada like hoboes, which was one of her fantasies."

"So I stole some money from my mother and took off with Bobby in the middle of the night, and we got halfway to Toronto when the police were waiting for us at one of the stops."

"Neil did what we should've done, Lulu," said Andy. "You would've done the same."

"I never would!" said Lulu.

"Lulu, you were just a kid."

"It was betrayal, pure and simple."

"What do you think, Mary?" asked Andy, sure that she would agree with him.

"Aye, it was betrayal all right," said Mary from the seat behind him.

"You agree with me?" asked Lulu.

"Oh, yes. People have been killed for less than that."

Lulu crossed her arms and gave Andy a smug look.

"We're not talking Northern Ireland and the Provos," said Andy. "The worst you could call him was a snitch, and what kid hasn't snitched on another?"

"I never did," said Lulu. "I would never snitch on a friend. I thought our friendship was sacred."

"I don't know," said Andy, "I guess I'll never understand women."

"That's because you're a man and men are weak," said Lulu.

"Don't get like that with me, I wasn't the one who snitched on you."

"Only because you hadn't the guts."

"So," said Mary, "this boy who betrayed you will be there tonight?"

"He's a good man," said Andy, "and Lulu's giving you the wrong idea about him. Anyway, he wasn't like us. He was from a rich family, went to private schools. He wasn't brought up like us. And what Lulu is neglecting to tell you is that she had a crush on him."

"I never!"

"It was as obvious as the freckles on your nose."

"I wasn't the least interested in boys at that age."

"You're remembering what you want to remember," said Andy. "Ask Kevin, he'll agree with me."

"Kevin knows I hated Neil's guts."

"Sure, afterward. But at the time Kevin and I used to talk about it."

"You talked about me behind my back?"

"You didn't have us completely under your thumb, Lulu. Sure we talked about you. We didn't understand much about sex in those days, but even we could see the sparks between the two of you when you were together. To tell you the truth, we were envious."

"Get out of here!"

"It's true. Sometimes the two of you made us feel left out."

"This is all blarney," Lulu said to Mary. "If anything, Neil and I were always in competition. We were always trying to outdo each other."

"And you say I'm talking blarney?" asked Andy. "You were the competitive one, with all of us. Neil just humored you. Furthermore, in a lot of ways you and Neil are exactly alike. Either one of you could talk anyone into anything, and the hell with the consequences."

"And Kevin? What's he like?" asked Mary.

"This is ridiculous," said Andy. "The way we're talking, Mary is going to be expecting a couple of kids. This all happened twenty years ago. Only Lulu is still obsessed with her childhood."

"No way," said Lulu. "I couldn't wait to grow up. And as soon as I did, it was out of that house for good."

"You'll like Kevin," Andy said to Mary. "He's good-looking and funny and charms all the women. In case you're getting ideas, though, he's also married."

"If you could call that a marriage," said Lulu.

"It's lasted ten years, hasn't it?"

"Only because Kevin has always been lazy."

"I don't know what you have against Caroline. She's always great when I go over there to dinner."

"You like anyone who cooks for you."

"And you would dislike anyone any of us married. You want us to still be a gang with everyone else outsiders."

"Well, I like your gang sight unseen," said Mary, who Andy figured was trying to make peace from the back seat. "Aren't they making a wee house just for me?"

"Well, just do me one favor," Lulu said to Andy. "Don't leave me alone with Neil."

"Kevin and I will be there with you."

"All right," said Lulu, "just see that you are."

LULU INTRODUCED MARY to Patrick Flanagan as her friend from Dublin. The bartender, with eyebrow cocked, put on his best brogue when he said, "Mary Moore from Dublin, is it? And what would you be doin' with the likes of Lulu and her rabble-rousin' friends?"

"And aren't all Irish rabble-rousers?" Mary countered.

"Sure and you'll all be wanting a bit of the brew," said Patrick, pouring them each a draft on the house.

Andy found them a table way off in a corner, and they saw the others come in before they were seen. Lulu saw Andy doing a double take and turned around to see a sheepish-looking Kevin followed by the redoubtable Caroline, with Neil bringing up the rear.

"What in the hell?" said Andy, looking once again.

"What's the matter?" asked Mary.

"It looks like Kevin has brought his wife," Lulu told her. That wasn't quite acceptable, but then who was she to be complaining when she had included Mary? Although what Kevin ever saw in that useless, social wife of his, Lulu couldn't figure out. She hadn't thought Kevin was so shallow as to go for only looks. And as far as Lulu could tell, looks were the only thing Caroline possessed in any discernible quantity. Not that she'd seen much of her since the day they got married, but she'd heard enough about her to know.

In the general confusion of introductions, Neil managed to sneak the chair next to Lulu and was already seated before Lulu could do anything about it. She saw Neil giving Mary a quick once-over, and Kevin give her a slower look, then Patrick was by their table, ostensibly to take their order, but giving them all the once-over.

"If ever I saw a group that looked to be up to no good," he muttered.

"We're just having our usual beer," said Kevin.

"And naturally you have to be dressed all in black to enjoy a beer," said Patrick. "If I didn't know you better, I'd be suspicious you were off to do a second-story job."

To Lulu, they didn't look like a group of criminals sitting around the table; they looked like three couples out on dates, and she didn't like that at all. Kevin was sitting with his wife, Andy was by Mary and looking half-enamored of her already, and Neil was by her side. How all this came about she didn't know, but she didn't like it.

"How've you been?" she asked, looking across the table at Caroline. She hadn't seen the woman for two or three years and then it had been at some boring suburban Christmas party at Caroline and Kevin's house.

Caroline didn't attempt to mask her dislike of Lulu when she replied, "What you really want to know is what I'm doing here."

"What *are* you doing here?" asked Lulu.

"What we're all doing," said Neil. "She came along to help."

"And your friend?" countered Caroline, "what's she doing here?"

"You mean Mary?" asked Lulu. "Mary is going to move into the house we're putting up. Mary is homeless."

She had half expected Caroline to recoil in distaste at the news. Instead she looked properly intrigued.

Mary smiled. "I'd the misinformed notion that everyone in the States had a house and a car and a telly."

"Ah, well," said Caroline, secure, Lulu supposed, in the knowledge she had all three, "you have your freedom. Don't take that lightly." It seemed a curious thing for Caroline to say.

"I never take that lightly," said Mary.

The beer arrived, and Andy, as usual, took over as the peacemaker. "So, Neil, have you decided on a location?"

"Since when has Neil been appointed—" began Lulu, but Andy talked right through her.

"Neil is our American History buff, Lulu. We thought it only fitting that we pick historical sights. The better to get our message across."

"Nobody told me about this," said Lulu, feeling compelled to complain since she hadn't been informed, but actually liking the idea quite a lot. If they wanted to make a statement, was there a more fitting way?

"Do you like the idea?" Neil asked her.

"Yes," admitted Lulu. "Yes, I like the idea quite a bit. Use the historical sites where the revolutionaries fought for freedom, a freedom that now means not enough housing for the poor."

Kevin said, "From a public-relations point of view, it's ideal. We ought to get great coverage on it. We were thinking of starting off with Bunker Hill."

"Yes," said Lulu. "That's perfect. A perfect spot for the homeless."

"I didn't know you were anticipating publicity," said Mary, suddenly sounding tentative and rather shy.

Lulu could've kicked herself for forgetting about Mary's illegality. Of course, publicity would be the last thing she'd want.

"Could we do the first one a little more privately?" asked Lulu, looking around the table to gauge the reaction. "Just to see if it flies?"

"I think we should go for all the publicity we can get," Neil argued. "Maybe we can shame the authorities into doing something major about the problem."

"The thing is," said Lulu, "the first house is going to Mary, and I don't think it's fair to force her into publicity she doesn't want. I mean, our major concern should be for the feelings of the homeless."

"You're right, of course," said Neil. "We'll find some place a little more private for tonight. There's a small park by a library out on Salem Street that would be just the thing. Relatively safe, secluded, not apt to cause a stir. I used to live out that way, and I'd use the park to read in sometimes. Hours would go by, and I'd never see another person."

"What do you think, Mary?" asked Lulu, managing to interrupt Neil before he talked them all to death.

"It sounds perfect," said Mary.

Andy, who lived in that area himself, looked pleased.

"But after this, I say we go for the publicity," said Kevin.

Caroline smiled. "You and your publicity. Don't you get enough of that with the Celtics?"

"A public-relations director never gets enough of it," Kevin informed her.

"For that location, I don't think we have to wait until the middle of the night," Neil said. "I don't know about the rest of you, but I can't wait to get started."

Lulu felt a surge of emotion go through her. The excitement had been building up all day, and now she could barely contain it. "Yes, let's do it now," she said.

There were grins all around the table.

"With a quick trip to the rest room first," suggested Caroline.

Caroline and Mary got up, and Lulu followed them. She hated to be seen following Caroline's lead in anything, but the truth of the matter was, she could never drink beer without having it immediately followed by a trip to the toilet.

They passed the bar on the way to the ladies' room, and Lulu couldn't help noticing the man, half-turned on the bar stool, who was watching their passage. He looked like a rock star or a clone of a sixties radical, with dark blond curly hair to his shoulders and small, round, gold-rimmed glasses perched halfway down his nose. Behind the glasses there was the glint of green.

She saw him give Caroline an admiring glance, then ignore Mary as his gaze zeroed in on her. The corners of his mouth turned up, revealing two dimples. Feeling like Cinderella trailing after her two glamorous sisters, Lulu paused and half turned to see if there was someone behind her who was the object of his smile. When she turned back, his grin had widened.

Charmed that such an appealing man was singling her out for his attention, she grinned back and then was about to say something when he turned his attention back to the bar.

When she got to the restroom, the door to the one stall was propped open. Mary was retching into the toilet as Caroline handed her moistened paper towels.

"What's the matter?" asked Lulu.

"She's sick," said Caroline.

"Yes, I can see that."

Mary's head lifted. "It's the beer on top of the excitement. I'm sorry."

"Do you want to go back to my apartment?" asked Lulu.

Mary stood up and flushed the toilet. She took one of the towels and wiped off her face. "Oh, no. I'm fine now. I would not miss this for the world."

"Are you sure?" asked Lulu, pushing past Caroline and putting her arm around Mary's shoulders. "Maybe you're coming down with the flu."

Mary shook her head. "I'm just not used to the drink. It's been a while. Really, I feel much better now."

"The fresh air will do you good," said Caroline.

"It's the sense of adventure, of excitement," said Lulu. "I used to feel like this when I was a kid." The only difference was in those days it was always her and the boys. It felt a little strange to be embarking on this adventure with two other women in tow.

Particularly Caroline, who was probably going to turn out to be a big pain in the kazoo. Well, if it got too cold or to be too much work or even too exciting for Kevin's hothouse wife, Lulu guessed that Caroline could always wait for them in the car.

This was something the Rooftop Gang could take care of all on its own.

As they finished up in the washroom, Mary said, "I really do feel the need of some air. Would you mind if I went straight out to the car?"

"I'll go with you," said Lulu. "Caroline can tell the guys we'll be outside."

"I like your gang," said Mary when they got outside. "And Caroline seems like a caring person."

"Umm," said Lulu, not committing herself to a position on Caroline.

"And your Neil is the handsome one."

"Neil? He's not mine, and I never thought of him as handsome."

"He's got the kind of dangerous looks that are hard to resist. He reminds me of that movie star of yours, the one who played the FBI man. Sean Connery was also in it. *The Untouchables*, that's the name."

"You mean Kevin Costner?" asked Lulu.

"Aye, that's the one. Your Neil looks just like him."

"He just looks rich, that's all."

"No, that's not it. I've met his type before. He's the kind you want to follow, and damn the consequences."

"You're perfectly welcome to follow him," said Lulu.

"You two are bound so close even I could see it, and me a stranger to all of you."

"I hate to accuse a nice woman like yourself of being full of blarney," said Lulu, "but you are."

"I think he's the reason you've never got married."

"The reason is, I grew up seeing firsthand what a bad marriage was like and saw no reason to follow in my family's footsteps."

"Didn't your parents stay together, then?"

"They stayed together," said Lulu. "Not because of any love between them, though. They were both good Catholics and took the sacrament seriously. In other words, they were scared of going straight to hell."

"You two are meant for each other," said Mary. "And if you don't end up together, it will be tragedy for both of you."

"Tragedy was the day I met him."

"Andy was right, you're just alike."

"I repeat," said Lulu. "Blarney. Pure blarney."

"And that's how tragedies come to be, Lulu. By people not seeing what's in front of their noses."

Lulu could see in front of her nose, all right, and it wasn't Kevin Costner she was seeing, either.

Chapter Four

It was a tight fit in the cab of the truck, with Neil and Caroline squeezed together on one side so that Kevin could get to the gearshift. Except for Kevin occasionally asking for directions, no one had said anything since they left the bar. There had been an air of excitement in the bar that Neil was sure could be felt by everyone. They were off on an adventure that could possibly affect all of their lives.

Neil could see that Kevin hadn't changed much since they were kids. Then he had raced his bike around corners with little regard for oncoming cars, weaving in and out of traffic, blowing a whistle he wore around his neck to warn pedestrians that he had no intention of stopping. Now he was doing the same thing with the pickup, only these days he was using the horn rather than the whistle, and his ability to judge distances seemed to have had diminished, only maybe it was just that he wasn't used to driving a truck. Since Caroline, who was sitting between them, didn't seem upset by her husband's driving, Neil decided to quit worrying and relax. Anyway, the guy was still alive, so he must be doing something right.

"She's impossible, she never changes," said Caroline, breaking the silence. Her words sounded thoughtful rather than complaining.

Neil felt the smile spread across his face. "You must be talking about our Lulu," he said, adding, almost to himself, "the little sweetheart."

"Who else?"

"You just don't know her," said Kevin, and Neil thought his friend had probably spent the last ten years justifying Lulu to Caroline. "Do I take a left here?" he asked Neil.

"No, next corner," said Neil. "Is Andy still behind us?"

Kevin glanced at the rearview mirror. "Yeah, he's still keeping up."

"I don't have to know her," said Caroline. "I've never seen her that she hasn't been rude to me."

"You're right," said Neil. "She hasn't changed. She doesn't know how to be subtle, and she doesn't know how to get along with other women, unless she's changed radically since I knew her. I don't remember her ever playing with girls. Hell, I don't remember her ever acting like a girl. Which was all right as far as we were concerned because none of us felt comfortable around girls." He was thinking out loud more than anything else.

"She seems to like that Mary," said Kevin.

Neil nodded. "Sure, and probably all the homeless women she works with. She's always been great with the downtrodden, or what she perceives as the downtrodden. But did she ever have any girl friends when she was a kid?"

"She didn't need 'em," said Kevin. "She had us."

"She still has you," Caroline muttered.

Kevin said, "You're still thinking of her as twelve, Neil. She had some female friends in high school and college. No one close, but she got along with them."

"You've got about two more blocks to go," said Neil. "It's dead around here at night. The most we're going to get is some guy walking his dog. Maybe we should have waited until later when all the dog walkers are asleep."

"We would've been too drunk later," said Kevin. "We probably would've put up a three-sided house, and no one would've wanted to live in it."

"Is this what you did when you were kids?" asked Caroline. "Run around breaking the law?"

"Sometimes, on a very small-scale. Mostly we saw ourselves more as avengers of justice," said Kevin.

"When we weren't being spies," said Neil.

"Or cowboys and Indians," added Kevin. "Although I guess that came before you met up with us, Neil. I don't remember playing cowboys and Indians with you.

Neil chuckled. "By the time I met up with you guys, you were too sophisticated for cowboys and Indians."

"I don't know about you, Neil," said Caroline, "but Kevin's not too sophisticated *now* for cowboys and Indians. I think he bought a VCR just so he could watch old westerns."

"Hasn't Kevin told you about when we were kids?" Neil asked Caroline.

"He won't tell me a thing. For all I know, he could've been born college age."

"Well, ask away, I'll tell you."

Kevin slammed on the brakes and pulled over to the curb. "Out," he said.

"I think we can park closer than this," said Neil.

"I mean *you*," said Kevin. "We swore a blood oath when we were kids never to reveal what we did, and now you're offering to break that oath."

Neil started to laugh.

"It's not funny," said Kevin.

"If you only knew how childish you sounded," said Caroline.

"I forgot about that blood oath," said Neil. "Sorry. My lips are sealed."

"I'll believe that when I see it," said Kevin.

"I don't believe you two," said Caroline. "Blood oaths!"

With a screech of rubber, Kevin pulled back onto the road. He flashed Caroline a grin of triumph.

Neil could remember Lulu with that prized possession of hers, that damned Swiss Army knife that she carried with her everywhere. She had made them all cut their arms, then transfer the blood to one another while vowing undying loyalty to the Rooftop Gang, which included a pledge never to reveal their secrets. At the time he'd been excited about it, not only having his friends' blood running through his veins, but the fact that he now had Irish blood mixing in with his own, which was something no one else in his family had. It made him special. He remembered thinking at the time that it created a real bond between them, especially between him and Lulu. It had felt very romantic, a feeling he had never had prior to that day. Still, it was hard to believe that Kevin was still taking it seriously twenty years later. The scar on his arm had disappeared long ago, and he'd completely forgotten about it. He wondered what else he'd forgotten.

"On the right," Neil said.

Kevin pulled over to the curb and shut off the engine. A moment later Andy pulled up behind them and parked.

"You want to stay in here with the heater on while we unload the stuff?" Kevin asked Caroline.

"Why would I want to stay in here?" asked Caroline.

"I don't know, I just thought—"

"Well, you thought wrong," said Caroline. "I'll bet you wouldn't ask Lulu if she wanted to stay in the truck."

"Yes, but Lulu wants to be out there bossing everyone around," said Neil, getting a laugh from Caroline.

"My God, treason in the ranks already," said Kevin, opening the door to the truck and climbing out. "I won't tell Lulu you said that."

Caroline put her hand on Neil's arm as he reached to open the door. "I take it you're not as enamored of Lulu as Andy and Kevin are."

"Oh, I wouldn't say that," said Neil.

"It doesn't sound like it."

"Andy and Kevin were never enamored of her. She scared them to death. She didn't scare me."

"But you're enamored?"

Neil shrugged. "I don't know how to answer that, Caroline. This is the first time I've seen much of her in twenty years. I was always drawn to her, though. I'll admit that."

"So was Kevin."

"No. They were just buddies."

"That's where you're wrong," said Caroline. "They went together all through high school."

"I didn't know that."

"He's still in love with her."

"I think you're wrong about that." But he wasn't sure, of course. Perhaps that's why Lulu was still single at thirty-two and why Kevin appeared to be in a bad marriage. And yet he didn't get the sense when they were together that Lulu and Kevin were anything more than good friends. If anything, she seemed closer to Andy, albeit in a sibling sort of way. Anyway, he preferred to think that she was waiting for him.

He got out of the truck and walked around to the back where Kevin was lifting down the tailgate and pulling aside the tarp to get at the building materials. Neil moved to help him, and together they wrestled the sides of the house out and got them standing up and leaning against a convenient tree.

"What can I do?" asked Caroline, joining them.

"You can carry the toolbox," said Kevin.

"I can carry more than that," said Caroline, giving a tug on the roof section and pulling it out by herself. "I'll carry this."

"That's too heavy for you," said Kevin. "Let one of the guys carry it."

But Caroline already had hoisted it up and balanced against one shoulder, and appeared to be holding it effortlessly.

"I'm impressed," said Neil.

"She lifts weights," said Kevin, sounding scornful. "Says it gives her strength, but I notice she always makes me carry the groceries. Waste of time for a woman, if you ask me."

"What is?" asked Lulu, coming up next to them.

"Lifting weights," said Kevin. "Building muscles."

"But it's all right for men, of course."

"Of course," agreed Kevin.

Lulu shook her head. "I thought I beat that nonsense out of you at eight, the first time we arm wrestled."

"That's when we were kids and you were still bigger than me," said Kevin. "Want to give it a try now?"

Andy stepped between them. "We don't have time for games, folks. Let's get to work."

"I bet I could still beat you," Lulu told Kevin. "You might be big, but you're sure not in shape."

Kevin laughed. "Like you are? I don't see you belonging to any health club, Lulu."

Andy physically separated them, taking each by an arm and moving them apart. "Come on, boys and girls, no fighting in the ranks."

"I challenge you later at Flanagan's," said Kevin.

"You're on," said Lulu, and Neil wondered at his attraction for a woman who still sounded like a ten-year-old tomboy. Did that make him as juvenile as she sometimes acted? Were he and Lulu socially retarded to the age of twelve?

With the three men carrying the structure and the floor, Caroline carrying the roof, Lulu dragging the door behind her and Mary bringing up the rear with the toolbox, they walked down a path through some trees and ended up in a small clearing. Some of the light from the street lamps filtered through the foliage, and the moonlight added to it. Neil didn't think they'd even need to use the flashlight.

"This is a good location," said Neil. "What do you think?"

"Nice," said Lulu. "Secluded. Maybe no one will spot this one for a while."

"It's like being out of the city," said Andy. "And there's even a park bench to sit on."

"It's a darlin' place," said Mary. "You can almost sense the wee folk hiding behind the trees."

"Well, the wee folk aren't going to put it up, so let's get started," said Kevin. "Why don't you women sit over there on the bench while we get the structure up."

Neil laughed out loud at the way Lulu's back immediately went up. "Where did he get this attitude?" Lulu asked Caroline.

"I thought he was born with it," said Caroline.

Lulu shook her head. "He didn't used to be that way."

"It's going to take all of us, anyway," said Neil. He started to pull the floor over so that it would be partially protected by the tree. It would offer some shade in the summer, if the house was still standing, by then. Andy moved to help him, and they got in it place. "How about this location?" he asked Mary.

She shrugged, as though leaving the decision up to him. He wondered about her for a moment. She seemed a shy, fey creature, someone out of a fairy-tale book and not well grounded in the real world. She also seemed unlike any homeless person he had ever come across. He could see that Andy was strongly attracted to her. He could appreciate her appeal and yet couldn't feel any himself. A tough little tomboy seemed to have spoiled him for the more feminine variety of women. He liked Caroline, though, and thought Kevin a damn fool for not appreciating her.

They all helped to carry the main structure over and unfold it to put it in place. The four sides were fitted together with hinges. Only the floor and the roof had to be nailed into place.

The house was a six-foot-high structure of inch-thick plywood that would have formed a perfect cube, except that Neil had designed it with a slanted roof so that snow would slide off. Instead of windows, he had decided, at the last minute, to place a plastic skylight in the roof: it would let in light but ensure the privacy of the occupant.

The original members of the Rooftop Gang each took a hammer and nails and staked out one side of the house, kneeling on the ground to nail the sides to the floor.

For a minute there was only the sound of nails being pounded into wood, and then Neil heard Kevin curse, curse again, and then Caroline say, "Here, let me do it for you, you're such a klutz."

Neil looked around, expecting fireworks. It really surprised him when Kevin handed the hammer over to his wife. It surprised him more when he saw the skill and efficiency of Caroline, who quickly finished her side and moved on to help him. He had a feeling she didn't have the guts to offer help to Lulu. She was good, so good she could get a job in construction anytime.

Andy was also getting help with his side from Mary. And if the men didn't watch their step, the women were really going to show them up on this job.

Neil finished his side and walked around to inspect the others' work. Caroline's nails had been perfectly spaced, a very professional job. Lulu, who was just finishing, had bent a few nails in her eagerness to get the house finished, but she had put in enough to hold it firmly. Andy's were fine, but he worked so slowly and methodically that Mary was doing half his work for him, and doing it even better.

Neil wondered if the way someone hammered nails was any indication of character.

The roof was lifted by the men and set in place. Then Andy and Kevin held it still while Neil and Caroline nailed it down. Lulu and Mary took off somewhere while this was going on, but before the last nail was hammered in, Neil saw them return carrying a folding cot and several shopping bags. They set them on the bench, and then Mary went over to see how they were doing.

She was a beautiful woman, Mary Moore, and Neil wondered again why he wasn't attracted to her. Andy obviously was, despite the fact she was completely different from Lulu, whom he had always idolized. Neil supposed half the reason was that he wasn't attracted to victims. He felt sorry for them, he even wanted to help them, but as far as attraction went, he was compelled toward survivors. Whether Mary would turn out to be survivor or not he had no way of knowing, but he had a feeling Lulu had been one from birth. It was the spirit in her that drew him, the indomitable spirit she had possessed as a child and that was still evident in everything she did. He had yet to find it that strong in any other woman.

When the roof was on, all that was left to do was to hang the door. Andy tried his hand at it first, but soon gave up.

Neil didn't think it looked so difficult, but when he thought he had it on, the door refused to close properly.

Finally Caroline took over. In less time than it took the others to argue over it, she had the door hanging and the hasp on, and all that was left to do was for Lulu to cart the furnishings inside.

Neil could feel the elation in the air. From a theoretical house sketched on a napkin in a bar they had progressed, in only one week, to an actual house for the homeless. He could see it in the others as they exchanged smiles and patted each other on the back. And then Kevin picked up Caroline and swung her around. "Hey, we really did it!" he yelled.

Andy picked up Mary and gave her a spin, which was a pretty surprising thing for Andy to do unless he'd drastically changed since Neil had known him.

Neil turned to Lulu, who quickly backed away.

"Don't even think about it," she told him.

"Can I at least shake your hand?"

With a great show of reluctance, she held out her hand. He was just about to shake it when he thought the hell with it and instead grabbed her and spun her off the ground.

"It's not fair," said Lulu when he set her back down.

"What's not fair?"

"We used to all be the same size."

"That's what happens when girls and boys grow up," Neil told her.

"Well, it's still not fair, and I don't like it."

"You like it, all right."

"Damn it, Neil, why don't you ever take anything I say at face value?"

"Because it's the subtext I find interesting."

Lulu folded her arms across her chest. "Would you just answer me one thing, please, and no subtext?"

"Ask away," Neil said.

"Why, now, did you have to show up?"

"You mean, why did I walk back into your life now?"

"Just answer the question."

"I figured I'd given you enough time to grow up."

"Of all the hypocritical—"

He reached out and ruffled her bangs. "Well, I didn't want to wait until you were too old to enjoy me, now did I?"

"You insufferable—"

"I'll be damned if it's not still there. Quit fighting it, Lulu, it's a losing game."

"It's you who's lost it, Neil," said Lulu, turning away.

"It's not over till it's over," said Neil, getting in the last word, as usual.

Lulu walked over to Caroline. "Good work, Caroline," Lulu complimented her, an unusual enough gesture in itself, but most surprising when directed at Caroline. "If you hadn't been along, we'd have been here until dawn trying to get that door hung."

"There's nothing to hanging a door," said Caroline, her words not endearing her to the men.

Neil watched the way Andy was watching Mary. If he were the one interested in her, could he just leave her there for the night to fend for herself? Not that the neighborhood was dangerous, but there would be certain biological functions that she'd have to contend with in a public park that weren't going to be easy for her. He thought he'd probably be tempted to persuade her to come home with him, but in the end he wouldn't go through with it because he'd want to leave her with her independence and dignity. It wouldn't be easy, though.

SHE LOOKED SMALL AND LOST to Andy. He thought about her spending the night cold and alone in the small house. He could suffer through it himself if he had to, but a woman shouldn't have to be put in that position.

"How do you like your new home?" he asked Mary.

"It's like a gift from the heavens."

"Never mind the heavens, it's a gift from your friends. Are you sure you'll be all right on your own?"

"Don't go worrying about me, I'll be fine. How could I not, in a darlin' house like that. And Lulu's given me her sleeping bag, so I'll be as snug as a bug."

"My grandmother used to say that," Andy told her. "'As snug as a bug in a rug.'"

"Aye, so did my granny. I suppose all Irish grannies say it."

Andy saw a light go on inside the structure. He reached for Mary's hand, and they walked together over to the doorway of the house. Inside, Lulu had set up the cot with the sleeping bag on top. On top of the sleeping bag was a flannel nightgown, and alongside the cot was a folding TV tray with a Coleman battery-operated lantern on top. Beside the lantern was a stack of paperback books and a hand-carved angel in wood that looked as if it came from Mexico. It was painted in primary colors, and the face had a cheerful smile, unexpected in an angel. Lulu had even put an old, chenille bathroom rug on the floor next to the cot and was just now screwing a large hook into the wall by the door so that Mary would have somewhere to hang her clothes.

Then Lulu pulled out a cardboard tube from one of the shopping bags.

"What's in that?" he asked her.

"The last and the best," said Lulu, smiling a mysterious smile. "This is a housewarming gift I bought for Mary."

"You shouldn't have done it," said Mary. "You've already given me too much."

"Ah, but this is for the soul," said Lulu.

"And what's the angel for, if not the soul?" asked Mary.

Lulu grinned. "I'm talking about your Irish soul."

She pulled something out of the tube, and Andy saw that it was a poster. He hoped it wasn't something tacky like a Last Supper that glowed in the dark. Although, for all he knew, Mary might like something like that. His grandmother would have liked it.

Lulu reached into her pocket, pulled out some thumb tacks, then spread the poster on the wall. Not recognizing the people, Andy said, "Who's that?"

"Who's that?" asked Lulu. "Where have you been, Andy?"

Andy shrugged.

"So it's to be U2 for my soul, is it?" asked Mary, looking pleased at Lulu's choice.

"You know who they are?" Andy asked Mary.

She smiled at him. "They're Irish, aren't they? How could I not know?"

Lulu handed Mary a key. "This is to be padlock. No one will be able to break into the house, the good job we did on it."

"I wish there was some way I could thank all of you," said Mary, her voice breaking a little.

"You can thank us by coming back to Flanagan's and doing a little celebrating with us," said Kevin. "We'll have some proper food and a few brews."

"Thank you," said Mary, "but I'd rather stay in my new house. I'm afraid if I leave it, when I come back the leprechauns will have become jealous and stolen it away for their own."

"Not with that angel to guard over it," said Lulu.

"You don't have to worry, we'll bring you back," said Andy.

"I'm really weary and would like nothing more than to crawl into my sleeping bag and shut my eyes."

When she wouldn't be dissuaded, everyone lined up to give Mary a hug and wish her well, then they headed back to the street, leaving Andy alone with her.

"I'll truly be all right," said Mary, "but I appreciate the concern."

"I know you will," said Andy. "We wouldn't have set you up in a dangerous place." He debated a moment and then asked, "Do you have any money?"

"Enough until I find work."

"I hate to just leave you. You don't even have a phone."

"Lulu said she'd keep in touch."

"I was hoping I could keep in touch, too."

"I'd be glad of it, Andy."

"I was wondering...tomorrow's Saturday, would you care to have dinner with me? Unless you have other plans."

"It would be a great pleasure to have dinner with you."

"Shall I come by around seven?"

"I shall look forward to it."

He thought of kissing her, didn't have the guts, and was pleasantly surprised when she reached up and kissed him on the lips. It was a fleeting kiss, but all the sweeter for it. Then he waited while she went inside and put the bar in place.

When he got back to the car, the others had left and Lulu was leaning against it, looking up at the sky. No rain tonight, and no snow; the stars were all out in force. Maybe Mary would be able to see them through the skylight.

"I FEEL LIKE DANCING and singing and shouting," Lulu said to him. "We did it, Andy. We actually did it!"

"It makes you feel good, doesn't it?"

"It makes me feel wonderful. I haven't felt this good in years."

"Me, too."

Lulu gave him a closer look. "I have a feeling, my friend, that your good feelings have more to do with Mary Moore from Dublin than with the house."

"I think they're all tied in together."

"I feel the same way," said Lulu. "It's a real dividend that the first house we put up is for someone we know and care about."

"And it doesn't hurt that Neil's along, too."

"Just what did you mean by that, Andrew Keely?"

"I saw the two of you together."

"Then you must have seen we were fighting."

"One of these days you're going to realize that you and Neil fighting is like anyone else making love."

"What is it with you? Are you suddenly afraid I'm going to end up an old maid or something?"

"Not anymore."

"Thanks a lot, Andy."

Andy unlocked the car for her, then went over to the driver's side. He got in, reminded Lulu to fasten her seat belt, which was something she was wont to ignore, then started the car. "I feel like we shouldn't leave."

"Mary will be fine. She's stronger than she looks, Andy. She's been on her own for some time now."

"She's having dinner with me tomorrow night."

"Good. I'm going to take her over a few things tomorrow, including some groceries. And I'm going to ask around at a few of the rectories and see if they need anyone to cook or clean."

Andy could use someone to cook and clean. And to decorate his loft. And to be there for him when he came home at night. He began to picture Mary doing those things, and he liked the picture. He would take it slow with her, not scare her away. If everything went the way he'd like it to go, pretty soon there would be an empty little house for some other homeless person, and he wouldn't be alone anymore.

It was strange. All these years he had been looking for a clone of Lulu, and then, when he finally fell for a woman, she was about as different from Lulu as he could imagine. Instead of a brash, assertive American woman, he had found himself a sweet, soft-spoken, old-fashioned girl from across the sea.

THE ROOFTOP GANG PLUS ONE walked into Flanagan's looking as though they had just heisted a Brinks truck and gotten away with a million dollars each. Kevin was feeling so good he felt like buying drinks for the whole bar, which he mentioned to the others, but Lulu told him to cool it, that they were acting suspicious. She reminded him that in any Irish bar there was a percentage—usually high—of Irish cops. And they didn't want to raise any suspicions. Not that a sober cop would give them a problem, but a cop with some brew inside of him was another matter entirely.

They stopped at the bar for a fast beer before getting a table. "To the Rooftop Gang," Andy sang out, holding up his glass to the others.

"And to Caroline," added Neil.

"Damn right," said Lulu. "We could've used you in the old Rooftop Gang," she told her.

"I was more into horses at that age," said Caroline, surprised by Lulu's comments.

"Horse shows and all that?" asked Lulu, and Kevin just knew that Lulu was picturing Caroline in perfect jodhpurs, a shelf full of trophies in her bedroom.

"It was more like me and my brothers playing at Jesse James and the gang on horseback," she said.

Kevin could almost see Lulu mentally revising her opinion of Caroline yet again. It was something he hadn't known about her, either. For some reason neither of them ever talked much about their childhoods. Jesse James and his gang—that sounded pretty good. He wondered if he would've preferred a horse to a bike at that age. He tried to picture the Rooftop Gang on horses, but it didn't work. He was pretty sure none of them had ever been near a horse, except maybe Neil. But Neil had never mentioned them.

Kevin noticed the long-haired guy at the bar watching Lulu. The guy looked as if he belonged in another era or another bar. "You've got an admirer," he said to Lulu, nudging her in the side.

Lulu glanced over and then lowered her eyes. "Knock it off, Kevin," she said.

"Want me to invite him to join us?"

Lulu sneaked another look. "No, I want to celebrate."

"Maybe he'd like to celebrate with us."

"Leave her alone," said Caroline. "Anyway, this is a private celebration." Then she took a good look at the guy watching Lulu. "He is pretty cute, though."

"That's your idea of cute?" Kevin asked her. "He looks like a musician."

Andy said, "He looks like one of those guys in that poster, Lulu."

"He doesn't look anything like the guys in U2," said Lulu.

"In case you hadn't noticed," Caroline informed Kevin, "a lot of women are attracted to musicians. If Sting was over at the bar admiring me, you wouldn't catch me by your side for long."

"That's telling him," said Neil.

"Sting?" asked Kevin. "I didn't even know you liked Sting."

"I don't tell you everything."

Neil got everyone's attention by saying to Lulu, "Would you fancy me more if I hung a guitar around my neck?"

"I'd fancy you more with a noose around your neck," said Lulu.

"This is a cruel woman," said Neil. "A cruel heartless woman who deserves her fate."

"And what might that be?" Lulu asked him.

"A cold bed on a winter's night."

"For your information, I have an electric blanket," said Lulu.

"I've got to tell you," said Caroline, "it's not the same."

"I say let's get a table," said Andy. "I don't know about you guys, but I'm about starved."

They headed for the back of the bar and found their regular table empty. Patrick came back and said, "The usual?" and they all nodded but Caroline.

"What's the usual?" she asked Kevin.

"Roast beef platter."

"With *your* cholesterol?"

"Shut up about that," he said to her, but Andy had already picked up on it.

"Your cholesterol high?"

"I'm trying to get it down," said Kevin.

Caroline ordered some broiled chicken and a salad and made Kevin feel guilty the entire time he was eating the roast beef and mashed potatoes with gravy. Once a week wasn't going to kill him, was it? The rest of the week he stuck to what the doctor had told him to eat, which was chicken and fish, chicken and fish, until he almost gagged at the sight of them. And he had managed to get his cholesterol down in the last six months.

"This is the best thing we've ever done," said Lulu, smiling at those around the table.

"I know you're not talking about the food," said Caroline.

"Don't you all feel good?" asked Lulu. "I mean, we actually housed one of the homeless. I've never felt this much satisfaction from my job. We may give women beds, but we sure don't give them back their self-respect." She glanced around the table with a mischievous look. "If we do one a week, that'll be fifty-two a year."

"That wouldn't take us any time at all," said Andy. "I bet we could do two a week, or even three."

"Cluster housing," said Neil. "That way they'd be in groups and less likely to get thrown out."

"We're talking a lot of money, though," said Kevin, knowing that Lulu wouldn't be able to afford her share on the salary she got.

"I was thinking about that," said Andy. "My company could pay for them. We're always donating money to different things—mostly for tax purposes, of course—but I'd rather put it in our own project."

"You're not going to be able to write this off," said Neil. "This isn't like saving the whales. We're not a charitable organization."

"Then let's become one," said Lulu. "How about Rooftoppers, Inc.? We could incorporate."

"I think we'd have a lot of trouble being approved as a nonprofit corporation," said Neil. "Anyway, doing it legally would hold up what we want to do."

"That's not the way to look at it anyway," said Andy. "Our purpose isn't to do it legally. But I'd still like to pick up the tab for the materials. My company's making more money than we know what to do with."

"Are we going to be proud or are we going to accept his offer?" asked Kevin, knowing that it would probably be Lulu who would object.

But she surprised him. "Sure we're going to accept," she said. "It's about time one of you capitalists started doing some good."

"I'd like to donate some paint," said Caroline.

"What do you mean, *you*?" Kevin asked her.

"I mean *me*," said Caroline. "I have my own money, which you never want me to spend."

"We don't need paint," said Kevin.

"Well, I think you're wrong," said Caroline. "Aesthetically speaking, plywood doesn't make it. I think the authorities would be much less likely to tear down a good-looking house than one that looks jerry-built."

"Are you insulting our first effort?" asked Neil. "What do you say, gang? Are we going to let her get away with that?"

Caroline smiled. "I'm just saying it would look better with a couple of coats of paint."

"Dark green would be nice," said Lulu, "and it would blend into the scenery. Maybe a white roof to keep it cooler in the summer, and some white trim on the door."

"It's going to really slow us down to put a couple of coats of paint on," said Andy.

"I'll paint them during the week," said Caroline. "I don't have anything better to do."

"You know what we could also do?" said Lulu. "We ought to be able to pick up six-foot pieces of carpeting cheap. Stuff they have left over from jobs."

"Wall to wall carpeting?" asked Kevin. "Are you nuts?"

"Why not?" asked Lulu. "As it is, they're going to get splinters from the floors."

"Next you're going to want appliances, maybe a bathroom added on," said Kevin, seeing this becoming a full-time occupation for all of them.

Lulu's eyes widened. "I never thought of that. What's Mary going to do for a bathroom?"

"What do any homeless do?" asked Caroline.

"I guess use public facilities," said Lulu.

Andy said, "Well, there's a public library next door."

"Look," said Neil, "we can't do everything for them. They're going to have to figure those things out for themselves."

"So where are we going to put up the next three?" asked Caroline.

"We?" asked Kevin.

Caroline gave him a sweet smile. "You don't think you're leaving me out, do you?"

"I say we go back to our original plan and use Bunker Hill," said Neil. "Make a real statement this time."

"Bunker Hill," said Lulu, her eyes shining. "Oh, I love that."

"To Bunker Hill," said Andy, raising his glass. They all joined in the toast.

FOR TEN YEARS LULU HAD BEEN feeling sorry for Kevin. To hear him talk, his wife was always complaining about something, particularly about his Friday nights out with the gang. Lulu had often wondered why Kevin didn't leave her, just walk out of the marriage. Now, in the space of one evening, all her beliefs about that marriage were being challenged. She found herself, almost against her will, liking Caroline. She would almost say—and this really felt like treason—that she liked her better than Kevin. Certainly Caroline had been a lot more fun to work with and much more enthusiastic about the project than Kevin had been.

She had always gotten the feeling that one of the problems with the marriage was the fact that there weren't any children. Kevin, in roundabout ways, had led the others to believe that this was because Caroline didn't want children. This could still be true, of course, but Lulu was beginning to suspect that the one who didn't want children was Kevin, who behaved, at least around his wife, rather like a child himself. Perhaps he didn't want competition when it came to her attention.

At any rate, she was glad Caroline was going to be involved in their housing project. Without her, Lulu doubted whether any of the houses would even end up with doors. She also liked the suggestion about the paint. Maybe she and Caroline could go over someday and paint Mary's house for her. And put in some carpet. And maybe a few other things Lulu had stuck away in her apartment that she didn't need.

She was sorry when Kevin said something about being beat and making it an early night. She had been prepared to stay until the bar closed, celebrating with her friends. She was still too excited about the whole thing to go home and go to sleep. And she was also going to miss the bedtime talk with Mary.

"Hey, you can't cut out on us this early," said Andy, when Kevin got up from the table.

"Just let me visit the rest room before we leave," said Caroline, also getting up.

Lulu followed her into the ladies' room. "I was thinking..." Lulu said, taking the stall next to Caroline.

Caroline's disembodied voice wafted over the partition. "Listen, I hope you didn't mind my coming along."

"You were great," said Lulu. "You should've started coming years ago."

"Thanks. My idea of a good time isn't getting drunk, though."

"That's 'cause you don't work. When you work all week, you fell like letting off steam by Friday night."

"I'd like to work, but every time I suggest it, Kevin has a fit."

"So don't listen to him."

"I'm thinking of going back to school the first of the year for a teaching certificate. I think I can get everything I need in one semester. Don't mention it to Kevin, though. I haven't told him about it yet."

"I think that's great," said Lulu. "What I was thinking was, would you want to paint Mary's house with me?"

"I'd love to. Do you want to do it tomorrow?"

"Won't Kevin mind?"

There was the sound of two toilets flushing, and then both women came out and walked over to the sink.

"Kevin won't even notice," said Caroline. "During football season, he never leaves the TV set. I'll just set out some junk food and leave."

"Good. I'll call you in the morning."

When they left the ladies' room, Kevin was waiting by the door. Lulu said good-night to them, thinking Neil had already gone outside. Lucky for her, because now she wouldn't have to bother being polite and saying good-night to him. She really hated having to be polite.

As she walked by the bar, the long-haired guy who she'd seen early that evening said hi. She debated for a moment whether to return the greeting. If she had been all alone, she wouldn't, as it would amount to a pick-up. But since she was obviously with friends, and Andy was at the table waiting for her, she didn't see how it could hurt anything to be friendly.

"Hi," she said, getting a grin from him. He really was cute, and she was half-tempted to drag him back to the table with her. But then she and Andy would have to curtail the conversation about their adventure, and she didn't want to have to do that. Anyway, she wasn't looking for a man.

She'd just gotten rid of one not two months before, and she was still enjoying the freedom.

When she got back to the table she was sorry she hadn't invited him along as Neil was still sitting there.

"I'm giving him a ride home," said Andy, seeing her look.

"Do you mind?" asked Neil, his eyes challenging her.

"Of course not," said Lulu, lying and having the satisfaction of knowing he knew she was lying. "I was sorry they left so soon, I still feel like celebrating."

Neil looked hugely amused.

"Great," said Andy, "let's order us another round."

ANDY DIDN'T KNOW what to do. Another beer hadn't seemed to help. Something had gone out of the celebration as soon as Lulu had returned to the table to find Neil still there. Andy tried to revive the spirit of the occasion, but he wasn't getting any help. Neil looked remote; Lulu looked as though she'd rather be anywhere else. Both of them weren't saying anything, which, for the two of them, had to be an all-time first.

"Hey," said Andy, inspiration having hit, "remember that time you two got locked in the boiler room and we didn't find you for six hours?"

Lulu didn't blush. Lulu didn't know the meaning of *blush*. But she turned a lighter shade of white than her usual winter hue. Neil looked surprised and then gave a bark of laughter.

Andy backed down. "I said something wrong, am I right? One small attempt at nostalgia, and I screwed it up."

"I thought we'd die of the heat," said Neil.

"Heat?" asked Andy. "It couldn't have been from the boiler because it was the middle of summer."

"That's just it," said Neil. "It was in the nineties outside and over a hundred in that boiler room. And being locked up with Lulu created a little more heat."

"Shut your mouth, Neil," said Lulu.

"I just meant you were madder than hell, that's all. You blamed me for getting us locked in."

"We couldn't figure out where you two had disappeared to," said Andy, happy now that he had gotten the ball rolling. "I mean, a simple game of hide-and-seek, and we couldn't find either of you. I finally had to go home to dinner."

"Locked in there with no food and no water," said Lulu, some of the color returning to her face.

"What'd you do in there for six hours?" asked Andy.

Dead silence.

"Hey, come on, what's the big secret? You were only twelve, it's not like anything happened."

"We fought," said Lulu.

"Yeah, I guess you could say that," said Neil.

Andy wasn't buying that. "You fought for six straight hours? Well, yeah, I guess I can believe that. You're still fighting."

"We fought while we tried to figure a way out," said Lulu. "Unfortunately, there wasn't one."

"If you hadn't gone in there in the first place . . ." Neil began.

"If you hadn't been so stupid," said Lulu. "That was my hiding place. I had been saving it for the right time. I had the door ajar and was hiding behind the boiler, and then you came in and shut it. I couldn't believe how stupid you were."

Neil shrugged. "What did I know about boiler rooms? I lived in a house."

"Poor little rich boy," muttered Lulu.

Neil unexpectedly laughed. Andy could remember the time when Lulu could really get to Neil with that remark, but it wasn't working anymore.

"Right," said Neil. "Locked up with the biggest juvenile delinquent in South Boston." That brought a smug look to Lulu's face.

"You were no angel," she said.

"Compared to you? Compared to you, I was the Virgin—"

"Now, now," cautioned Andy, "let's not get sacrilegious."

"What do you expect of a Protestant?" asked Lulu.

It was almost like old times, thought Andy, smiling at the two of them.

Chapter Five

Andy pulled up in front of an old building in a bad part of town and stopped. Neil looked out the window at the neighborhood. So this is where Lulu lived. There'd been countless times he'd thought of driving by, but he never had. Just as there'd been countless times he'd picked up the phone to call her and then changed his mind. It had never seemed like the right time. If he kept waiting for the perfect moment, though, it would probably never happen.

"I'll call you," Lulu said to Andy, then half turned to say good-night to Neil. He noticed that she didn't meet his eyes, just said the words in his direction, then quickly opened the door and got out. As though she could escape memories that easily.

Andy watched her as she walked to her building. Neil was surprised Andy didn't just walk her to the door and wait until she was inside, but he guessed Lulu had discouraged that kind of behavior in the past.

"I'm getting out here," Neil said, coming to a quick decision.

"Here?"

"I want to talk to her."

"That's up to you," said Andy, "but if I know Lulu, she'll slam the door in your face, and you'll be stuck in the cold trying to find a taxi. And that isn't any easy thing to do in this neighborhood."

"We need to talk."

Andy nodded. "I agree with you. I just don't think this is the right time."

"Well, as you said, maybe she'll slam the door in my face, but I have a feeling if we don't talk now, it's going to be too late."

He pushed the seat back forward and got out of the car. Andy wished him good luck before driving off.

By the time he got to her door, she was already inside. He should have moved faster. He knocked loudly on the door, then heard her unlocking it on the other side, saying, "What did I forget now?" And then she had the door open and was staring at him.

"We have to talk," he said, but she was already pushing the door shut. He caught it before it closed and put his weight against it, forcing it open, and then he stepped inside. It wasn't the kind of thing he usually did. In fact, it was the kind of behavior designed to half scare a woman, particularly in the city, but he knew it wasn't going to frighten Lulu. Anger her probably, but not frighten her.

She took a step back from the door, arms folded across her chest, lower lip jutting out. "What do you think you're doing, Neil?"

"I just want to talk to you."

"It's late, can't we talk some other time?"

"No."

"If this has to do with the boiler room—"

"You know it does."

"I don't want to discuss it."

"I know you don't, Lulu. But it's that and a lot of other things, and we've wasted too many years and too much time not talking about it."

She looked frightened for a moment. She should look frightened. He felt frightened. It was always a scary thing when you put your emotions on the line.

Feeling unsure of himself but trying not to show it, he stepped past her into the room. If he hesitated now she'd demolish him. What he had to do was be in control and take charge quickly. That was the only way to handle Lulu, that and outtalking her, which he used to be pretty good at.

He looked around. He had been curious about how she lived for a long time and now, when he thought of her, he'd be able to picture her in the right setting. That was important to him. When he did sketches of her now, he'd be able to fill in the background.

There was a black cat playing dead on the couch, shelves full of books interspersed with fantastical angels, a dusty Red Sox pennant on a stick stuck in a vase in lieu of flowers, dusty blinds on the windows, a tweed couch, an antique rocking chair painted black and a round wood table under the windows with two black metal folding chairs. As small and as cluttered as it was, it felt like a home. Lulu had built herself a little nest. He thought it would be more Spartan, and he realized that all these years he had actually been picturing her living in their clubhouse.

She was still standing by the door as he took off his jacket and threw it down onto the rocking chair. "Are you going to be hospitable, or are we going to face-off like two boxers?"

There was a flicker of movement around her mouth. Dead serious as she could be about a lot of things, there was always that underlying sense of humor.

He picked up the cat and moved it to the center of the couch, then sat down in the corner. His rear end was going to end up covered with cat hair, but he didn't care. The cat was still playing dead, but the seat of the couch was warm from its body, which felt good in the cold room. He stretched his arm along the back of the couch and watched to see what Lulu would do next. Unless she had changed, it would be something unexpected.

Keeping her jacket on, as though for added protection, she pulled back some louvered doors, revealing a kitchen area. He waited for her to reach for the tea kettle, but instead she opened a cupboard and brought out a bottle of whiskey.

"I've had enough to drink," he told her.

"I haven't."

"Do you have to be drunk to talk to me?"

"Yes."

"You turned cowardly in your old age?"

She ignored him. She took out a jelly glass and poured herself a shot, quickly downing it. Then she carried the bottle and the glass over to the couch and put them on the coffee table. She went around the room, turning on lamps, and then she switched off the overhead light. The room looked better in the lamplight. Was she going to put on soft music next? Not likely, if he knew Lulu.

She sat down on the other end of the couch, the cat between them. She could have taken one of the chairs, but he was pretty sure she was trying to prove she had nothing to fear from him. Well, that was an error in judgment on her part.

He reached for the bottle and took a long swallow. It was smooth and warming and went down easy. "Why don't you take off your jacket and make yourself at home, pet?"

Her eyes flashed for a brief moment at his use of the word *pet*, but then she ignored him, her hand going behind the cat's ear to scratch. He could hear a low, rumbling sound and realized it was the cat purring. He hadn't thought of it for a long time, but the cat he had as a kid had sounded like that. Puff had always slept in his bed at night, attacking his feet whenever they moved and invariably ending up on his pillow by morning. Once he'd gotten fleas from his cat, who was a hunter during the day. He reached over now to give the cat a little pat or two, and Lulu's hand instantly retracted.

"You might as well get comfortable because I'm going to be here a while," he told her. "Cute place you got here—a little more homey than I would've figured it."

Narrowed eyes lifted to his. A defiant look, no doubt meant to scare him off. The pupils of her eyes were growing larger, turning the hazel to pure black. It was a trick she'd learned as a child, and it amused him that she still used it. It was supposed to be her intimidating look. It had scared the others, but it had never scared him.

"We're not locked up this time," she said.

At the memory, he felt a smile drift across his face.

SHE WAS REMEMBERING, TOO.

They'd all been twelve that summer, except for Andy, who would have his birthday in September. They were going into seventh grade and didn't consider themselves kids anymore. They didn't think of themselves as teenagers, either. Teenagers were kids who started to act silly. Girls started liking boys, boys started liking girls, and everything changed as a result. They all agreed they wanted to be grown-up, but none of them wanted to be a teenager in between.

The summer when Lulu was twelve consisted of endless days of over-ninety-degree heat and very little rain to cool things off. It was so hot on the roofs of the buildings that by noon the tar stuck to their shoes, and if they didn't move fast, they got stuck. The clubhouse was stifling, and use of it was out except for in the evening and early morning, and as a result, they took to the streets more than they had in previous years.

Hide-and-seek was a favorite game of theirs that summer. They didn't play it the way they'd been taught, which was indoors. They were too old to get excited about hiding in closets or under beds. Instead, they marked off a nine-block square of South Boston, a location everyone but Neil knew intimately, and they played it more like a complicated war maneuver than like hide-and-seek.

To be "it" was to be the commanding general. Instead of counting to one hundred, the person who was "it" would be tied up in the clubhouse. This allowed the others the time in which to hide. Once out of his ropes, "it" would be allowed the use of binoculars and a bike. Once "it" found the first one hiding, that person would be "it's" deputy and have to follow the leader's commands. The way they played it, a good game could last for hours.

Those hiding also had rules to follow. The first rule, of course, was the nine-block stricture. The second rule was that they each had to change hiding places every thirty minutes. The third rule was they had to hide alone.

That summer those hiding would seek out the coolest spots, and Lulu thought she had found one that was perfect. The few times she wasn't with the gang she would use her time to check out new hiding places. They used rooftops; they used alleys. There was a school playground that had been used several times. They would occasionally use a store, although the owners usually chased them out. This particular hiding place had never been used, and Lulu was waiting for the perfect occasion.

The day in question, Kevin was "it." As far as Lulu was concerned, he was the most formidable "it," except for herself. Neil might have been better at it than Kevin if Neil had known the neighborhood as well, but they had lived there all their lives and knew it almost as well as they knew their apartments. Andy wasn't a very good "it." Andy wasn't very good at hiding, either. Andy didn't like being alone.

They started the game at two in the afternoon that day and placed a three-hour time limit on it. This meant that at five o'clock, whether they had been found or not, they were to assemble in the clubhouse.

They tied up Kevin, securing him well enough to allow them a good ten minutes to get away. Then they all scattered. Lulu took off across the rooftops, guaranteed to shake Andy, who usually tried to follow her. Andy was scared to jump between roofs. At the end of the block she went down the fire escape and came out on the street. She headed west another block, then went south two blocks.

She made a quick stop on the way to get an orange drink and some bubble gum. Then she casually strolled into the apartment building, opened the door to the basement and headed down.

The door to the boiler room was ajar, just as it had been the first time she found it. It was dark in the boiler room but not too dark to see. The room didn't have windows, but the rest of the basement did, high up, so that enough light filtered through the dirty glass and leaked into the boiler room.

She sat down a crate and opened her can of orange soda. She rolled the can across her forehead to cool herself off, then took a long drink. The basements were usually several degrees cooler than outdoors and damp, but the heat wave had gone on so long even the basements were getting too hot.

Not more than a couple of minutes later, she heard footsteps on the stairs leading to the basement. Thinking it was the super and that he'd throw her out if he found her, she quickly ducked behind the boiler. She didn't think it likely that he'd come in there in the middle of the summer, but she wasn't going to take the chance of blowing her perfect hiding place.

She heard someone walking across the basement floor in the direction of the boiler room. She held her breath, afraid the sound of her breathing would give her away. Then two things happened at once. The door to the boiler room slammed shut, and she found herself in total darkness. She was just about to yell out, "Hey, you locked me in here," when she heard someone trying the door. Only whoever it was was trying it from the inside, which meant she was no longer alone in the boiler room.

Warnings from the nuns about men who molested little girls entered her consciousness, but she forced the thoughts back out. She wasn't even sure exactly what *molesting* meant. No one messed around with her, though; if some guy even tried, she'd scratch his eyes out.

Lulu threw the can of soda in the direction of the door. It hit the metal door with a crash, then she heard the can fall to the floor and roll around.

Then she heard someone laugh, and that really scared her. She was closed up in a small, dark room with someone who found it funny. It was probably some maniac who would try to kill her next. It could even be another Boston Strangler.

She slowly stood up, reached into the pocket of her jeans and drew out her Swiss Army knife. She pulled out the largest blade and held it in front of her. If anyone tried to attack her, he was going to get a gut full of metal.

"Who's in here?" asked Lulu, and was pleased to hear her voice sounding steady and even a little threatening.

The low laugh came again, this time from a different direction.

She turned to face the sound of the laugh. "I've got a knife on you. You've got to the count of ten to open the door and get out of here. One..."

"Sorry, Lulu, but it won't open."

"Neil?"

"It looks like it automatically locks when you shut it."

"You stupid jerk!"

"I didn't do it on purpose."

"What're you doing in my hiding place, anyway?"

"I was in a tree across the street when I saw you come in here. I just thought I'd check out where you were hiding."

"That's not the way we play the game, Neil. You know you aren't allowed to follow me."

"Well, that's tough, isn't it?"

"You cheated!"

"So what're going to do about it?"

She kicked the wall in frustration, managing only to end up with a sore toe. "That door can't be locked. The super'd get locked in."

"You try it, then, if you're so smart. It feels locked to me."

Lulu put her knife away and, feeling with her hands, made her way over to the door. She felt herself stepping in something sticky and remembered her orange drink. She tried the doorknob, but the door wouldn't open. She rattled the knob around, but nothing happened. "Great. We could be stuck in here till next winter."

"I doubt that," said Neil.

"Maybe if we threw our weight against it."

"It's metal. That door weighs a ton."

Lulu tried throwing her weight against it anyway, but the door didn't even move. It was about as effective as throwing herself against a brick wall. And now, to make things really perfect, her shoulder was sore, too.

"Yeah? Well, you think of something if you're so smart, Neil."

"Try picking the lock with your knife."

Pleased that he assumed she knew how to pick locks, Lulu took the knife back out, opened one of the smaller blades and tried to find the lock. "I don't think there's an opening on this side," she told him.

She heard him come up beside her, then felt his arm brush against hers as his hand moved over the door. "What's in here besides the boiler?" he asked her.

"A crate I was sitting on."

"That's it?"

"That's all I saw."

"No window?"

"If there was a window, Neil, we'd be able to see."

Neil chuckled.

"What's so funny?"

"I don't think Kevin's gonna find us."

"You better hope he does."

"Kevin won't think of it. Kevin figures you to be always hiding outdoors. When he's looking for you, he looks behind every bush and up every tree."

"I figured he did, that's why I came here. As soon as I found it, I knew he'd never look here."

"He knows Andy always hides on the ground."

"Andy doesn't like heights. The first time we went up on the rooftop, we had to practically carry Andy up."

"We could always try to get the boiler to work," said Neil. "The people in the building would complain fast enough if they started to get heat in the middle of the summer."

"I don't know anything about boilers, and we can't even see. And I know for sure *you* don't know anything about them."

"How do you know that?"

"Because you live in a house. I bet you've never even *seen* a boiler."

"Was that a can you threw at me?"

"Yeah, my orange drink. Thanks a lot. Now I'll probably die of thirst."

"We ought to bang on the door with it."

"No one's going to hear us down here unless the super comes down for something."

"Well, I sure hope Kevin's a little sharper today than usual. I don't know if he'd figure us to be down here."

Lulu felt her way over to the other side of the room. She was tired of standing in sticky stuff. She found the wall on the opposite side and slid down to sit on the floor. It felt several degrees cooler sitting on the floor than standing up.

"What're you doing?" Neil asked her.

"Making myself comfortable."

"Maybe we should yell or something."

"You yell, I don't feel like it."

"Hey, anybody out there?" Neil yelled a couple of times, and then she heard him walking over to where she was sitting. The shoe came to a stop against her leg. A moment later he sat down next to her.

"Better be careful," she told him, "there are probably rats down here."

"If there were rats down here you wouldn't be hiding here."

"I'm not afraid of rats."

He laughed.

"I'm not. I'm not afraid of spiders, either, and there's probably black widows around."

"If you're trying to scare me, Lulu, you're not succeeding."

"I'm just warning you, that's all."

"So you're not scared of anything, is that it?"

"That's right."

"Then why'd you throw that can at me?"

"It wasn't because I was scared." Lulu remembered her bubble gum and took it out of her pocket. She opened a piece and put it in her mouth.

Neil said, "I smell bubble gum."

"You want a piece?"

"Sure."

She handed him a piece, and they spent a couple of minutes getting it soft and then blowing a few bubbles. Lulu didn't think it was as satisfying, though, when she couldn't see how big the bubbles were.

"You want to arm wrestle?" she asked him. It was boring just sitting there. It was like being in school when she'd rather be out playing.

"Why work up a sweat? It's already hot enough in here."

"You chicken?"

"When have I ever been chicken to arm wrestle you?"

"Well, I'm challenging you." She pushed herself away from the wall and rolled over onto her stomach. "Come on. Two out of three."

"You're going to lose."

"You wish!"

"In case you hadn't noticed, I'm a lot bigger than you this summer."

"That doesn't mean you're stronger."

She felt his arm move up against hers, and then they clasped hands. She'd been doing a lot of chin-ups on the playground the past year, and she didn't think that he was going to beat her just because he'd grown a couple of inches.

"Ready?" he asked.

"I'm ready."

She tried to put all her body weight behind her arm. Neither arm moved, and she could feel sweat popping out on her face. It was strange not being able to see him, just feeling the force behind his arm and knowing that only inches away the sweat was probably pouring off his face. She knew he was smiling. He always smiled when they arm wrestled.

"This is weird," she said.

"You mean in the dark?"

She nodded, then realized he couldn't see her. "Yeah. It seems strange."

"You have a boyfriend?" he asked her.

The question surprised her so much she stopped straining for a moment, and in that split second he slammed her arm to the cement floor.

"That wasn't fair," she shouted.

"You gonna be a sore loser?"

"What'd you ask me *that* for? You threw me off."

"Bull. I'm stronger than you, that's all."

"The hell you are!"

"I'm shocked, Lulu. Is that the kind of language you learn in Catholic schools?"

"I know worse than that."

"Really? Let's hear some of it."

Still grasping hold of his hand, she lifted their arms back up. "Come on, two out of three."

She beat him the second time, and then the third. She had a sneaking suspicion on the third try that he gave in too easily, except that Neil never gave in too easily.

"You want to try some real wrestling?" he asked her, his voice sounding a little different.

"There's no way we can wrestle in the dark with a boiler taking up most of the room."

"We can try."

She let go of his hand sat back against the wall. "I don't feel like it."

"You're not going to give me a chance to win at something?"

"Why'd you ask me if I had a boyfriend? That's really weird."

"A lot of kids at my school are going steady."

"You get in trouble with the priest if you go steady at St. Catherine's."

"What about Kevin? Do you like him?"

"He's my best friend, of course I like him."

"Do you like him as a boyfriend?"

"What's the matter with you, Neil? You get really strange in the dark, you know that?"

"Let's wrestle."

He touched her arm, and she moved a few inches away from him. "Get away from me!"

"What're you afraid of, Lulu?"

"I think you're freaking out. You afraid of the dark or something?"

"I'm not afraid of the dark."

"Then let's talk about baseball or something."

"Let's talk about boyfriends."

"What's the matter with you? You wouldn't be talking like this if the other guys were around."

"You're right."

"Then why are you doing it?"

"'Cause I don't think of you as one of the guys."

She scrambled to her feet and leaned against the wall. "I hate you! Why'd you lock us in here?"

She could hear him getting to his feet, and she pressed her back against the wall, folding her arms across her chest.

"I didn't do it on purpose."

"Maybe you did."

"What're you afraid of, Lulu?"

"Not of you, that's for sure."

He laughed. "You know something, Lulu? You're not going to be a boy when you grow up."

She was hearing her worst fear verbalized. "I'll be whatever I want."

"You don't have a choice in the matter."

"Shut up, Neil Blessing. I don't want to listen to you!"

"You can act as tough as you want, but you're still a girl."

"You're wasting your time, because I have my hands over my ears. I can't hear a thing you're saying."

She felt his hands on her shoulders, and she tried to get away from him, but he had her pinned to the wall. "Let go of me, you *Protestant*!"

She heard him chuckle. "Is that supposed to be an insult?"

It was about the biggest insult at her school, but she could see it didn't bother him. "I swear, Neil, when we get out of here you're going to be sorry."

"You ever kissed a boy, Lulu?"

"You try and you're dead!"

She could feel his breath on her face, and she turned her head and yelled, "Help! Let us out of here!"

"No one's going to let us out, Lulu. We'll probably be locked up here forever."

She started pounding his back with her fists. "You better hope we're not found, because you're going to be in deep trouble when we get out."

"Who you going to tell? Kevin? Andy? You going to tell your mother?"

There was no one she could tell. She'd die rather than tell someone some boy wanted to kiss her. It was the most humiliating thing that had ever happened to her. She started to stamp on his foot, but it only made him laugh.

"All right," she finally said. "You want to wrestle, it's okay with me." And when she pinned him to the floor she'd slam his head against the cement. Maybe it would knock him out and she could yell for help.

No, she wouldn't yell for help. That would be chicken, and she wasn't chicken. Neil might be acting weird, but he was her friend and she wasn't afraid of him.

He backed up, his hands coming off her shoulders and resting on her forearms. She moved away from the wall and faced-off against him. Lightly touching each other on the arms, they circled warily, each waiting for a move. Only it was hard to determine when to make a move when it was so dark that the only proof she had that he was even there was by touch.

"What're you waiting for?" he asked her.

"I'd hate to throw you against the boiler and kill you by accident."

"A minute ago you were ready to kill me."

"A minute ago I wanted to barf, all that talk about kissing."

"I only asked a simple question."

"Well, it's none of your business."

"I don't think you've ever kissed a boy."

"Shut up, Neil, or I *am* going to throw you into the boiler."

"Wouldn't you like to see what it's like?"

"Wouldn't you like a punch in the mouth?"

He started to laugh, and when she heard it, she grabbed his arm, twisted her foot around his ankle, and they went tumbling to the hard cement floor. She felt one of her elbows scrape but was more concerned with trying to pin him down. She grabbed one of his arms and tried to twist it, but in the next moment he was grabbing both of her wrists and pulling them above her head, then rolling her onto her back and straddling her. Her arms were thrust down hard against the floor, and she bit her lip to keep from yelling out.

"My point," said Neil, his voice coming eerily out of the darkness.

He was sitting on her stomach with both hands holding her wrists. She could smell him but she couldn't see him. She was being flooded with feelings, and she was too angry to determine whether they were good feelings or bad. They were strong, though, so strong she could barely speak.

"Two out of three," said Lulu.

She could feel his breath against her face.

"Get away from me, you *pervert*!"

She felt herself getting warm, and she felt her legs getting weak. It was very much the way she felt when she got the flu, only this time it felt good.

She felt something move softly across her cheek. By the time she figured out it was his mouth, he was kissing her. She clamped her lips tight and stopped breathing. It didn't last long, and when he lifted his mouth off hers, she wondered what was the big deal. She'd rather chew bubble gum.

"You're supposed to move your mouth a little," he told her.

She refused to speak.

"Try moving it this time," he said, and then he was kissing her again. She didn't move her mouth, but she relaxed it. She felt him letting go of her wrists, and she knew she could push him off of her, but for some reason she didn't want to. She wanted to stay there with Neil on top of her and continue feeling good. She hoped Kevin didn't find them, because she wouldn't mind feeling like that the rest of the day.

After a while he stopped and got off her. She could feel him laying down on the floor beside her.

"Will I have a baby?" Lulu asked him.

"Of course not."

"You're lying. The girl next door to me was always kissing boys, and then she had a baby and got sent away to her grandmother's."

"Lulu, you don't get a baby from kissing."

"Are you sure?"

"Don't they teach you *anything* in Catholic schools?"

"It was a sin, though."

"It was just a kiss."

"You're not Catholic. You don't have to go to confession. Now I'm going to have to confess it to Father Ryan." What if Father Ryan told the nuns and everyone found out about her? She'd die if that happened.

"Lots of people kiss. My parents are always kissing."

"I don't believe you," said Lulu, who had never seen her parents kiss.

"Lulu, don't you know how you have babies?"

"Do you know?"

"Of course, I know."

"Will you tell me?"

"Ask one of your girl friends."

"I don't have any girl friends. The girls in my school are really stupid."

"Then ask your mother."

"She wouldn't tell me."

"Well, I'm not going to tell you, either."

"Then how am I supposed to find out?"

"Look, I'll tell you when we're older, okay? I'll tell you when we're both sixteen."

"You promise."

"I swear."

"Okay, but it's your fault if I have a baby."

"Lulu? Now listen, don't get scared, but there's something I want to tell you." She felt him shifting around next to her, and then he said, "The thing is, I'm pretty sure I love you."

"You're crazy, Neil Blessing! Totally crazy. How could you even say something like that?"

"I mean it. I've thought about it a lot. You know, during the winter, when I don't see you, I think about you all the time."

"So what? I do that, too." As soon as school started in the fall, she counted the days until summer vacation when the gang would be together again. It was Neil she counted the days for, though; she saw Kevin and Andy every day of the year.

"When we grow up, will you marry me?" he asked.

"Get out of here, you weirdo!"

"Will you?"

"First of all, I'm not *ever* getting married,"

"Why not?"

"I don't want to."

"Do you love me?"

"You can't force me to answer that question."

"That means you do."

"It does not!"

"It does so!"

"If I did, I wouldn't tell you."

"I know you do. Every time I'm with you I know it. I can just feel it."

Lulu was pretty sure she loved him. She certainly liked him a whole lot better than she liked her parents or brothers, so that must be love. And the very happiest days of her life were when she was with him. Was that love?

"I know we're just kids, but I'm going to still love you when we grow up," said Neil. "You're just right for me, Lulu. And I'm right for you."

She felt his hand next to hers, and then it moved to take hold of it. She didn't try to pull hers away. The world wasn't going to end just because she let him hold her hand, was it?

"I wish we were grown-up now," said Lulu. "I wish we could live in the clubhouse and never go home." She turned toward him and put an arm across his chest, resting her head on his shoulder. It felt good to be close to someone.

He put his arms around her and pulled her closer. "Promise me something, Lulu. Promise me you'll never forget today."

"That'd be pretty hard to do."

"I'll love you forever, Lulu."

"Okay."

"Okay what?"

"You know."

"Tell me."

"I'll love you forever, too. But you better not tell Kevin and Andy, or I'll swear you're a liar and I'll kick your face in."

And then she began to feel a little silly having Neil's arms around her, and she rolled on top of him and quickly pinned him to the floor.

"Two out of three?"

Chapter Six

Lulu unzipped her jacket, then pulled it off and threw it across the room. It landed, pile side out, on top of Neil's in the rocker, setting the chair in motion and getting a rise out of Mohammed, who jumped down from the couch and went over to inspect. A moment later he was circling atop the jacket, his claws kneading the pile, preparatory to settling down for his thousandth snooze of the day.

"You want to wrestle?" Neil asked her. "Two out of three?"

She slid down in the couch, stretching her legs out on the coffee table and crossing her ankles and, in the process, nudging over a pile of magazines. She needed to throw them out. She didn't even know why she kept them around. After the first ten minutes of looking through them, she invariably put them down and never picked them up again. She'd take them to Mary. It would give her something to do when she was all alone.

"Well?" said Neil, as though his question had been anything other than rhetorical.

He was wasting his time. They weren't locked in a boiler room now. They were in her house, and she was in charge. He could give her that cool, gray gaze from now until next week and she'd still be in charge.

It felt almost as warm as that day in the boiler room, though. She ought to get up and open a window, let out some of the steam heat, but she was too tired. She just wanted to sit still for a moment and relax. And get rid of Neil as quickly as possible.

"We're not kids anymore, Neil."

"I think we are."

She sighed. "What's that supposed to mean?"

"It means we seem to be stuck at age twelve with each other. Maybe every other part of our lives has progressed in the last twenty years, but emotionally, with each other, we're still twelve years old."

She was almost too tired to answer. Maybe she'd just close her eyes and let him talk on and on, if that's what he wanted. Maybe he just liked to hear himself talk. He thought she was still twelve years old? Right now she felt more like seventy.

"Maybe *you* are," she said, the words an effort.

"Now you even *sound* twelve."

"I'm not the one who wants to wrestle." She heard it herself then, the querulous sound of a kid looking for an argument.

"I meant that metaphorically." A smile crept up the corners of his mouth. "Well, maybe I didn't. Some of my best memories of you have to do with wrestling of one sort or another."

He was more honest than she was. She prided herself on her honesty, what some people preferred to call bluntness, but when it came to feelings, he was always up-front about his, and she was always relegating hers to the area of subtext. Right now she could feel his presence with as much definitude as if they were wrestling on the floor, but she'd cut her throat before admitting it. Just his being in the room with her seemed to be raising the temperature. She leaned over and untied her shoelaces, then kicked off her Nikes.

"Maybe we're still twelve years old with each other," she said, "because we haven't talked in twenty years."

"Nonsense."

"It is *not* nonsense!" When she pictured him in her mind, he was still that twelve-year-old. It was because she hadn't watched him grow up, as she had with Kevin and Andy. He'd gone from being twelve years old to being this grown man, with nothing in between. It was like that movie with Tom Hanks—what was the name of it? *Big*. It was just like that. She was looking at a grown man, but she was still feeling the presence of the boy.

He wouldn't let it alone. "It's because nothing was resolved. It's because the natural progression was brought to an unnatural halt."

"It's because you betrayed me." She blurted it out and then was sorry. He should've known without her spelling it out. It diminished her for having to do so.

"That was undoubtedly the way you perceived it—"

"I perceived it that way because that's what it was."

"There are many different forms of betrayal, Lulu."

"Oh, God, am I going to hear a treatise on betrayal now? Come on, Neil, just say what you mean."

"We were in love."

"We were *twelve*!"

"We were still in love."

"We loved each other, yes. We all loved each other. I still love Kevin and Andy."

"It was different."

She reached down and grabbed the bottom of her sweater and began to lift it over her head. She saw the startled look in his eyes, which would no doubt disappear when he saw she had a T-shirt on underneath it. What did he think she was, some kind of exhibitionist? Sure enough, when the sweater was off, he was back to looking normal.

What could she say that would be guaranteed to get him mad? Making fun of him would probably do it. Men didn't like being made fun of. For that matter, *she* didn't like it, either. "Haven't you been in love since then, Neil? Haven't you had girlfriends? Don't you have someone now? It wasn't different, it was just a kids' thing. My God, you make it sound like *Romeo and Juliet*." She started to laugh at the whole idea.

He didn't even smile. "Lulu, we had something perfect, and your acting like you don't remember doesn't change that."

"I can't believe I'm hearing this. Are you telling me you've been hung up for twenty years on some crush you had when you were a kid?"

"Be honest, Lulu. Are you telling me you haven't?"

She worked at her socks with her toes until she had them off. A flick of her foot, and they fell off the coffee table. Undressing seemed to be easier than getting up and opening the window. Why was it so hot in here, anyway? Had her cheap landlord finally decided to give them some heat?

She looked at Neil and smiled, putting a little pity in the smile. "Neil, I hate to demolish the fantasy you've been sustaining, but I've hated your guts for the last twenty years." She broadened the smile, really giving it to him.

He gave her a mocking look. "And you're trying to tell me you haven't been as hung up as I have?"

"No. Not hung up. I haven't actively hated you every day since then."

"But some days."

"Oh, yes. Some."

"Don't try to convince me that you'd hate someone twenty years over a childhood slight, because it won't wash."

She felt tired. She'd been up over eighteen hours, putting up the house had taken all her energy, and now he wanted to sit around and reminisce when all she wanted to do was fall into bed. That'd teach her not to open the door without asking who it was first.

If she swung her legs up onto the couch, shoved the throw pillow under her head and closed her eyes, she'd be asleep. Just like that. No counting sheep, no nothing. Closing her eyes was all it would take. Except then she'd be asleep and he'd still be in her apartment. She didn't want him to watch her sleep. She didn't like being watched.

Summoning up every bit of energy she had left, Lulu got up and headed for the kitchen.

"Where're you going?"

"To make some coffee. Otherwise this conversation is going to put me to sleep." She filled the teakettle with water and lit the stove. She took two mugs from the dish rack and spooned in instant coffee. One mug was cream-colored and had a picture of a cable car on it. Andy had brought it to her from San Francisco. The other one was white and said Life's a Beach. She liked them both. She didn't want him to drink out of either of them. "How do you take it?"

"A little milk."

She leaned against the sink while waiting for the water to boil. She saw him stand up and walk over to her bookshelves. He lifted a papier-mâché angel and seemed to be examining it. He set it down and picked up another. He better be careful, guardian angels didn't like Protestants. At least that's what she'd been led to believe.

"So many angels. Is there a reason for them?"

"They're guardian angels."

She saw his finger move lightly over the gold-leaf trim. He had good hands, slim and strong. They were twice the size of hers. She didn't think she'd be able to beat him at arm wrestling these days. Then again, she didn't have much occasion to arm wrestle these days. He might still think of them as twelve years old, but she considered herself an adult.

"Are you in need of guardian angels?" he asked her.

"Everyone could use one." Or two. Or three. Although what good they were doing her at the moment she couldn't figure out.

"But so many?"

She shrugged and turned to the stove. She was so tired she could barely keep her eyes open. Maybe after his coffee he'd go home and leave her in peace. She wasn't ready to spar with him. She needed to gather up her defenses and plan a point of attack. She needed to be able to summon up all the things she'd held against him all these years. At the very least, she needed to be wide-awake.

The kettle began to whistle, and she turned off the flame and filled the mugs. Mohammed roused himself and joined her by the stove, his body winding around her legs. Her being anywhere in the vicinity of the kitchen was a signal to him that there was a possibility he was going to be fed. Nine out of ten times he was wrong. She fixed the coffee and carried the mugs to the coffee table.

Neil returned the angel to the shelf and appeared to be scanning the titles of her books. He was as tall as the bookcase. He could easily see the top, which she couldn't see so never dusted.

"Sit down, Neil, and drink your coffee."

"Still trying to give me orders, Lulu?"

"And stop making something of everything I say."

He moved the jackets from the rocking chair onto the floor and sat down, ignoring the coffee. He stretched out his legs and began to rock. She looked at him and tried to picture the boy of twelve. He was taller, of course, but he'd suddenly been tall at twelve, too. He'd grown inches that school year when she hadn't seen him. The light brown hair was now cut a little better and worn a little shorter. At this hour he had the appearance of needing a shave, and that was certainly a difference. The biggest difference might have been that in those days they were always in summer clothes. If she gave him a shave and dressed him in cutoffs and a T-shirt, would he still be the boy of twelve? If she gathered her hair in pigtails, would they suddenly be transported back in time?

The essence of what she remembered about him was certainly still there. He had a presence, something she had thought of as being cool when he was a kid and now became a sort of dignity. He had never acted silly when the rest of them had been in the mood to cut up. He had always stood back a little from that kind of behavior, and, as a kid, she had supposed all Protestants were like that. He didn't scream or yell or fall to the floor laughing; he didn't participate wholeheartedly in their burping contests. Except for that time in the boiler room, he had always held some part of him inviolable, and it was that part, that untouchable part, that she had been drawn to. She didn't have it herself and had wanted to learn it from him. One thing hadn't changed, though: he still had a big mouth.

"Have I changed?" he asked her, and she realized she had been staring.

"Yeah, you need a shave."

He acknowledged this with a nod. "You've changed. You no longer have that effervescent quality you had as a kid. You seem calmer, not as happy."

"I've never thought of my childhood as being happy," said Lulu.

"You never whined or complained. You never seemed bored. I never saw you cry, not even when you broke your arm."

"That was the only good part of my childhood, the Rooftop Gang. I was happy then. When you didn't see me, though, when I was at home—then I wasn't happy."

"I didn't know that."

Lulu shrugged.

"I wish I had known."

"It wasn't important. Anyway, there was nothing you could've done about it."

"So why aren't you happy now?"

"I'm happy," said Lulu. "I'm just not as happy as you remember because then it was as though I was saving up all my happiness for those times. Now my whole life's okay, so I don't have to go from being wildly happy to wildly unhappy."

"Maybe feeling the highs and lows is better. Maybe that's the only way you really experience life."

"Believe me, it's not better."

She took a sip of coffee, wishing he would pick up his and finish it off so she could go to bed. She was still warm, and she wondered what he'd do if she were to suddenly remove her T-shirt. Would he attack her? Would he run for the door? No, he'd probably double up laughing when he saw she was wearing an undershirt beneath it. She'd gotten her way with her mother after all; she never had actually needed a bra. She almost laughed out loud at the thought.

"Do you have a boyfriend?"

"What is this, a walk down memory lane?"

"Are you seeing anyone?"

"What do you think, if I had a man in my life I'd be wildly happy again? I haven't found that going with someone improves the quality of life."

"That's a pretty cynical statement."

"Then I guess I'm pretty cynical. And if you believe it does, then why aren't you married?"

"I don't think you want to go into that."

"You mean *you* don't."

"I'm not about to marry anyone but you, Lulu."

She started, spilling some of her coffee down the front of her T-shirt. At crucial times of her life, she always seemed to be spilling something on her T-shirt. "Then I guess you're never going to get married, are you?"

"Want to take it from the beginning?"

"Your coffee's getting cold, and when you finish the cup I'd like you to leave."

"The first time we met?"

"It's late, and I have to be up early in the morning."

"It was pure fate that meeting, there's no other explanation for it."

She got up and grabbed his mug and carried it over to him, holding it out at arm's length. "Here, drink it up, and then you better be going."

He took the mug from her and glanced at the picture before setting it down on the floor beside the chair. "It's not coffee we're discussing." He held out his hand, and she backed up. "You want to arm wrestle, Lulu?"

"I want you out of here."

"Two out of three?"

"We're not children anymore."

"I'm very aware of that. Being adults would give arm wrestling a totally new meaning."

She folded her arms across her chest. "I think you're coming on to me—"

"Oh, I'm definitely coming on to you."

She picked up his jacket from the floor and dumped it on his lap. "Why don't you call me on the phone sometime and we'll talk?"

"I have a pretty good idea you'd hang up on me."

"And you'd be right. And if you're not an idiot, I would think that would tell you something."

"It tells me you're afraid to talk."

"Neil, it's the middle of the night, I'm tired and this isn't going to get us anywhere."

"You want to go to bed, is that it?"

"Yes."

He gave her a wicked smile, one she didn't remember from his boyhood repertoire. But then there was nothing boyish about this smile.

She moved farther away from him. "Is it sex that you want from me?"

He pushed back in the rocker and seemed to be considering his answer. "That's a part of it."

"A part of it?"

"I want a great deal more than sex from you, Lulu. I want your soul."

Her eyes moved quickly to the shelves.

"Are you looking for your guardian angels to protect you?"

And why weren't they, now that she needed them?

"They're supposed to look out for you, aren't they?" he asked. "But coming between us wouldn't be looking out for you. I think the angels are as clear on that as I am."

"If you think you're going to force yourself on me again—"

"Want to talk about that day in the boiler room?"

"No!"

"Sit down on the couch, Lulu. Make yourself comfortable. I'm going to tell you a little bedtime story, and then I'm going to leave."

"You promise you'll leave?"

"I promise."

She warily circled the rocking chair once, then went back to the couch and curled up in a corner, pulling the afghan down from the back of the couch to cover herself with. When Mohammed returned to the couch, she pulled him up into her lap for a further layer of protection. She was dying of the heat, but she suddenly wanted as much between her and Neil as she could get.

He waited until she was settled and then he spoke. "It was pure chance I met you at all, Lulu. That day was the first time I'd ridden my bike to South Boston. It wasn't an area I knew at all, and I had no reason for being down there. In fact my mom would've had a fit if she knew where I was because that was one of the areas I was supposed to stay out of."

"Too bad you didn't listen to her."

"I was riding around aimlessly. I came to a stop at a red light, and there was a fruit stand right there on the sidewalk. I saw this kid—you—grabbing apples and shoving them down your shirt. And then the man who owned the fruit stand caught you at it, and you started to run, followed by two boys. I had trouble keeping up with you on my bike. You were like a blur, with pedestrians scattering along your path. I'd never seen a girl run that fast."

"I could beat you, if you recall."

"Will you shut up and let me tell it?"

"Well, I could."

"You probably still could. So I followed you, and I was thinking that it was all right you stole the apples because you were poor kids and probably didn't get enough to eat. And

I started feeling like a real do-gooder, like maybe I'd toss you a quarter or something, and then, a couple of blocks from there, you and your friends started throwing the apples at the tires of cars that were passing. You didn't eat one of them. And you were laughing like crazy, like it was the most fun in the world.''

"It was pretty fun," said Lulu, remembering the noise an apple made as it flattened against a tire.

"Anyway, that's when I stopped. I wanted to get to know you."

"And got punched for your trouble."

"There was something about you, something defiant, that really got to me. I'm not going to call it love, Lulu, because we were ten years old, but there was something there. I was drawn to you. I had to meet you, I had to get to know you, and then, when I did, I couldn't stay away."

"You just had more fun with us."

"Look, I had friends in my neighborhood. I had access to swimming pools and tennis courts, and my dad had season tickets to the Red Sox. It was you. There wasn't anyone like you in my neighborhood, that's why I hung out with you. I even talked my parents out of sending me to summer camp with all my friends."

"All kids get crushes, Neil. You're supposed to grow out of them."

"I had girlfriends in high school. And college. But as soon as I saw you at Kevin's wedding I knew what had been missing, what those other girls were lacking. I kept looking for you in all of them, and I never found it."

"Well, I'll tell you, Neil, I might find all of this touching if you hadn't betrayed me."

"I'd do it again."

"Like hell!"

"I'd do it again in a minute, Lulu. If I thought you were going to leave the country and I was never going to get another chance to see you, I'd do it again. Damn it, Lulu, I loved you, and you were ready to walk right out of my life."

"We were kids!"

"I don't care. I felt that way then, and I still feel that way."

"I wasn't walking out on you. I was running away from my home life."

"I didn't know that at the time. From where I was sitting, it looked to me like you were running away with some juvenile delinquent."

"He wasn't so bad. He didn't do anything we hadn't done, only he got caught at it."

"I wouldn't have liked anyone you ran away with."

"You know, I might take you a little more seriously if I didn't know that it's been ten years since we've seen each other and you've never made any effort during that time to get in touch."

"I've always known where you were, what you were doing."

"From Kevin?"

He nodded.

"I'll kill him!" She made an effort to sit up, then fell back against the couch.

"Oh, come on. We've remained friends, and it was just casual conversation, or at least as far as he was concerned."

"So why'd you pick now to suddenly show up?"

"Timing. Either I was going with someone or you were, and this time, when Kevin said you'd broken up with your latest boyfriend, it seemed like a good time."

"Did you think I'd be vulnerable without a man?"

"I don't see you as ever being vulnerable, Lulu."

"Well, you're right, and I'm not looking for a boy-friend, either, so you can just forget it."

"I know you, Lulu. I know you'd bite off your nose to spite your face, to use an expression my mother used to use."

Lulu grinned. "My mother always said the same thing."

"About you?"

She nodded.

"I did one thing you didn't like when we were twelve, and because of that, you're denying the fact that the attraction is still there and that neither of us has found anything half that good with anyone else."

"Speak for yourself."

"I'm speaking for you, too, because you're too chicken to tell the truth about it."

"I was never chicken."

"No, you weren't. So why are you now?"

"I think you have an overactive imagination, Neil Blessing, which isn't something I supposed Protestants had in any large quantity. You're romanticizing a wild, unhappy tomboy of twelve and projecting her onto the way I am now. I'm not the same person anymore. I'm happy in my job, I'm happy in my home life, and I'm quite content being single. I think you'd be bored with me these days."

"You were never boring."

"I'm telling you, I am now."

"Why don't we find out?"

"Why don't you just take my word for it?"

"Is that the way you want it?"

"That's the way I want it."

The motion of the rocker stopped, and he stood up. He reached for his jacket and put it on, then picked up the mug from the floor and carried it over to the sink. For just a fleeting moment she was sorry he was giving up. The old

Neil, the one in her memory, wouldn't have given up so easily.

She moved the afghan and Mohammed off her lap in one heap and got up. She'd see him out, lock up for the night and finally get to bed. She had won, but the victory didn't seem sweet.

He was buttoning up his jacket when she reached the door. Wanting to end the evening on an up note, she said, "It was great fun this evening, wasn't it?"

She saw confusion in his eyes.

"I mean earlier. That's the most fun I've had since I was a kid."

"I think you're a born anarchist, Lulu."

"Didn't you enjoy it?"

He nodded. And then, just when she thought she was safe, he pulled her into his arms.

"I thought we settled that, Neil!"

"We settled nothing," he said, then leaned down and tried to trap her lips beneath his.

She moved her face out of the way and began to push her hands against his chest, but he grabbed them up and pulled them behind her back. He was twice as strong as she was these days, and she felt pinned like an insect. She supposed she could yell out or kick him, but she wasn't going to give him the satisfaction of seeing her squirm.

She gave him a scornful look. "Up to your old tricks, I see."

"It seems the only thing you understand is force."

"Yes, and I understand it for what it is—it's a form of rape."

"It's no more rape than when you used to pin me to the floor with one of your wrestling holds."

He brought his head toward hers again, only this time she faced him off, and when his mouth met hers, she pulled in her lips and allowed him nothing. Eyes open, she watched him trying to melt her with his mouth, his own eyes watching for her reaction. She glared into his eyes and saw a look of amusement cross his face.

He broke away and let go of her wrists. "One kiss, Lulu. One real kiss, and if you're still fighting me off after that, I'll never bother you again." He grinned wickedly. "What are you afraid of?"

"I'm not afraid of you!"

"Nonsense. You could've given me a friendly good-night kiss, and I would've been on my way. You could've laughed it off and made me feel a fool. But fighting me off, the way you have, makes me know you're afraid of what would happen if you really let me kiss you. You're dead afraid, Lulu, because it might be just the thing you've been longing for."

"I swear, you talk more than the Irish."

"That's an invitation if I ever heard one."

Lulu didn't like being on the defensive. She liked to call the shots, make the moves. Why was she leaving it up to this idiot, who was going to stand by the door all night talking about it?

She wished he weren't so tall. She wished they were the same height, the way they used to be in the days when she was still tall for her age and hadn't stopped growing. He was watching her, as though trying to read her mind now. Well, she'd give him something to think about.

She reached her arms up around his neck, straining on her toes to do so. And then she pulled his head down and tilted her face, and it only took closing her eyes for her to believe they were back in the boiler room and she was being kissed for the very first time. Only this time she knew what she was doing.

Then his mouth began to move, and the shock to her senses was astonishing. Oh, yes, she had felt things back then, but at the time it had felt like the flu. Now it was the way she always knew it should feel but never had with any other man. The feeling was so strong she might faint. Maybe this little experiment of hers hadn't been such a good idea after all.

His arms went around her and drew her up so that her feet were off the floor and she was being pressed back against the door and pressed in by his body. And then he was lifting her up and carrying her over to the couch. This wasn't the way it was supposed to be. He was supposed to be walking out of the house about now.

She heard an annoyed cry from Mohammed as he was crowded off the couch, and then Neil was sitting down none too gently, and she was still in his arms, half on his lap. She was afraid to open her eyes because if she opened them, it would be the same as admitting that she was going along with all this nonsense. It would make her responsible for her actions.

Nevertheless, she opened one eye just a fraction and saw that his also were closed. It was better that way. If they were in the dark, then they could still be in the boiler room and innocent of what they were doing. But if they opened their eyes, they would know what they were doing and have to stop.

One of his hands moved between them, and she shifted a little to give him room. His hand moved up under her T-shirt and undershirt, and she could feel its warmth on her bare flesh. As his tingling fingertips traced figure eights across and around one nipple, she felt herself shudder, and with the shudder, she also felt a loosening, as something within her began to say yes to what was happening between them. His other hand moved between her legs and began to rub against the fabric of her jeans. She heard herself gasp, felt her mouth open involuntarily, and then something powerful took over, overwhelming her, and everything turned black. She felt herself floating in space, but it wasn't a blue space with fluffy clouds passing by, it was more like falling into a black hole, and guardian angels were calling to her, calling her name.

"Lulu? Are you all right?"

She heard his voice but didn't want to answer. She wanted to keep falling, deeper and deeper into the endless black hole in the universe.

"Lulu?"

The blackness began to disintegrate, and she saw light in the distance, as though filtered through a screen.

"Come on, Lulu, will you answer me, please. You're scaring me."

It took a great effort but she managed to open her eyes. Neil, looking concerned, was gazing down at her.

"What happened?" she asked.

"I think you passed out."

She struggled to sit up, but he held her down. "I couldn't have passed out. I've never passed out in my life." Did he mean *faint*? Did he really believe she was the kind of woman who fainted?

"Maybe you were holding your breath. You used to do that when we were kids."

Lulu couldn't remember holding her breath. She could remember his hands on her, though, and how the excitement seemed more than she could bear. Now she was having trouble remembering why she hadn't wanted those hands on her to begin with.

"Has this ever happened to you before?"

"No," she said, then wished she hadn't said it so quickly. It wasn't good to let him think he had so much power over her that he could make her pass out by just touching her. It was rather incredible, though. She thought she was well versed in sexual things, but she hadn't known you could lose consciousness from sheer pleasure. It was astonishing. It was surely a gift from the angels.

Neil was going on and on. She heard him saying, "Well, I know you didn't pass out from hunger, because I watched you eat. And the last thing you drank was coffee."

As usual, his mouth was working overtime. Hadn't he known there were more important things to do than talking? Wasn't he ever going to shut up?

"Do it again," she said.

"What?"

"Make me pass out."

His hand reached out to push her bangs back off her forehead, and she realized how wet her hair was. Maybe it was the flu after all. Maybe she was feverish. Wouldn't it be strange if everything she was feeling was due to an illness and not due to Neil at all?

His hand was fooling with the buttons on her jeans, and then he was opening them and his hand was sliding down inside her bikini panties. She gasped as his fingers slid inside of her, her eyes going to his and seeing how carefully he was watching her. Was he afraid she was going to pass out again? Did he want her to?

She felt a shudder rack her body as his strong fingers stiffened and his thumb began a circular motion. She felt the darkness closing in again and closed her eyes to meet it. And then, abruptly, the movement stopped.

She opened her eyes and saw him smiling down at her. "Do you love me?" he asked her.

"No." But even she could tell it was a halfhearted no.

He tilted his head. "No?" His hand withdrew from her jeans, and the action felt as horrible and as final as an amputation.

"Maybe," she allowed.

"At least you'll admit to an attraction."

She couldn't very well not admit to it when what she wanted most in the world was for his hand to resume its magic. "I guess so."

"Could we be a little more unambiguous?"

"What do you want from me, Neil?"

"I told you what I wanted."

"You're not getting my soul!"

His fingers moved across her mouth, softening the stubborn lines. "Oh, I'll get it, all right. It's just a question of when."

He gently moved her off his lap and stood up. And then, before she could even think to stop him, he was at her door and opening it, and it wasn't until it had closed behind him that she finally summoned the strength to move.

She stood up and fumbled with the buttons on her jeans until she got them fastened again. With the thought that he might still be outside her door, she opened it and looked out, but the street in front of her building was empty. He couldn't have gotten a taxi so fast; he must have walked. She realized she didn't even know where he lived.

Mohammed stuck his head out the door, and then retreated into the warmth of the apartment. Lulu shut the door and locked it.

She felt numb. She felt tired and hung over and feverish, and if this wasn't the flu, if this was what love felt like, then she wanted no part of it. He was a manipulator, that was all. He manipulated her when they were kids, and he was doing it again.

But why was it that her body responded so strongly to his manipulation and never to that of other men? What was it about him that bound her to him in ways she hadn't imagined? It was nonsense to think there was only one man in the world for her and that was the very one she could never trust.

Her body had betrayed her tonight just as truly as he had betrayed her twenty years ago and would again if she gave him the chance. He walked out of there with the smug certainty that she was in his power now. Well, she wasn't in his power; she was in no man's power. And he would find that out the next time he tried to use that particular brand of magic on her.

He wanted her soul, did he? Well, her soul wasn't up for negotiation. And what kind of man was it who spoke of wanting souls, anyway? Maybe there really was a devil, and maybe Neil was it. Maybe that bogeyman the nuns had warned them about, had instilled that fear of, was after all at work in the world today, and maybe no amount of guardian angels could ever keep her safe. And maybe she had better go back to that church she had thought she'd outgrown and go down on her knees and ask for all the help she could get.

Too tired to bother washing up or even making up the couch, Lulu lay back down and pulled the afghan around her for warmth. She was cold now, shivering. It was as though when Neil left he took all the warmth with him.

She could feel her body trembling. She reached for the bottle of whiskey and poured herself a shot. She needed something to stop the shaking. Something to stop the coldness. She had the glass to her lips when she wondered whether her father had had his own devils he had tried to defeat with his drinking.

She thought she heard a laugh and looked around the room. The guardian angels seemed to be smiling at her. They were all smiling and mocking her. Was it their laughter she heard? Were they really guardian angels, or were they fallen angels, like Lucifer, here to help the devil get her soul?

Very quickly she decided she wasn't her father and she didn't need whiskey. She set down the glass and closed her eyes. And what was the matter with her, anyway? She wasn't some superstitious lass from the old country who believed in leprechauns and the devil in the form of a man. More likely she was becoming sex starved in her old age and the first man to excite her in years was throwing her for a loop.

To hell with Neil and his talk of love. She'd not be possessed by any man. Maybe she did love him, so what? She still wasn't going to forgive him.

Chapter Seven

Her dreams were in Technicolor—dreams of Neil with horns and a tail and a chorus line of guardian angels tap-dancing around her living room. Sometimes Neil dancing with them, his bare, red, disfigured feet doing silent shuffle-hops on the worn, beige carpeting. After a night of them, Lulu awakened with a horrendous headache, raw throat, stomach cramps and what she could only surmise was a temperature of a hundred and ten. Despite feeling as though she'd been run over by a truck that had then backed up and run over her again, she was vastly relieved to find out that it was, after all, the flu and not love that ailed her. That was her first thought, and where it came from was a mystery.

Her second thought was that she was dying. She was sure of it. She wasn't going to last the day. She might as well just stay where she was on the couch and wait for death to pick her up and carry her off. On the other hand, if she could make it to the bathroom, she could take something for her headache.

She tried to sit up and got as far as lifting her head. Even her neck hurt. She used her hands to shove herself up a little. She heard plaintive cries from Mohammed, always alert to her first movement of the day. "In a minute," she thought she said to him, but she didn't hear any sound. She tried to swallow, but there wasn't any saliva in her mouth.

She slowly moved her legs off the couch until her feet touched the floor. She stood up. It was even worse standing up. Either she was swaying and the room was standing still, or the other way around. Making her way around the edges of the room so that she had the walls to hold on to, she eventually arrived at the bathroom.

She opened the medicine cabinet while at the same time avoiding any glimpse of herself in the mirror. Looking into the mirror was bad enough on a regular morning; there was no point in staring death in the face.

The bottom shelf held three kinds of toothpaste—all three brands purchased on sale and none of them to her liking—and a plastic container of dental floss. She told herself her mouth would taste much better if she brushed her teeth. But just moving a toothbrush around her mouth required more energy than she thought she had at the moment.

The second shelf was filled with useless junk. Junk she never used and should've thrown out but kept in case of some future need. She even spotted one of Mohammed's catnip mouses among the junk.

The third shelf held everything she owned that could conceivably make her feel better, but it wasn't much. Thank God for Andy, she had aspirin. She never used it, but she kept it there for his frequent headaches, computer-induced. It took her more time than she thought she had left to live to open the child-proof top. When she did get the top off, she put it on the second shelf with the rest of the junk. It wasn't as if aspirin had to be closed up so it wouldn't go bad, she thought.

She poured herself a glass of water and downed three aspirins, the third one catching in her throat for a moment and tasting worse than her throat already tasted. There was also an opened package of Contac. She got three colds each winter, and she found that with Contac she didn't have to miss any work. It might not be for the flu, but it couldn't hurt. She took one twelve-hour capsule.

She felt worse when she left the bathroom than when she had walked in, but with faith in the pharmaceutical companies of America, she knew she would soon feel better.

Hanging on to the walls again, she made her way to the kitchen. Mohammed was making little high-pitched sounds, reminding her of the castrati, of whom he was one. She couldn't face opening a can of cat food. Just the smell of it on a normal morning made her stomach turn over. Instead, she tore open a package of Tender Vittles and shook them into one of his dirty bowls. She left it on the counter. Mohammed was quite capable of jumping onto the counter, and she wasn't at all capable of bending over.

Instead of jumping, Mohammed walked to a corner to sulk. She knew him well enough by now, though, to know that in a few minutes he would forget what he was supposed to be sulking about and go in search of some food.

Then, with her last reserve of energy, she staggered back to the couch and collapsed on the cushions.

Something flashed across her mind and then disappeared. When it happened again, she knew there was something she was supposed to be doing, something important. She tried to remember what it was, but the effort was making her headache worse. She closed her eyes and dozed off and woke up a couple of hours later remembering what it was.

She got up, staggered to the bathroom, took two more aspirins and three glasses of water and then got back on the couch with the phone and dialed Kevin's number.

"Let me speak to Caroline, Kevin." She thought she had said all the words, but only the last one was audible.

A pause. "Who is this?"

"Lulu."

"I can barely hear you."

She put a little more breath behind the words. "I can barely talk. Put Caroline on, okay?"

"You want to talk to Caroline?"

"Please."

There was another pause, and then she heard him calling Caroline. It occurred to her that she had never phoned Caroline before. The woman had been married to her best friend for ten years and not once had she ever even asked how his wife was. No wonder he sounded surprised when it wasn't him she wanted to talk to.

"Hi," said Caroline.

"I'm dying."

"Kevin said you seemed to be losing your voice."

"The flu."

"It's going around. Well, listen, save your voice and take two aspirins and get into bed."

"Already did."

"Don't worry about Mary. I'll go over there on my own, if you don't think she'll mind."

"Don't think so."

"I'll give her house a coat of paint, and I've got a winter coat I never wear that I thought she could use. How about if I come by and see how you're doing?"

"Not up for it," said Lulu.

"I could fix you something to eat."

"Thanks, but I'd rather sleep at the moment. Appreciate it, though." His wife was certainly more accommodating than Kevin had ever been.

"Okay, then, I'll give you a call later and tell you how it goes."

"Caroline?"

"Yes?"

"Have you ever mistaken the flu for being in love?"

There was loud laughter from Caroline's end. "You sound feverish to me, Lulu."

"I am."

Lulu hung up the phone and pulled the afghan over her shoulders. The flu. Just what she needed. And why did she have to get it for the weekend? This meant her laundry wouldn't get done, her groceries wouldn't get purchased and her bills wouldn't get paid. On the other hand, she felt marginally better. She wasn't so certain anymore that she was going to die.

She knew where she got it. It had been going around the homeless shelter for weeks. She hoped Neil would get it; it would serve him right. For what, she wasn't quite sure, but for something. She hoped Mary didn't get it. How did the homeless survive something like the flu? It seemed inconceivable.

She tried to remember the night before. She could remember putting the house up. She could remember later, at Flanagan's, but not too clearly. She thought she remembered Neil being in her apartment, but that didn't make any sense. Why would Neil be in her apartment? Who invited him there?

The thing she remembered most clearly was waking up in the middle of the night, in between nightmares, and being convinced of two things: that she was in love with Neil and that he was the devil. It was scary enough awakening in the dark in the middle of the night and feeling terrible without also having those kinds of thoughts. It must have been the nightmares, a result of her fever.

And all this thinking was making her headache worse again. Once more she closed her eyes.

The phone rang a little after noon. Lulu woke up, put it to her ear and managed a faint hello.

"Forget about your soul. I've been thinking it over and I've decided I'll settle for your body."

The voice sounded somewhat familiar. Not familiar enough, however, to be saying something like that to her. "I beg your pardon?" she muttered rather inaudibly, wondering if she should just hang up on whoever it was.

"How about dinner at my place tonight? I'm cooking. And then, after dinner, maybe we could do a little passing out."

"You've got the wrong number," said Lulu, slamming down the phone. Then, in case he got the wrong number twice, she took the phone off the hook. Her head still hurt, and a ringing phone didn't help.

NEIL CLEARLY HEARD THE PHONE being slammed in his ear, but he still held it for a minute, not convinced it had really happened.

Then he had the embarrassing thought that perhaps he had dialed the wrong number. He had assumed it was Lulu at the other end, but the woman—if it had even been a woman, and he sure couldn't tell by the voice—hadn't really sounded like Lulu.

Lulu had a low voice, but this one had been even lower, and strange. If it hadn't been Lulu, then that was certainly a peculiar thing for him to say to the woman. That talk about passing out—maybe she thought he was referring to drugs. Not that people generally passed out from drugs, although someone not familiar with the effects of drugs might think so. It could even have been construed by a stranger as being a lewd phone call. How embarrassing.

Actually, he thought it would get a laugh out of her. He was pretty sure if it had been Lulu on the other end he would have gotten a laugh. He thought it was funny, all that talk about bodies and souls. He had thought so the night before, but she hadn't laughed. Telling her he wanted her soul? Could she really take that seriously? Were souls something you weren't supposed to mention in casual conversation with a Catholic? No, not Lulu. He was sure he could say anything to Lulu.

He dialed her number again, this time slowly. He got a busy signal.

He was feeling good today. Actually, he was feeling more than good, he was feeling on top of the world. Not only had Lulu just as good as admitted to loving him, but she had passed out from ecstasy at his touch. He was finding that pretty incredible. He had never had a woman complain about his lovemaking, but he sure never had one faint from the pleasure, either.

He smiled just remembering it. Admittedly at first it had scared him just a tad. He couldn't quite picture having a relationship with a woman who'd constantly pass out at his touch. They hadn't even done that much. They would never get to the actual making love part if she passed out during the foreplay.

Then he realized that what happened had been the culmination of twenty years of repressed feelings that had finally exploded. He could understand that. Just that kiss had nearly wiped him out on the spot. It was beautiful. It was larger than life. It reinforced his feeling that they were meant for each other and no one else would do.

So she wasn't about to open up completely and pour out her heart the first time they were alone together. She was protecting herself, that's all. He could understand that. She didn't have to say she loved him, anyway. He could see that easily enough by her reaction. You didn't pass out from casual sex. To get to that state, you had to be madly in love along with it.

He had left when he did because he had the feeling he was rushing things. All he really meant to do was talk to her last night, but when the talking didn't work he took it from there. He'd rather go slowly. They had a lot of years to catch up on, and you couldn't condense twenty years in one night, particularly when that one night had started so late. He could tell she was exhausted, and he had been tired, too. Tonight would be different. Tonight would be like their first real date.

He wished he'd been the one to date her first. But since he missed out on high-school dates and dances, college parties, all the rest, he wanted things to be so perfect now that it would be as though they'd never dated anyone else in the interim. He wanted to wipe all memories of other men out of her mind so that she was completely focused on him. Just as he was on her.

He also wanted to make her faint dead away from desire again. God, that had been something. He'd never felt that much power over anyone in his life. He had a feeling he could easily get addicted to that.

He picked up the phone and tried again. Still busy.

They'd wasted a lot of years and for no good reason. One thing was for sure, he wasn't going to waste any more time. If he had his way, they'd be married before Christmas.

He wondered if she'd want a wedding. He didn't care either way. He tried to picture Lulu in a wedding dress and then realized he'd never seen her in a dress in his entire life. In fact he'd never seen her in anything but jeans. In fact seeing her in a dress might be as much of a shock as seeing Andy or Kevin in a dress, and probably as likely.

Oh, hell, she must have a dress. Every woman owned a dress. He'd ask her if she'd wear one tonight.

He picked up the phone and dialed again.

"Caroline?" yelled Kevin. "Hey, will you get me a beer, honey?"

Kevin reached for more potato chips and instead ended up scraping his fingernails across the bottom of an empty pottery bowl, managing to get salt under every nail. He sucked at the salt and watched as Penn State scored their third touchdown of the game. After the extra point, he lifted the remote control and turned off the sound, his eyes still on the commercial. It was a beer commercial, which accentuated his thirst.

He realized what he was doing and took his fingers out of his mouth. He wasn't even supposed to be having salt.

"Hey, Caroline, you in the kitchen?"

What was the matter with that woman? Was she getting hard of hearing?

He shoved himself out of the crumb-filled recliner, stuck his head out into the hallway and yelled up the stairs. "Hey, Caroline, you up there?" When he didn't get an answer, he took the stairs two at a time and looked into each bedroom. No Caroline. Not in her sewing room. Not in the bathrooms, either.

He went back downstairs and pulled the curtains across the bay window in order to see outside. Her car wasn't in the driveway. He let the curtains fall back into place so that the light from the windows wouldn't get reflected in the TV screen. Now where had she disappeared to just when he wanted another beer?

Andy was working on a software program for a chain of dry cleaners. Normally he would be finding it fascinating, but today he kept seeing Mary's face on the computer screen. When it got so that he was imagining two of her faces on the screen, side by side, both of them smiling at him, he saved the program and turned off the computer.

The faces were still there, so he closed his eyes. One of the faces winked at him, and he realized that what he was seeing was an exact replica of a Doublemint Gum commercial he used to see all the time. Only the women on the commercial had been blondes.

He wanted to see her. He wanted to talk to her. Since he couldn't, he wanted to talk to Lulu.

Andy tried to get Lulu on the phone for over an hour and kept getting a busy signal. That wasn't like Lulu. She didn't like talking on the phone. He finally had the operator try the number and was told the phone was off the hook.

Andy felt a little worried. It wasn't that Lulu couldn't take care of herself, it was that Andy was a worrier. He imagined all kinds of scenarios in which Lulu's phone would be off the hook. He didn't like any of them. He finally called Kevin.

"Hey, buddy, did you see that touchdown?" Kevin asked him.

"I'm at the office."

"On Saturday?"

"What can I tell you? Listen, Kev, you talked to Lulu today?"

"Yeah, for a sec. She called Caroline."

"Is Caroline there?"

"What's this with everyone wanting to talk to my wife today?"

"I was just a little worried about Lulu, that's all. Her phone's off the hook."

"Her cat probably knocked it off, he's done it before. Anyway, Lulu can take care of herself."

"Yeah, I know."

"Well, Caroline's disappeared, so maybe they're together."

They talked a little about football, and then Andy hung up. He had a pretty good idea where Lulu and Caroline were, and it was exactly where he'd like to be, only he thought he ought to wait until evening, when he told Mary he'd pick her up. He didn't want it to look as though he were rushing things.

On the other hand, it wouldn't hurt to just drive by and see what was happening. It was on his way home, and it was a public street, wasn't it?

LULU COULDN'T SEEM to stay awake, but she didn't like the dreams she was having. If she didn't know she had the flu, she'd begin to think she was having a religious experience. But she'd never heard of people having visions of the devil. If she started seeing the Virgin Mary, she'd quit taking aspirins and call a priest.

Why did she keep dreaming about the devil, and why did he look so much like Neil? And angels all over the place, fighting him for her soul? She sure hoped it was only the twenty-four-hour flu because she didn't think she could take much more of this.

THE STREET WAS CROWDED with cars parked for the library. Andy circled the block twice looking for a parking space and finally had to park a block away.

He got out of his car and walked back to the park. When he got there, he noticed something in daylight that he hadn't realized at night, and that was you could see Mary's house from the street. Somehow he had thought with all the trees she'd be hidden, but the trees were bare, and the house was clearly visible. So was the group of people outside the house.

He didn't see Lulu but he saw Caroline, and she had a spray can in her hand and was painting the house. Andy didn't know whether that was a good idea. The bright white roof and door sure stood out a lot more than the natural wood would have. The door looked like a beacon. It was pretty, though; he liked the dark green with the pure white.

There were several other women there, but no one he recognized. Mary was either in the house or not around.

"Hey, Caroline," he said, coming up beside her and getting a little white paint on him that was being deflected from the house by the wind. "What're you doing?"

"Lulu and I thought it would look better with a coat of paint."

"Where is Lulu?"

"Home with the flu."

"I knew there was something wrong when I kept getting a busy signal."

"I'll stop by when I'm finished here," said Caroline, "and see if she needs anything."

"You don't need to," said Andy. "I'll go by. I have an extra set of her keys. I'll pick up some cat food and get her some ginger ale." He leaned in close to her to whisper, "Who are all the people?"

"People from the neighborhood, and they've been so nice and welcoming to Mary. Some brought her food, a couple of women brought her clothes, and one woman invited her over to her house to take a shower, which is where she is now. They all loved the idea of houses for the homeless."

"That's great," said Andy, feeling jealous that everyone in the world was helping Mary except him.

"They're forming a group to adopt this particular house. I think Mary will be well taken care of."

"Maybe we should put a couple more up in this park," he said.

"I have an idea their group might do that themselves. Wouldn't that be great, Andy, if we started something? If groups all over the city started putting up houses, there wouldn't be any homeless anymore."

"And this place isn't even big," said Andy. "Just think how many could go up in Boston Common?"

Caroline took hold of his arm and drew him away from the other people. "Andy, there's something you ought to know."

"Is it about Mary?"

"There was a reporter here when I got here, and someone was taking pictures of the house."

"I guess there was no way we could keep this a secret."

"I talked to him. I hope that's all right. He wanted to talk to Mary, but when she found out he was a reporter, she went inside and put the bar up and refused to come out until he left."

"She's shy," said Andy.

"Will the others be upset I talked to a reporter?"

"Did you give him your name?"

"No."

"What did you say?"

"Well, he asked me who put up the house, and I told him I'd heard it was the Rooftop Gang."

"Did you tell them you were one of the gang?"

"No, they didn't ask. I think they assumed I was one of the people from the neighborhood. Most of them talked to the reporter, too, and they were all in favor of the house being here. I don't think we'll have a problem with that."

"I wouldn't worry about it, Caroline. We knew the newspapers would find out about it. Just so long as they don't know who we are, we'll be able to keep doing it."

LULU WOKE UP BRIEFLY when Andy came in her door. He walked over to the couch, looked down at her and said, "You don't look so good."

"I'm dying," said Lulu.

"You're such a baby when you're sick."

"I know."

"Well, don't worry, I'll feed Mohammed for you. And I brought you some ginger ale that I'll leave on the table in case you get thirsty. Have you taken your temperature?"

"It's a hundred and ten."

He gave her a doubtful look. "Did you actually take it or is that a guess?"

"A guess."

"Thermometer in the bathroom?"

She nodded.

She saw him disappear into the bathroom, then come back with her thermometer in his hand. He shook it down and stuck it in her mouth.

"Andy?"

"Don't try to talk with that thing in your mouth." She watched as he went to the kitchen area, got out clean bowls and fed Mohammed. He was using cereal bowls, not cat-food bowls, but Mohammed wouldn't care. Andy turned on the water, and she saw he was washing the dirty dishes in her sink. He even dried them and put them away in the cupboard, which seemed strange to her. Why dry dishes when you could set them in the drainer and they'd dry all by themselves?

He came back, took the thermometer out of her mouth and squinted at it.

"How much?" she asked.

"A hundred and two. You're improving already." He disappeared into the bathroom again and this time came back with the aspirin bottle and a cold washcloth, which he used to wipe down her face. For a few minutes she felt cooler.

"You want the TV on?" he asked her.

"I can't seem to stay awake."

"There's a couple of games on."

"Turn it on, but I'll probably sleep right through them."

She watched as he moved the TV stand closer to the couch, then tuned in one of the games. The sound of the announcer's voice was soothing.

Andy said, "Sleep's probably the best thing for you. Listen, why don't you move over to the chair for a minute, and I'll make up the bed for you."

"You don't have to do that."

"You don't want to sleep on a couch when you're sick. Come on, I'll help you."

Being extremely gentle, he helped her up from the couch, but instead of leading her to the chair, he led her to the bathroom.

"I don't need to go to the bathroom," said Lulu.

"Lulu, you're sleeping in your jeans. That can't be comfortable. Go on, put those pajamas on I saw behind the door. Do you need any help?"

Lulu shook her head. "I can do it."

After she changed into the pajamas, she realized her stomach felt a lot better out of the tight jeans. And her clothes had been soaked with sweat. She threw them all in the bathtub and pulled the shower curtain across so that Mohammed wouldn't jump in to sleep on them.

When she came out, her bed was made up, and it looked a lot better to her than the couch. Andy held the comforter aside as she crawled in, then pulled it up to her chin.

"Now that's a proper sickbed," said Andy.

"What would I do without you?"

"You'd survive, in your own stubborn way."

"Andy? Why was Neil here last night?"

"He said he wanted to talk to you."

"What about?"

"You asking me? I wasn't here. So, did you talk?"

"Yeah, I guess so."

"Give him a break, Lulu, he's a good guy."

An image of Neil with horns and a tail flashed through her mind. "I keep having nightmares about him."

"That's guilt. I told you at the time you should confess it."

"I had nothing to confess!"

"You tried to kill him."

"I did not!"

"You almost pushed him off the roof."

"I wasn't trying to kill him, I was just trying to beat him up. And there's no point in confessing something you don't feel guilty about."

"Obviously you feel guilty or you wouldn't be having nightmares."

"I don't think that's it. I don't know why I'm having them, but I don't think it has anything to do with that. I keep dreaming of the devil, and he's trying to get my soul."

"You want me to get a priest over here?"

"Don't you dare, Andy! And I don't think it's very nice of you to yell at me when I'm on my deathbed."

"I was just kidding you. Listen, you have nothing to feel guilty about, so why don't you get some more sleep."

She watched him pull the blinds and light the small lamp, then her eyes closed and she drifted off.

NEIL FINALLY CALLED THE OPERATOR, said it was a life-or-death emergency and asked her to cut in on Lulu's conversation. Several hours on the phone was ridiculous.

The operator told him that the party's phone was off the hook and that it had already been reported. He could only think of two reasons for her phone being off the hook. Either that had been Lulu on the phone and she didn't want to talk to him again, or she was in some kind of trouble. He decided to drive by her place to find out for himself.

KEVIN HEARD THE FRONT DOOR slam and yelled out, "Where the hell have you been?"

She looked in from the entry hall. "What do you want, Kevin?"

"Where the hell you been?"

"Out."

"Out? Just like that? No explanation? Why didn't you tell me where you were going?"

"Why do I have to tell you where I'm going?"

"'Cause I might worry about you, that's why. I looked all over for you."

"When? When you wanted another beer?"

"I can get my own beer. You just disappeared."

"I went into the city."

"On a Saturday?"

He waited for an explanation, but none was forthcoming. "What's for dinner?"

She came into the living room and sat down on the arm of the couch. She said, "I thought we'd go out."

"If you wanted McDonald's, you should've picked it up."

"I meant to a restaurant."

"Ah, Caroline, that means I'd have to change my clothes. Why don't you just fix some lasagna?"

"I feel like going out."

"Well, I don't feel like it, okay?"

Caroline got up and walked out to the hall closet. He watched as she put on her shearling coat, grabbed her handbag off the hall table and then he heard her open the door. Before he could ask where she was going, the door slammed shut.

LULU WAS DREAMING that someone was pounding on her door, trying to break it down. When she looked at the door, she saw that she could see right through it. On the other side, lifting his pitchfork to batter in the door, was the devil. He was naked and the same color as a freshly boiled lobster.

She looked around the room for help and saw the guardian angels crouched behind the furniture, trembling. She knew they were going to be no help to her at all.

"Let me in, Lulu," the devil kept shouting. "Lulu, are you okay?"

She was okay now, but she wouldn't be so okay if the devil got inside the apartment with her. If he got in there, she was in danger of losing her soul. She saw Mohammed crouched in a corner and hissing at the devil. And then Mohammed turned to her and said, "You forgot to feed me."

Lulu yelled out, "This is a dream, you're all in a dream, this isn't really happening." She thought everything would dissolve, like in a movie, but the devil kept pounding and the cat kept hissing. Only the guardian angels were doing a fade-out.

NEIL COULD SEE THE LIGHT in the window and could hear the sound of the television. He couldn't distinguish any actual words, not enough to tell what she was watching, but he could hear the laugh track clearly enough. There would be a low murmuring and then the sound of raucous laughter.

He went back to her front door again and began pounding. She was in there, he knew it, and she must be able to hear him. Why did she have the phone off the hook? Why was she refusing to answer the door? Was it possible that he had completely misread her last night?

Even if he had—and he certainly wasn't ready to admit that, not the way she had melted in his arms—this wasn't her way. The Lulu he knew would come to the door and tell him to get lost, not hide inside her apartment like a fugitive.

Why was she doing this? Was this some punishment she had devised in retaliation for what she perceived as his betrayal of her? Did she lead him to believe she loved him last night, then decide to demolish him today? Well, if that was her plan, it was effective. He was becoming frantic at the thought that she was inside and he couldn't get to her.

Wait a minute. What if she wasn't in there at all? What if she had gone away for the weekend and left the light and the television on to fool some would-be thief? Was he out here making a complete fool of himself? Was he doing nothing more than probably scaring her cat, who was no doubt cowering inside at all the racket he was making?

He knocked one more time, less loudly, then rubbed his sore knuckles. This was ridiculous. He was acting like a kid who wasn't getting his own way. She wasn't home; she couldn't possibly be home. Adults just didn't behave that way.

He turned away from the door and headed for his car.

ANDY KNOCKED ON THE DOOR without thinking, ending up with white paint on the knuckles of one of his gloves. He took it off, folded it up with the paint part inside, then shoved it in a pocket.

He heard the bar being lifted, and then the door opened. The Coleman lantern shed enough light so that he could see the two men inside the house with Mary. They looked to be in their sixties, dressed plainly in work pants and worn jackets, both squatting on the floor with their backs to the wall. One was wearing a brown tweed cap.

"Good evening," said Mary.

"Are you ready to go?" asked Andy, not knowing whether to acknowledge the men's presence or not.

She stepped outside and closed the door after her. She was wearing a red wool coat that was too big for her, but her black hair looked beautiful against the collar.

"Those men were admiring my house, so I said they could use it until I returned home."

"They're homeless, then?"

She nodded.

"They might steal your things."

"I have nothing to steal," said Mary, as he opened the car door to let her in. He waited while she settled herself, then closed the door.

He was worried about her. She could return that night and find the door barred against her. In that case, though, Andy would simply take her home with him. It would be the only thing to do. And then, after spending one night there, what would prevent her from staying on indefinitely?

"YOU WENT OUT TO EAT?"

Caroline nodded. "It was wonderful. It's been years since I had lobster."

"You went to a restaurant?"

"Of course, I went to a restaurant. They're not serving lobster at McDonald's."

As she walked by him, on her way upstairs, he said, "You ate by yourself?" Maybe that's what this was all about; maybe she was seeing some guy.

"Of course, I ate by myself. I enjoy dining alone."

Kevin stared at the television screen, but his attention wasn't on it. How could she enjoy eating all alone? He hated eating alone. He never ate alone. If he didn't have someone to eat lunch with, he called out for a sandwich and ate it at his desk. He knew she went to movies alone sometimes, which he'd always thought odd, but eating alone? In a decent restaurant? It seem inconceivable to him.

"Hey," he yelled after her, "you telling me you've already eaten, and I'm sitting here starving, waiting for you all this time?"

ANDY COULDN'T REMEMBER TALKING about himself at such length to anyone. He would ask Mary a question, and she would deflect it back to him, and he would find himself telling her everything there was to know about him. About his family, about the Rooftop Gang when they were kids, about dropping out of Boston College in his second year and, with two other young computer geniuses, starting up their own computer company, about the economic miracle in Massachusetts that was largely due to companies like theirs.

Mary was a wonderful listener. She wanted to know everything they had done as children, smiled when he was trying to be amusing, asked incisive questions about his business and didn't have any of the annoying mannerisms of other women he had dated, such as listening to his answers while scanning the room for more interesting people. She made him feel like the most fascinating man in the restaurant.

But despite how much he talked and despite how many courses they ate, it was still early when the bill was brought to their table. He could take her home, but she wouldn't be able to invite him in. She couldn't say, "Do you want to come in for a cup of coffee?" because there was nothing for her to prepare coffee with, just as there would be nowhere for him to sit.

As he escorted her out of the hotel grill, he said, "Would you like to see where I live?"

It was the kind of question that usually elicited a raised eyebrow or a knowing smile, but Mary simply said, "I would like that."

LULU WOKE UP around eleven in the evening. Her pajamas were soaked, her skin felt cool, and she was starved. The news was on TV and she got up, found she could walk without holding on to the walls and turned it off. She was feeling a little weak and her head was buzzing, but she was no longer so certain that she was going to die.

Since she hadn't been to the grocery store, she knew there was nothing much in the house to eat. Some stale bread, a few slices of Velveeta, maybe a couple of cans of soup covered with dust at the back of her cupboard behind a few cans of cat food that Mohammed didn't care for. Nothing she particularly felt like. She started to feel very sorry for herself. Sick as she was and nothing in the house to eat. And she was starved.

She put the phone back on the hook and called a pizza place that delivered and ordered spaghetti, salad and a double order of garlic bread. She changed her mind and made it a triple order. While she waited for her food to arrive, she washed her face, ran a comb through her hair, looked for her clean flannel nightgown, didn't find it, and remembered she had given it to Mary. She put on a clean T-shirt, instead, one that came down to her knees. Then put on her robe so the delivery boy wouldn't get any ideas.

She'd lost a day. It seemed strange to go from Friday night to Saturday night with nothing but wasted time in between. A picture flashed through her mind of her and Neil on the couch in a rather compromising position. Now where had that come from? Why was she suddenly thinking about Neil? She tried to get the picture back so she could concentrate on it, try to make some sense of it, but it wouldn't come. For that brief moment it was there, though, she was sure she'd been on Neil's lap. She must be hallucinating or something. In her worst dreams she didn't get on some guy's lap.

She felt like some music. She rummaged through some loose cassettes and found one by U2. When she put it in her stereo and the first beats were heard, she remembered the poster she had bought for Mary. She hoped Mary was doing all right. If she felt well enough tomorrow, she'd go by to see her. Maybe take her out to brunch, if there was somewhere in that neighborhood that served brunch. It wouldn't be a bad idea to explore the neighborhood, see where things were. That's what she would want to do if she moved into a new place. Maybe there'd be someplace nearby where Mary could get a job, be able to walk to work. She should've spent more time trying to line Mary up with a job. She'd get on it Monday, make a few calls around to see if she could come up with anything. Wait a minute, was this Saturday night? Andy was seeing Mary tonight, wasn't he? Maybe Andy could help with finding her a job.

Lulu went to the window and separated two of the slats and looked out. She didn't see any legs walking into view. Where was the food? At eleven o'clock at night they couldn't be getting that many orders. How long did it take them to dump some spaghetti into a carton and carry it one block? Didn't they know she was starving to death?

"WHAT A GREAT HUGE PLACE you have for yourself," said Mary, walking the length of the loft and pausing to look at the view of downtown Boston through his floor-to-ceiling windows. "Ah, that's a lovely sight." She took off her red coat and let it drop to the floor.

Andy picked up the coat, shook it a little in case it had gotten dust on it, then carried it to the closet and hung it up. He liked the way it looked hanging next to his black overcoat. The coats looked good together, like a couple.

Andy came up beside her. "I haven't gotten around to furnishing it yet. I keep getting different ideas about what I want, but then I never have time to actually go look at furniture."

"Sure and you could put a dozen of my houses in here and have room left over."

Did she think he was greedy to have so much space? He hadn't really needed the space; what he'd needed was a tax write-off. "You're more than welcome to put your house in here," he said to her.

She smiled at him and leaned against his arm. He carefully arranged his arm around her shoulders, and she didn't move away.

"Could I fix you a cup of coffee, Mary?"

"I couldn't take in another thing, Andy, but thank you all the same."

"Would you like to hear some music?"

"The quiet is lovely."

He was at a loss as to what to suggest next, but then she moved around to face him, pressing her body up against his and lifting her arms to pull his face down close to hers. He realized, with a surge of unexpected delight, that he wasn't going to have to suggest anything after all.

NEIL WATCHED THE ELEVEN o'clock news, then went out to get the Sunday papers. He got back chilled from the drop in temperature and built a fire in the fireplace. He poured himself a glass of blackberry brandy, then took a seat on one of the Chesterfield couches that flanked the fireplace and pulled out the sports section.

He tried to concentrate on an article on Mike Tyson, but he couldn't read about fighting without Lulu coming to mind, so he finally set aside the newspaper and decided to call her one last time. It was late, but since it was the weekend and she didn't have to get up early to go to work, he figured it would be all right.

He figured it was the right thing to do. You didn't just make a move on a woman and then not call her for forty-eight hours. Not if you hoped to see her again.

This time he didn't get a busy signal.

LULU MANAGED TO SHOVEL a mound of spaghetti into her mouth and pick up the phone on the first ring. She sucked most of the spaghetti down her throat without chewing and said a mumbled, "Hello?"

"Lulu?"

"Mmm." She didn't recognize the voice. At this hour of the night you ought to at least be able to recognize the voice. She lifted another forkfull of spaghetti.

"This is Neil."

The spaghetti, which has been halfway into her mouth, fell out and dripped all over the receiver. Some of the tomato sauce went down into the little holes. She tried to lick it back up before any more of it spilled in her lap.

"Lulu?"

"Yeah, I'm here."

"I heard a strange noise."

"So what's up, Neil?" She got a flash of her and Neil on the couch again and choked on the spaghetti going down her throat. She set the phone down for a minute while she reached for a swallow of coke.

When she picked the phone back up, he was saying, "Did I catch you at a bad time?"

"Yeah, you did."

"Well, I just didn't want you to think I hadn't called. I've been trying to get you all day."

Why would he think she'd think it was funny if he hadn't called? Did he think that now he was back in the gang, so to speak, they had to check up on each other daily by phone?

She said, "As far as I know, everything's okay with Mary."

"Mary?"

"Yeah, Mary Moore. The one living in our house."

"Oh. Well, I'm glad to hear that."

She picked up a piece of garlic toast, but just the smell of the garlic made her feel slightly sick, so she set it back down. She'd stick to spaghetti until she felt better. She all of a sudden flashed on a picture of her and Neil kissing. The problem was, it wasn't the same kiss they'd exchanged in the boiler room, she knew that for a fact. Because in the boiler room neither one of them had opened their mouths.

"Are you still there?" Neil was asking.

"Did something happen last night?" she asked him.

"What do you mean?"

She reached across the coffee table to get the Parmesan cheese and ended up dragging the front of her T-shirt through the plate of spaghetti. She was going to have to take a bath after this meal.

"Nothing. Never mind. Listen, Neil, I'm having trouble here talking. Could I get back to you next week sometime?"

"Next week?"

"Yeah."

"I was wondering if you'd want to get together tomorrow?"

"Tomorrow?"

"Yes. Tomorrow. Meaning Sunday."

"I'm going to be really busy tomorrow, Neil. Was it anything important?"

He was silent for a moment. "I guess not."

"Okay. See you, then," she said, and hung up the phone. As soon as she finished washing herself, she was going to have to do something about the spaghetti sauce all over her white telephone.

WAS SHE PLAYING GAMES with him? Was that it? He hadn't figured Lulu for the kind of kid who would grow up to be the kind of woman who would play games. Not those kind of games.

It was enough to make him wonder if he'd imagined the night before. The trouble with that was, he wouldn't have spent all day trying to get hold of someone who was a figment of his imagination.

One thing was for sure—nothing had changed. She had driven him nuts as a kid, and she was still doing it to him.

Chapter Eight

NEW GANG IN TOWN

Over the weekend a group of people calling themselves the Rooftop Gang erected a small house for the homeless in one of the city's parks. Neighbors who were interviewed said they supported the venture and were thinking of adding a few more. The stylish little house is already home to a female tenant who refused to be interviewed.

LULU READ THE ARTICLE TWICE. It was astonishing to see the name of their gang in print like that. She wanted to run out to show the other workers, yell out, "Hey, guys, I made the papers," but it was still a secret, and better that the people in power in the city didn't find out. And news, or even rumors, among city employees spread quickly.

She picked up the phone and called Andy, but was told he was at MIT on business. She tried Kevin's office and was told he was in a meeting. She left a message for him to call her back. That left Neil, and she didn't want to call him. Neil had acted peculiar on the phone.

She called Kevin's home number hoping that Caroline would be there. There was no answer, and she hung up. Why wasn't anyone around when she needed them? She was reading the article for the third time when her phone rang, and she grabbed it up.

"Margaret Boyd Center for Homeless Women," she answered, "Lenahan speaking."

"How are you, Lenahan?"

This time she recognized the voice. "Is that you, Neil? Did you see the paper?"

"What paper?"

"This morning's. There's an article about us in there."

"About you and me?"

"Oh, right, about our longtime feud."

"I don't have a feud with you, Lulu."

"It's about the Rooftop Gang. It must have been Caroline who talked to the reporter. She was the only one over there as far as I know. Or maybe Andy, but he would've said something."

"What page?"

"Second section, third page, but it would probably be faster to read it to you." She proceeded to do so. "What do you think?"

"I like it. The Rooftop Gang has finally gotten the notoriety it deserves."

Something occurred to her. "If you're not calling me about that, why are you calling me?"

"Do I have to have a reason?"

"What is it, you just like talking on the phone?"

"As a matter of fact, I don't."

"Well, neither do I, so why are you calling?" Lulu saw Janet go by the door, and she put her hand over the mouthpiece and yelled out, "Janet?"

Janet looked in her door. "Morning, Lulu."

"Any coffee out there?"

"Be ready in a minute."

"What did you say, Neil?"

"I didn't say anything. I heard you talking to someone else."

"Oh. Yes, I wanted coffee. So what did you want?"

"I heard of a job that might be right for Mary."

"Neil, that's fantastic!"

"Well, I'm glad you're able to summon up enthusiasm over something."

"What do you mean? I'm very enthusiastic about that article."

"One of my partners has a mother with Alzheimer's. He had a woman looking after her, but she's quitting. I guess it's hard to get someone to do that kind of work. He says she isn't all that bad yet, but he feels better with someone in the house with her during the day."

"That should be perfect for Mary," said Lulu.

"That's what I thought. I was thinking of driving by at noon and telling her about it, and I was wondering if you'd come with me. I barely know her, and she might not open the door to me."

Of course, she'd open the door to him. She knew very well who Neil was, but Lulu wanted to go by to see Mary, and this would save her taking two busses to do it. She hadn't gotten by there yesterday because she had still felt too weak to go out.

"All right," she said.

"Did that take a lot of deliberation?"

"I was just thinking."

"Shall I pick you up at noon?"

"Fine. I work at—"

"I know where it is."

"How do you know that?"

"I told you, Kevin keeps me informed."

"What are you talking about?"

"We'll talk when I pick you up, okay?" And then he hung up, leaving Lulu to wonder about that remark. Informed? Why in the world would Kevin keep him informed?

LULU WAS EXPECTING SOMETHING pretentious: A Rolls, a Mercedes, a BMW at the very least. But when she followed Neil out to the sidewalk, all she saw were the usual old wrecks that seemed to permanently reside on the block and a flashy motorcycle.

When Neil headed for the motorcycle, Lulu almost fell off the curb. She was so jealous she could die. All her life she'd dreamed of having a motorcycle. It wasn't fair. First that ten-speed bike, now this. She wanted to ask him if she could drive it, but stubborn pride prevented it.

He handed her a helmet.

"I'm not wearing that," she said.

"Well, I know you're not afraid of messing up your hair, Lulu, so it's got to be something else."

Not having any good reason except she didn't like to be told what to do, Lulu took the helmet and put it on. If she didn't, she knew he'd refuse to take her. If she was going to have to give in anyway, she might as well do it now.

"What're you doing with a motorcycle?" she asked him.

"I like them."

"You're not the type."

"Come on, Lulu, an old member of the Rooftop Gang not the right type for a motorcycle? Then who is the type?"

She conceded the logic of that with a quick nod of the head, then climbed on behind him. He started the motorcycle and then tore away from the curb, taking a right at the corner with the cycle on such a tilt that she laughed with pleasure.

She only wished they weren't in the city. She wished they were out on a highway where he could get up some speed and not have to stop at lights all the time. Nevertheless, she loved it. The wind on her face, the roar in her ears, the feel of all that power between her legs—it was better than sex. And if she started saving a little money every week, maybe in a year or so, she would be able to get one for herself. Except she'd been saying that for years, and she still didn't have the money. Why didn't Andy have one of these? She knew if Andy had one she'd be able to use it. She'd start dropping hints the next time she saw him.

At one red light, Neil turned around and yelled something to her.

"What?" she yelled back, lifting up her helmet so that she could hear him.

"I said, do you want to stop for lunch or do you want to wait and take Mary out to lunch?"

"Let's wait," yelled Lulu.

She was sorry when he pulled up in front of the park; she could have gone on riding like that all day. She got off and found her legs were a little shaky. She took off the helmet but carried it with her so that everyone would know she rode a motorcycle. She saw Neil was locking his up to the bike.

"It looks wonderful," said Lulu, spotting the green-and-white house through the trees.

"Who painted it?" asked Neil.

"Caroline. She did a good job, didn't she?"

"She can paint my house anytime," said Neil.

Lulu knocked on the door, saying, "Mary, it's me. We came by to see how you're doing."

She heard a footstep on the floor inside, but the door didn't open.

"Mary? Listen, we want to take you out to lunch. Are you dressed? If you're not, we'll wait."

"It's me with her, Mary—Neil. The house looks great!"

A moment later they heard the bar being lifted, and then the door opened a crack. "What do you want?" a gruff voice asked them.

"Where's Mary?" said Lulu.

"There's no Mary here."

Lulu pushed on the door but it wouldn't budge. "It's Mary's house, what happened to her?"

"It's my house, and you're trespassing."

Neil moved in front of Lulu and shoved at the door. He got it open, and Lulu saw a grizzled old man, dressed in rags and reeking of liquor.

"You don't belong here," said Lulu. "We put up this house for a friend."

The man staggered back into the house and sat down with a thump on the floor. He reached for a pint bottle and lifted it to his mouth. Bleary eyes kept watch on Lulu.

"The house was empty," said the man. "I took possession."

Lulu saw that the U2 poster had been ripped off the wall and now lay crumpled on the floor. The cot and lantern were gone, probably pawned for the bottle, but the sleeping bag was still on the floor. The angel was also gone.

Neil looked at Lulu. "What do you want to do?"

"Let's go get lunch," said Lulu.

"Just one thing," said the man, waving his bottle at them. "Next time you build one of these houses, put in a peephole or something. That way a person doesn't have to open the door to every bit of trash that comes by."

They were back on the sidewalk when a woman in a jogging suit stopped and said, "Did you know the woman who lived in that house?"

"Yes, she was a friend," said Lulu.

"She was a sweet woman. We were going to watch out for her," she said. "I live over there, across the street."

"What happened to her?" asked Lulu.

"I don't know. We didn't see her all day yesterday, and then last night that drunk moved in. Some of the neighbors are thinking of calling the police. This isn't that kind of neighborhood, you know."

"What kind of neighborhood?" asked Neil.

"The kind the homeless congregate in."

"A sweet, young woman is all right," said Lulu, "but not an old drunk. Is that it?"

"Come on, Lulu, let's go," said Neil, and she got back on the motorcycle behind him.

A few blocks later he pulled up in front of a diner and parked. "This okay?" he asked her.

"Fine."

This time she let him lock up her helmet. "That makes me so furious," she said to Neil, following him into the diner.

They took a seat in one of the booths, and Lulu glanced at the chalkboard that listed the specials of the day.

"What do they think, that the homeless should all look like Mary?" he said.

"Although I must admit, Neil, if I'm going to be honest, that I wouldn't have invited *him* to stay in my apartment. And we probably wouldn't have had him with us at Flanagan's." Although, she thought, her father, if he had lived this long, would have probably resembled that man by now.

"You can't blame people too much, I guess," said Neil. "Their children most likely play in that park."

"Well, what's the answer?"

"I don't know. But I think we should continue putting up the houses."

"But not in residential neighborhoods."

"He was right about one thing, though; the house should have a peephole of some kind. I'll put that in the next models."

"Maybe like we had in the clubhouse," she said.

"I wonder what happened to Mary," he said.

"I'd be more worried if I didn't know she went out with Andy Saturday night."

"That I didn't know about," said Neil. "I'm glad to hear Andy's not so shy around women anymore."

"The thing is, he is. I'm amazed that he'd get her to stay over on a first date. And more than one night."

"Maybe Mary's a fast worker."

"That's a terrible thing to say. She's a sweet woman, and I even had the feeling she was a virgin."

"They're still that strict in Ireland?"

"The Irish priests and nuns sure are. Give me an easygoing Italian any day."

The waitress came by and placed a coffeepot on the table. Lulu ordered soup and a grilled cheese sandwich, and Neil ordered the turkey special.

Lulu poured the coffee. "I like this place. How did you know about it?"

"I didn't know about it. I was hungry, and it was the first place I saw."

"I didn't think it was your kind of place."

"What kind of place is mine?" Neil asked her.

"Oh, something a little fancier."

"They frown on motorcycles at fancy places."

Lulu grinned. "That surprised me, too."

"I could see it did."

"I figured you for something like a Mercedes."

"Well, that shows you're perceptive, because I also have one of those. Only for when it rains or snows, though."

"And do you live in some fancy house on Beacon Hill?"

"I think most people live in what they can afford, Lulu. You no doubt can afford that apartment you live in. I can afford a house on Beacon Hill. That derelict we just left can afford that free house.''

"You live all alone in a big house?"

"Yes."

"Doesn't that make you feel guilty?"

"Not in the least. Do you want to see it?"

Lulu was silent.

"Why don't you come by tonight, and I'll fix you dinner?"

"You cook?"

"I can cook steaks."

Lulu made a little chart in her mind. On one side, Side A, she listed grocery shopping and a frozen dinner. On the other side, Side B, was a free steak dinner in the lap of luxury. And she was very curious about where he lived. "Okay," she said.

"You know something, Lulu? This is our first date. Crazy, huh? We should've been doing this years ago."

"Date?"

"It's about time, wouldn't you say?"

"This isn't a date, Neil."

"What would you call it?"

"I'd call it having a friend over to dinner."

"I don't cook for friends."

"Maybe we ought to forget about it," she said, suddenly wondering if the lunch they were having was also a date.

"You scared to come over to my house?"

"No, I'm not scared. Why should I be scared?"

"I think you're chicken."

"Well, you're wrong, as usual."

"All right, you win, I'm having a friend over to dinner, okay? Does that make you happy?"

"Just don't forget it."

"You're not about to let me, are you?"

"And I'm not chicken."

"Okay, whatever you say. I'll pick you up after work."

"You don't have to pick me up."

"Lulu, do you have a car?"

"No."

"Then tell me, would you rather take the bus or ride on my motorcycle?"

She conceded that she'd rather ride on his motorcycle.

"And we can stop by, and you can feed Mohammed first, if you want."

He even knew her cat's name. Just how long had he been there Friday night?

SHE HAD MESSAGES FROM EVERYONE when she got back to the office. She called Andy first, dying to know about him and Mary.

"Lulu? I've been trying to get you."

"I've been trying to get you."

"Mary is—"

"Staying with you, I know."

Andy was silent for a moment. "How'd you know that?"

"Because Neil and I drove by, and there's some old drunk living in the house."

"Do you mind?"

"That you're living with Mary, or that there's a drunk living in the house?"

"I guess we've got to expect all kinds. Even I might stay drunk if I was homeless, who knows?"

"Neil heard of a job for Mary," said Lulu, and told him what she knew.

"I don't think so," said Andy.

"It sounds perfect, and the pay's good."

"We're living together, Lulu."

"You mean *really* living together?"

"We're in love. Or at least I am, and I think it's mutual."

"I think that's wonderful, I'm crazy about both of you, but wasn't it a little sudden?"

"I think it happens like that. The right one comes along, and that's it."

"I'm amazed. Does Kevin know about it?"

"I told him, but he's got an attitude."

"An attitude?"

"He thinks she wants to marry me to get citizenship."

"Well, I know that's not true because I know her views on it. I'd say she fell for the Keely charm."

"You want to come by tonight? Have some dinner with us?"

"I'd love to, Andy, but I promised Neil."

"I'm glad to hear that."

"It's just dinner, my friend."

"That's what I thought about Saturday night."

"Tomorrow, okay?"

"Great. Oh, Lulu, I didn't even ask you how you were. You feeling okay?"

"I think it was just a twenty-four-hour bug. I feel fine today. And thanks. Thanks for coming by. I don't remember much about your being there, but I appreciate it."

"Anytime. You know that."

MORNINGS WERE HECTIC in the center, what with feeding the women, sending them on their way and then cleaning up before the next contingent arrived. The middle of the days was quiet, the time when Lulu took care of the paperwork involved, all the forms in triplicate and the up-to-date files that city agencies required. Around four the tempo picked up again as the first women began to arrive for the night.

This day was worse than usual. At four-fifteen Lulu was notified that one of the other women's shelters had had a fire and it was deemed uninhabitable for at least the next twenty-four hours. In the interim, Lulu's shelter was to handle some of the overflow.

Lulu was on the phone to one of the restaurants that donated surplus food to the shelter, trying to talk the manager into doubling the amount today, when Caroline walked into her office carrying a matched set of American Tourister luggage and looking gorgeous in a tan leather coat lined with fur and a matching hat.

Lulu raised a brow, motioned for Caroline to sit down and went on arguing with an equally harassed Mr. Manero, who had three waiters out sick and a chef who was threatening to quit unless he got a raise. When he finally promised he would send over whatever he could spare without shortchanging his customers, she hung up and said, "You interested in being a waitress this evening? If so, I can get you a job."

"No, thanks," said Caroline. "I'm tired of being a waitress." She took off her coat and hung it on the coat rack near the door, then settled herself gracefully into a chair on its last legs.

"You going down to Florida early this year?" Lulu asked her, referring to the vacation condo Caroline and Kevin had in Boca Raton.

"I left Kevin." She smiled as she said it.

"I don't believe this," said Lulu, sure that Caroline was joking.

"I was wondering if I could stay with you while I look around for a place."

"Stay with *me*?"

"I know what you're thinking. You're Kevin's friend, and I have friends of my own. But my friends are all married, and the last thing they want is someone reminding them how fragile marriage really is. Feel free to say no, though. I can always go to a hotel. On the other hand, I was hoping to get to know you better.''

"Kevin would kill me!"

"Are you really afraid of Kevin?"

Lulu said, "Look, I'm going to say yes, mainly because I don't have time to argue with you. But I've got an emergency here, and I could use all the help I can get. Would you make some phone calls?"

"Gladly," said Caroline.

Lulu handed her the phone and a list of restaurants, told her what to do and then went outside to use the phone in the reception area. The funny thing was, she'd never had slumber parties with girl friends when she was a kid; now it seemed she was having one right after another.

LULU USUALLY GOT OFF AT FIVE, but she was still there at five-thirty when Neil walked in the front door, right behind a homeless woman. Lulu took one look at him and belatedly remembered he was picking her up.

"You forgot," said Neil, correctly reading the expression on her face.

"I know it seems impossible when I just left you a few hours ago, but we have a little problem here."

"Social Services sent me over," said the woman, handing Lulu a slip of paper.

"If you want to go down the hall and take a right," said Lulu, "there's coffee. Dinner in about an hour."

The woman took off down the hall, and Neil said, "I seem to catch you at bad moments."

"Actually, I'm almost done here," said Lulu, "but there's another problem. Come on in my office."

She headed down the hall with Neil behind her. Inside, her boots on the floor and her feet up on the desk, Caroline was just thanking someone and hanging up.

"Hi, Neil," said Caroline, and to Lulu, "I got us some barbecued chickens from a deli I called."

Neil looked from Caroline to the luggage on the floor. "Is something up?"

"Caroline's running away from home," said Lulu.

"Well, we'll have to build her a house. We certainly can't allow a friend to be homeless."

"I forgot," Lulu said to Caroline, "I'm supposed to be having dinner with Neil tonight."

"Aha," said Caroline. "Well, don't let me stop you."

"You're welcome, too," said Neil. "I'm just fixing steaks."

"We can just drop off her luggage," said Lulu, "and I'll feed Mohammed. You drove here, didn't you, Caroline?"

"Yes, I drove, and I wouldn't think of butting in on your date," said Caroline. "Anyway, I'd love a quiet evening alone. No dinner to cook, no *Monday Night Football*..."

"I always watch *Monday Night Football*," said Lulu. "And it's not a date."

"Not at all," said Neil. "It's not anything like a date, is it, Lulu? It's just one old friend having another old friend over to dinner."

"It sounds like a date," said Caroline, "unless they're calling dating something else these days. I wouldn't know. I haven't dated since college. Go on, Lulu, watch *Monday Night Football* with Neil. What's Mohammed?"

"A cat."

"I can feed the cat."

LULU HAD NEVER been inside a house like Neil's. The first thing that was unexpected was that nothing matched. She thought only poor people lived in houses where nothing matched.

There were other surprises. Instead of wall-to-wall carpeting, there were hardwood floors with patterned rugs in muted colors. Instead of original artwork, there were old maps framed under glass hanging on the walls in the hallway and in the living room. Instead of a sleek, pedigreed dog, there were a couple of nondescript striped cats who sniffed at Lulu's pant legs, detecting the smell of Mohammed.

"Just let me get them fed," said Neil, taking her jacket, "and I'll get started on ours. You know how to build a fire?"

"Sure," said Lulu, thinking even a Boy Scout could build a fire.

"Don't forget to open the flue."

"The what?"

Neil went over to the fireplace, reached inside and pulled at something. "Okay, it's all set. Just throw on a few logs and crumple up some newspapers."

Lulu got the fire lit and then went in search of Neil. She found the kitchen at the back of the house. It was about twice the size of her entire apartment. One of the cats was eating from a bowl on top of the counter; the other one was under the table with another bowl.

"They refuse to eat together," said Neil. She liked the fact that he didn't try to force some discipline on his cats. Not that discipline had any kind of effect on cats.

"You need some help?" she asked him.

"No. Fix yourself a drink, if you want."

"I was wondering if you'd mind my looking around."

"You want me to show you around?"

"I can do it myself."

"Sure, go ahead. I don't have any secrets."

"I wasn't looking for secrets. I just want to see how the rich live."

"This isn't how the rich live. The rich have maids to feed the cats."

"Well, either you have a maid or you're so neat you scare me."

"I have a cleaning woman who comes in twice a week."

"That's a relief," said Lulu, wandering out of the kitchen and down the hall.

In addition to the living room and kitchen, the downstairs had a formal dining room and a small den filled with bookshelves, a handsome secretary with glass doors and comfortable reading chairs. The second floor had two bathrooms, two extremely neat bedrooms and one bedroom with the bed unmade and clothes piled up on a chair. She walked inside for a closer look.

The bed was large with a massive headboard and footboard of dark wood. There were at least a dozen pillows piled up against the headboard. The sheets and comforter looked like faded blue denim, and she recognized them as Ralph Lauren. She wouldn't have recognized them except she had seen them in the store, had loved the look of denim and had subsequently priced them. She thought the price was totally out of line and remembered extending this view to the saleslady.

On one side of the bed was a large table that held a digital clock radio, a good reading light, a couple of books, a pile of magazines, a remote control and an old photograph of Lulu in a silver frame, taken when she was eleven. She knew that she was eleven in the picture because she had a cast on her arm. And, if she recalled correctly, the only reason he had managed to take a picture of her was because she couldn't take a swing at his camera with her broken arm.

On the other side of the bed was a pint-size refrigerator. She opened it and saw different fruit juices, a couple of cans of beer and some bar nuts.

On the wall opposite the bed was a TV set built into the wall. She thought she could very easily live an entirely satisfactory life in his bed with everything she might possibly need right at hand. The room even had an adjoining bathroom not visible from the hallway. She peeked inside, saw a bathtub large enough to comfortably hold four, and decided she was seeing, in person, her first hot tub.

She left the bedroom and climbed the stairs to the third floor. This was one, large room, four times longer than it was wide, with lots of windows. One end held a drawing table and a lot of artist's paraphernalia. She ignored that end. The other end, the one that interested her, had a pool table, a shuffleboard table and several antique pinball machines. Never mind the bedroom—this was where she wanted to live. There was even a big, comfortable-looking leather couch, another refrigerator, this one larger than the bedroom's, and an enormous TV set. Was he spoiled rotten or what? One person with all this? It was enough to make her a Communist.

When she got back downstairs, he was sitting on one of the couches by the fire, holding a can of Michelob. "Can I get you anything?" he asked.

She shook her head and sat down on the other couch. "Can I take off my shoes?"

"Take off anything you want."

She really didn't appreciate that kind of remark from him, but she undid her shoelaces and pushed her shoes off anyway, then curled her legs underneath her. "Two questions," she said.

"I can guess the first."

"Let's see you try," she said.

"You're wondering about the picture in my bedroom."

"It seems a little weird."

"It's not as weird as it seems."

"Come on, a thirty-two-year-old having a picture of an eleven-year-old who isn't even his daughter next to his bed?"

"It's only been there a few days."

"Right. And you just ran out and bought a silver frame for it."

"If you had bothered to take out the picture, you would have found another picture of a very nice-looking woman I used to go with. After meeting you guys at Flanagan's that first night, I came home and went through some old stuff I hadn't looked at in years, and I found that picture. Since it was the same size as the frame..." He let the words trail off as he took a sip of his beer.

"The next woman's going to think it's weirder than I do."

"There isn't going to be a next woman," said Neil.

Lulu tried to stare him down.

He merely smiled. "So what was the other question?"

"Can I rent your third floor?"

Neil laughed.

"I'm serious."

"I practically live up there. I only go into the office a couple days a week. The rest of the time I work up there."

"And play."

"Only when I have someone to play with."

Lulu thought it best not to touch that subject. "Andy ought to do something like that with his loft. He's got this enormous area, and it's practically empty."

"Maybe Mary will help him fill it up."

"Yeah. Maybe. Do you have a yard?"

"Sure. You want to see it?"

"Maybe later. What's out there?"

"It's mostly bricked in. I have furniture out there in the summer, but now it's all in the basement."

"Hey, Neil, you want to get married?"

"Is this a proposal?"

"Maybe. What do you say?"

"I say it's a little sudden."

"I never figured on getting married," said Lulu, "but it might be worth it to get this house. It's not like you don't have plenty of room for two people."

"Ask me again when you'd be willing to marry me if I lived in a shack."

"Let's see how you cook first," she said.

"All I can cook is steak. Hardly worth moving into a shack for."

HE WAS RIGHT, THE DINNER wasn't worth moving into a shack for. The steaks were overdone, the baked potatoes, cooked in a microwave, had the consistency of rubber, and his idea of a vegetable was canned string beans. Nevertheless, she ate it all. For dessert he had Dove bars in the freezer.

"You serve great dessert," she told him, starting in on her second bar.

He piled the dishes in the sink, ran a little water on them, then left them. "You want to watch the game?" he asked her.

"Only until halftime," she said. "Will you take me home at halftime? I want to talk to Caroline before she goes to sleep."

"Why'd she leave Kevin? Did she say?"

"I haven't had a chance to talk to her yet. She walked in during a crisis, and then you showed up."

"They probably just had a fight."

"I don't think so," said Lulu.

"No?"

"He acts like a real jerk with her sometimes."

"You're criticizing Kevin?"

"What do you think, that I think he's perfect or something? Kevin's got some real macho attitudes, and I don't know where he picked them up. He wasn't like that as a kid."

"You don't know where he picked them up?"

"No, I don't. Why, do you know? Was it at Harvard?"

"I always figured it was from you," said Neil. "He was always trying to act just like you. If you remember correctly, you were the one who always put girls down."

"Me?"

"Yes."

"But we were just kids then."

"Nothing's changed. You're still trying to run the world, Kevin's still trying to act like you and Andy's still trying to get everyone's approval."

"And what about you?"

"I'm still trying to get you alone in the boiler room."

Lulu marched out of the kitchen fast. "Want to watch the game upstairs?" she asked him.

He came up beside her. "You mean in bed?"

"No, I don't mean in bed. I mean in your playroom, or whatever you call it. And you can just knock off those kind of remarks with me, Neil. I thought we agreed this wasn't a date."

"I call it a playroom, and I call this a date."

"Well, you can call it whatever you want, but that doesn't make it so. And yes, I'd like to watch it in the playroom."

"I wouldn't."

"Why not?"

"Because the living room is more romantic. There's a fire going—"

"Romantic? Who needs romantic to watch a football game? Come on, Neil, let's go upstairs."

"I don't feel like shooting pool with you or playing shuffleboard or—"

"Well, maybe I do!"

"Then you can come back some other time, and we'll play. We'll make a play date, okay?"

She ignored him and headed for the stairs. She was on the first step and moving toward the second when he grabbed her by the wrist and stopped her. She turned around to yell at him and found their eyes were on a level and the look in his was wicked. Even as he was reaching out for her other wrist, she said, "Knock it off, Neil."

"Why?"

"Because we're buddies, that's why."

"Buddies?"

"Yes. Now quit fooling around."

"What's happened to you since I've seen you?"

"What do you mean?"

"You know what I mean. This wasn't the message I was getting from you last Friday night. Or should I say Saturday morning?"

She flashed on that scene on her couch again, and then on Neil as the devil in her dreams. "Forget last Friday night. I've had nightmares about that night, and they're really weird."

"You've had nightmares about me?"

"Several."

"Well, I've had a few dreams about you, but I wouldn't call them nightmares."

She was starting to grow uncomfortable standing there looking him in the eyes. She tried to step down and around him, but he blocked her. What was he trying to do, anyway, extract a price for that dinner? Maybe the Dove bars were worth a kiss, but the rest sure wasn't. So she'd kiss him, get it over with and then maybe they could watch the game. Anyway, she sort of felt like kissing him, but she wasn't sure why.

So when his lips moved toward her, she moved in herself, and when his mouth closed over hers, she leaned into the kiss and encouraged it. And wasn't it amazing how much he had improved his technique since that infamous day in the boiler room.

He let go of her wrists and put his arms around her, and she found hers just naturally finding their way around his neck. If this is what had happened on the couch, no wonder she kept remembering it. Kissing Neil was a memorable experience. She couldn't remember any man kissing her quite like this or her enjoying it half as much.

When he finally came up for air, his head moving back a little as he smiled at her, she said, "Wow, that was really something!"

"Wow? That's it? Just 'wow'?"

"What do you want me to do, lead a cheer?"

"I expected a little more than a wow."

What did he think she was going to do, run upstairs straight for the bed? This was their first time alone together and he hadn't even taken her out. She wasn't even exactly sure how she felt about him. She felt something, yes, but she'd have to do some heavy thinking about what exactly it was.

And while she was thinking all that, he moved in again, his arms tighter this time, moving her so close to his body she could barely breathe. And then his mouth once more found hers, and she shut her eyes and wondered how long before the game started. And then she figured it wouldn't hurt if they missed the first few minutes, particularly since it would be such a shame to stop such a dynamite kiss right in the middle. And then she stopped thinking and just went with the kiss and the way his body felt pressed against hers and the way he was trying to sneak a hand up underneath her sweater, which she supposed she should put a stop to, only it didn't seem worth the effort, particularly since his hand felt awfully good moving around under there like that, so good, in fact, that she was reassessing her thinking and figuring if they missed the entire first quarter she wouldn't really care. After all, a game was very seldom decided in the first quarter.

He did a really macho thing then, something she would ordinarily hate. He picked her up and held her in his arms and headed for the living room. She hated it that men could pick up women that easily, and she hated it that she was so small it was easy for him to do, but on the other hand, it felt kind of nice to be kissed all the way down the hall.

He sat down on one of the couches and arranged her in his lap. His lap? She was actually in his lap? Oh, this was embarrassing. She was not the type of person to sit around in some guy's lap, and he should know that. It felt good, though; it felt comfortable. And the length and power of the kiss was becoming more astonishing by the moment.

It was only when his hand began moving below her stomach that she managed to pull her mouth away from his, at the same time taking hold of the roving hand. Come on, it was much too soon for this. If she let him keep that up they'd for sure end up in the bedroom, and afterward she'd hate herself for being so weak. It would be nice if they could get a little reacquainted first. Date a little. That sort of thing. She wasn't really into instant sex.

"You okay?" he asked her.

"I'm fine, but could we cool it?" she said, moving off his lap and sitting next to him on the couch. She pulled down her sweater that had been riding up on one side.

"Feeling faint?"

She looked over to see if he was joking. He wasn't. "No, I'm not feeling faint. Why should I be feeling faint?"

"Well, I just thought..." He let the words trail off, looking a little embarrassed.

"What did you think? And why should I feel faint? That's about the weirdest question I've ever been asked."

"I don't know how you're feeling, but I'm—"

"Neil, do we have to analyze it? It was enjoyable, okay?"

"I feel like I'm with a schizophrenic or something. Do you have a dual personality I don't know about?"

Lulu moved away from him on the couch. "What is your problem, Neil?"

"I don't think it's *my* problem."

"I think I liked you better when you were twelve. At least you didn't sit around the boiler room analyzing the kiss."

"It's last Friday night I'm thinking about, not the boiler room."

"Could you be a little more specific?" So she kissed him on the couch, what was the big deal?

"Well, excuse me for being a little puzzled, but you've got to admit your response is a little different tonight."

"In what way?" She was almost afraid to hear.

"Look, I'm not complaining. I thought it was great. I'd never had quite that effect on a woman before."

She sure didn't like the sound of that. "*What* effect?"

"The way you passed out when I touched you."

Lulu sat very still for a moment. "I did *what*?"

"The way you lost consciousness. Look, I was feeling every bit as emotional as you were. I just show it in a different way."

"Are you telling me I passed out?"

"Oh, come on, Lulu, quit acting like you don't remember. We talked about it. You asked me to make you pass out again."

Lulu began to edge away from him. "You're making me nervous, Neil."

"You're making *me* nervous. I didn't imagine it, you know. What's so different about the way you remember it?"

Lulu sighed. "I don't remember it."

"Convenient amnesia, is that it? You regret letting yourself go, so you choose to forget it."

"I was sick."

He started to laugh, but there was no humor in it. "You mean like in *depraved*?"

"No, I mean like in the flu. I woke up the next morning with a high temperature and a sore throat and a lot of other things. I had a bad case of the twenty-four-hour flu, and I can barely remember your even being there. But I kept having these nightmares where you were the devil and you were trying to get my soul."

Dead silence from Neil.

"I know it sounds crazy, but I guess it was the fever."

"It wasn't the fever."

"It wasn't?"

"No. It was something I said to you, something about wanting more than sex from you. I told you I wanted your soul."

"That's a strange thing to say, Neil."

"I didn't mean it literally. What I meant was, I wanted love from you, not just sex."

Lulu quickly stood up. "I think I'd like to go home now, Neil."

"Now?"

"Yes."

"What are you running from?"

"You."

"For God's sake, Lulu, are you that afraid of love? Haven't you ever loved anyone?"

"Not the way you're talking about. The way you're talking about sounds like being buried alive."

"I'm talking about a total commitment, yes."

"I want to go home. I have to think about this."

"It's not something you have to think about. Either you feel it or you don't."

"That's not true, Neil. I only feel what I allow myself to feel, and I have to think about it first."

"That's a cop-out if I ever heard one. When did you start getting so chicken, Lulu?"

"You're really getting me mad, Neil, calling me chicken all the time. If someone doesn't want to go along with you, the only thing you can say is the person's a chicken. For your information, we're not kids anymore."

"I'm aware we're not kids, but I don't think you are."

"Okay, you want to act like kids? I don't want to play anymore at your house, Neil. I want to go home."

"So who's stopping you? I don't see you handcuffed to the couch."

"Thanks. Thanks a lot. You get me over here and then you won't even take me home."

"It's not a date. You can take your own self home."

"What's the matter, you afraid you're going to miss a few minutes of the game?"

"It wasn't the game I had in mind for tonight."

"I know it, and that was your first mistake!" She got off the couch and went to the entry hall, opened the hall closet and grabbed her jacket off a hanger. "Thanks for a great meal, Neil. Next time I'll eat with a *real* friend."

He didn't even get off the couch. "If you weren't too chicken to admit you loved me, we could watch the game like a couple of civilized adults."

"And if you can't tell the difference between love and sexual attraction, I don't know how the hell you ever got into Harvard."

"Have fun trying to find a taxi in this neighborhood."

Lulu slammed the door with all her strength and fury.

"LISTEN, DO YOU MIND if I turn the game on?" Lulu asked Caroline. "I can talk and watch it at the same time."

"What're you doing home so early?"

"We had dinner. Did you order in something to eat?"

"Yes, but what do you mean you 'had dinner'? Is that all? You just ate and then came home?"

"What'd you think it was going to be?"

Caroline shrugged. "I just thought it would be a little more romantic, that's all."

"Well, you and Neil think alike, then."

"What was his house like? What did you have to eat? What did you do?"

"Is this what it's like to live with someone?" asked Lulu. "Every time you come home you get questioned?"

"All right, be mysterious."

"His house was great, the dinner was so-so, and what we did was eat. What I want to know is, what happened with you and Kevin?"

"Nothing happened. I just had enough, that's all."

"Does he know you're here?"

"No."

"Caroline, he's going to be worried sick about you. He probably has the police out looking for you already."

"I left him a note. I said I wanted to get away to think for a few days."

"Think? About what?"

"About whether our marriage is going anywhere."

"So have you done any thinking?"

"I don't need to," said Caroline. "I thought it all out before I left. Ten years of looking after a man who's never going to grow up is quite enough. I'm going to start making a life for myself."

"Is marriage that bad?" asked Lulu. "Is it like being buried alive?"

"It doesn't have to be, Lulu. I let it happen. Someone like you, it wouldn't be like that. You're strong. You stand up for yourself. I just stood by and let him bury me until finally I couldn't even find myself anymore."

Lulu looked at the TV and saw that it was halftime and she hadn't even noticed. She got up and went out to the kitchen to put some water on. "You want some tea, Caroline?"

"Sure. You want me to unfold this couch so we can get in it and talk?"

"Sure. I'll just get into my pajamas."

When Lulu came out of the bathroom, Caroline, in a man's striped nightshirt, was setting out the tea on the coffee table. Lulu propped some pillows up against the back of the couch and climbed into bed.

"I was thinking while I was in the bathroom," said Lulu, "and I think Kevin could change. I think he would be crazy not to if it meant losing you. You still love him, don't you?"

"Kevin doesn't need to change. Kevin has everything he wants: his job, you guys, a wife and a home. I'm the one. I don't have anything besides Kevin. That was enough for a while, but it's not anymore."

"So you get your own life going, and then you see if you can work things out."

Caroline nodded. "What about you and Neil?"

"What about us?"

"You still going to hold something that happened twenty years ago against him?"

"You know about that?" asked Lulu.

"That's one of the few things Kevin told me. I think you're being stubborn, Lulu."

"It doesn't sound like a big deal, I know that. But it was a big deal then. Of all the people who could've betrayed me, Neil's doing it hurt me the most. I thought he was perfect."

"No one's perfect."

"But I thought he was. I don't know if kids can fall in love, Caroline, but it really killed me when he did that."

"I think kids can fall in love. And I don't think it's a co-incidence that neither of you has ever married."

"I've never even loved anyone else."

"Well, there you are. What are you going to do about it?"

"I don't know. I'm not going to do anything about it. Neil and I are two of the most incompatible people on the face of the earth. Just put us in the same room, and I can guarantee you a fight."

"You're great together."

"That's your idea of great?"

"You have spirited, wonderful fights. You have the kind of fights two people have who love and respect each other. Kevin and I have ugly, mean-spirited fights, the kind that slowly destroy a relationship."

"Look, I'll admit I loved him when we were kids. And I'll admit that the sexual attraction between us is strong. But I could never, ever love someone who betrayed me, and that's exactly what he did when we were kids, and nothing tells me that he wouldn't do it again. The subject is now closed, and I want to watch the rest of the game."

Watching football was easy and relaxing. Thinking about or even discussing Neil was guaranteed to raise her blood pressure. And her blood pressure had already been raised enough that night.

Chapter Nine

Andy came home from work and opened the door. He called out to Mary but could see she wasn't there even before he called. Not unless she sat around in the dark.

He pushed a switch, and the track lighting went on, going down one side of the room, across the back and up the other side. It was enough light for a night baseball game, and he dimmed it a little.

Except for the red coat in the closet there was no sign of her anywhere. She didn't seem to like the coat. She preferred wearing a couple of his sweaters under that thin black jacket of hers. No possessions lying around, no sign that she had eaten. The bed looked the way it had looked when they got up that morning. Their two coffee cups were still in the sink.

He changed into jeans and a sweatshirt. He hoped she'd be home soon because they were supposed to meet Lulu and Caroline at a new Japanese restaurant he wanted to try out. He bet she'd never had Japanese food, and it was going to be a real treat to watch her enjoy it.

He was getting a bundle of laundry together when she came in the door. She moved silently, giving him a small smile, that Mandonna's smile of hers that knocked him out.

"Hi. Where've you been?" he asked her.

"I went for a walk," she said.

"In the cold?"

She shrugged.

He knew she liked going for walks. She liked learning the neighborhood, finding her way around the city. Sometimes she went out at night for walks and wanted to go alone. He didn't want her to feel walled in, and he let her go, although his natural inclination was to accompany her.

"Want to try some Japanese food tonight?" he asked.

"What about Lulu? Weren't we going to eat with her tonight?"

"She's meeting us. I also invited Neil along. I think the two of them have been seeing each other."

Mary just nodded, coming up to him and leaning into his side. He put his arm around her. She was so small, so delicate. He wanted nothing more than to take care of her the rest of his life.

LULU AND CAROLINE PULLED UP just as Andy and Mary arrived at the restaurant, and not even waiting for the car to come to a complete stop, Lulu jumped out.

She said hi to Andy, then pulled Mary aside. "I'm sorry I didn't get by Sunday."

"I heard you were sick, Lulu. Are you all right now?"

"Fine, just fine. But, Mary, I'm so happy for you and Andy. You're exactly what he needs in his life."

Mary looked down a little shyly. "Aye, he's a good man."

"I just can't believe it happened so fast. That date with him must've been terrific."

Mary was starting to look distinctly uncomfortable. Lulu could see she was embarrassing her, but she had thought they had gotten close enough that she could say what she was feeling. "Well, I think it's great—just perfect. And that way you won't disappear from my life."

"I wouldn't be doing that, Lulu, in any case."

Andy came to claim Mary, taking her by the hand. "Could we continue this conversation inside?" he asked. "It's freezing out here."

Lulu noticed the way Mary melted against him, and she was disappointed in a way. She had thought Mary was more independent; more like her. Instead she was turning out to be the way Lulu always expected women to be, wrapping themselves up in some man's life rather than choosing to stand alone. She knew it was unfair to judge Mary by those standards, though, since Mary was all on her own: jobless, homeless and in the country illegally, to boot. In the same circumstances, Lulu might do the same, although she seriously doubted it.

Once inside, they were asked if it was four for dinner, and Lulu said yes.

"No," Andy corrected her, "it'll be five."

"Five? Who else is coming?"

"I asked Neil to join us."

Lulu shot him a dirty look. "How could you do that to me, Andy?"

"What's the matter?" asked Andy. "I thought you guys were seeing each other."

"We're doing nothing of the kind," Lulu informed him. "I had one dinner at his house, and that was enough."

"And lunch," said Caroline.

"Right," said Lulu, "but that was just lunch."

Andy grinned. "Well, I'm sorry if I put my foot in it, but I guess it's just one more example of betrayal," he said.

"I wouldn't exactly call it betrayal," said Lulu, backing down. It certainly wasn't on a par with what Neil had done to her. It was just inconsiderate, that's all.

"Well, do you think you can behave in a civilized manner when he shows up?" Andy asked her.

"I suppose so," Lulu grumbled.

Two tables were pushed together for them, and at the same time the waiter came by to take the drink order, Neil showed up.

Lulu had taken the seat at the end of the table. To her right were Mary and then Andy, to her left, Caroline. Lulu expected Neil to take the seat at the other end, facing her, but he surprised her by sitting down next to Caroline. Well, good—that way she wouldn't have to look at him.

Not that she hadn't already seen him, and he looked damn good. He was wearing a tan leather coat lined in shearling, and beneath it a cashmere sweater with his jeans.

After about five minutes of this arrangement, Lulu began to feel left out. Andy clearly had eyes for no one but Mary, and Lulu could tell they were holding hands under the table. Andy was whispering things in Mary's ear, and, judging by the soft smile on her face, they were things she liked hearing. Lulu wondered whether this was the way people in love acted. If so, she had never been in love. She was glad for Andy, but did he have to go so public with it?

She heard Caroline burst out laughing and glanced away from Andy in time to see Neil lean back and put his arm around Caroline's chair. Caroline was turned to him, still laughing, and Neil was looking at her in a way that Lulu didn't like. Neil had no business looking at Kevin's wife in that way, a way that said he was enjoying her company. Lulu began to get irritated. Personally, she couldn't care less whom Neil was amusing, but she felt she ought to put a stop to it for Kevin's sake. Not that she was siding with Kevin in this, but, after all, he was her oldest friend.

"What's so funny?" Lulu asked, realizing too late she had put all of her annoyance into her voice.

Caroline, still smiling, turned to look at her. "This guy's pretty funny, you know it?"

Lulu looked to Andy for help. Andy knew as well as she did that Neil wasn't ever funny. But Andy had his head close to Mary's, and they were both in another world. By the time she looked back at Caroline, she and Neil were reminiscing about Harvard.

The waiter brought them menus, and Lulu didn't even bother looking at one. There was no point in eating in Japanese restaurants if you didn't order sushi, and since that was what she was ordering, why spend time reading what else they had?

Andy was leaning close to Mary, explaining the menu to her, with Mary saying, "You order for me, Andy." Neil and Caroline ordered the same thing, which was something Lulu had never heard of. She finally said, rather loudly, "Well, guys, we ready for Friday night?"

Everyone turned to look at her as though she were interrupting something important. "Never mind," she said.

She had to admit Caroline and Neil made a good-looking couple. They also seemed to have a lot in common. They were both tall, both took an interest in being well dressed, both had gone to Harvard and both were from rich families. In fact, it probably would have saved everyone a whole lot of trouble if they had been the ones to get married right out of college. That way Kevin wouldn't be sitting home alone right now with a broken heart, and she wouldn't be getting more jealous of Caroline by the minute.

KEVIN FLIPPED THROUGH the channels, watching a little of this and a little of that, never pausing for more than a minute or two. He lifted up his can of beer, felt that it was empty and called out, "Mrs. Esposito?"

The woman, wearing an apron tied around her ample midsection, came out of the kitchen immediately. "Yes, sir?" she asked him.

"Could I have another beer?"

"Right away, sir," she said, and moments later she was carrying a cold beer into the living room and setting it down on the table beside him, taking the empty beer can back to the kitchen.

She paused in the doorway. "Dinner won't be ready for another twenty minutes. Would you care for something to snack on while you wait?"

Kevin beamed. "That would be great."

No more than two minutes later, Mrs. Esposito was back, this time with a plate filled with crackers and slices of cheese.

"Thanks," said Kevin.

"You're quite welcome, Mr. McCrory."

He could smell the lasagna cooking from here. If the lasagna was as good as everything else about her seemed to be, she was hired.

She was an older woman, maybe a few years older than his mother. Older women knew how to treat a man. He remembered how his mother always waited on his father, and never a word of complaint out of her. His father was the boss around the house, and his mother knew her place. Not like these modern women—like Caroline—who thought the two should be equal, even though he was the one bringing in all the money.

He was watching a special on Sports Channel when Mrs. Esposito came into the room again. "Would you like me to set up your dinner in here, Mr. McCrory?" she asked him.

"I can come out to the kitchen."

"There's no need," she said, "I can just as easily bring it in here. That way you can watch the TV while you eat."

She was amazing, she really was. And she was willing to come in every day and clean his house and have his dinner ready for him when he got home. And after dinner she'd clean up and then go home. It sounded like a perfect arrangement. She said she even ironed shirts. She didn't just take them out of the dryer and hang them up so that they were always somewhat wrinkled even though the label said they were wrinkle-proof.

She brought over a table and set it up in front of him. The lasagna smelled delicious. If it tasted as good as it looked, he had himself a housekeeper.

He picked up a fork to take the first bite. Mrs. Esposito was standing a foot or two away, as though waiting to see whether he approved or not.

He put it in his mouth. It was fantastic!

"This is great," he told her. "Even better than my wife made it."

"Was she Italian?" asked Mrs. Esposito.

"No."

The woman sniffed, as though it was ridiculous to think that anyone but an Italian could make lasagna.

"You're hired," he told her.

"Thank you, sir, and just call out when you're ready for seconds."

Kevin reached for another bite, a happy smile on his face. He wished Caroline could see him now. She probably pictured him crying his eyes out without her. Well, he'd show her. He was just like Lulu; he could get along without anyone.

LULU WAS BEGINNING TO FEEL as though she were out with two couples, one already madly in love and the other on their first date and getting that way. If she'd known this was going to happen, she would've invited along a man of her own. Not that she knew of anyone offhand. And why was this happening, anyway? For someone who claimed to have been in love with her since they were kids, Neil sure wasn't acting like it. It was the first time in her entire memory that she had ever been in a group of people that included Neil when his attention hadn't been focused primarily on her. She might have ignored him some of those times. She might have fought with him all of those times. But it didn't feel very good to be having him ignoring her.

What was the matter with her, anyway? Was it pure perversity on her part? Did she have to be the center of attention when he was around? Or had she liked that attention but refused to admit it?

She thought of getting up and walking out. She had a feeling if she did, no one would even miss her. So what was stopping her? Was she afraid to walk out? Was she *chicken*?

Hell no, she wasn't chicken. Let them stay and have a cozy, intimate meal; she had better ways to waste her time.

Grabbing her jacket as she got out of the chair, Lulu headed for the door. She pushed it open, not even looking back, and walked outside. She was acting like a child. Worse, she was acting like a spoiled child who wasn't getting her own way.

So what? she thought, heading down the sidewalk and wondering how she was going to get home. She didn't know of any buses in the neighborhood and didn't see any taxis cruising by.

She heard someone running up behind her, and then she was grabbed by the arm and spun around.

"What the hell are you up to now?" Neil asked her.

"Leave me alone."

"Are you always this rude to your friends, or was this a special occasion?"

She tried to pull her arm out of his grasp, but he wouldn't let go. She saw he had run out without even putting on his coat. "You're wasting your time, Neil, I'm not going back." She'd be embarrassed to death to walk back in after the scene she just made. She wished that for once in her life she had given more thought to her actions.

"Don't think I don't know why you walked out of there, Lulu."

"You don't know."

"*I* know. I'm just wondering if you do."

"I really don't like Japanese food."

"That's a lie."

It was a lie. She adored Japanese food. "I wasn't feeling well."

"When did that start, when Caroline and I began to talk?"

"I don't know what you're talking about."

"Caroline happens to be married, and I happen to be in love with you, not Caroline. God only knows why, though. You're as perverse today as you were when I met you."

"I think you and Caroline would be great together."

"What do you want to do, Lulu, have a punching match right here in the street? Do I have to beat some sense into you?"

"You better not try it!"

"Listen to you, you still sound like a child. I'm not ten anymore, Lulu, and I don't show my interest in someone by punching her."

"Maybe I do," Lulu conceded.

"I'm aware of that."

"You've got me all mixed up, Neil."

"I'm aware of that, too."

"I don't seem to be able to sort it out."

"Maybe I could be of some help. The attraction is mutual, you've got to admit that much."

"Oh, yes—I admit that."

"You're halfway in love with me now—at least—and you'd be all the way if you'd let yourself."

"I guess so."

"You *guess* so? Then what the hell is the problem?"

"How can I love someone I don't trust?"

He let go of her arm and stared over her head. "You're never going to forgive me for that, are you?"

"It's the worst thing that ever happened to me."

"Maybe you should've just pushed me off the roof that day."

Lulu was silent, very close to tears and fighting it.

"I give up," said Neil. "I always thought it would be right with us, but I guess it's never going to be. Come on back in, Lulu. I promise I'll never bother you again."

Feeling very much as though she had lost, Lulu followed him back into the restaurant.

"WHAT WAS THAT ALL ABOUT?" asked Caroline as they were driving home.

"I'm really sorry. I can't believe I did that."

"I said, 'Where did Lulu go?' and Andy said, 'Oh, she always walks out, don't worry about it.'"

"I swear, I haven't done that in years."

"And then Neil said, 'I'm going after her, but don't be surprised if I come back with a black eye.'"

"I feel really stupid. You're not going to believe this, but I was jealous of you."

"Oh, I know that. I was trying to make you jealous."

"You were *what*?"

Caroline laughed. "You might scare the guys with that tone of voice, but you don't scare me. Hey, it worked, didn't it?"

"Why would you do something like that?"

"So you'd realize how you felt about Neil, that's why. And I'll tell you something, Lulu—I don't think he's going to take that kind of behavior from you forever. Anyway, it beat having you two fight all through dinner."

"I don't know what to do," Lulu admitted. "I really don't."

"Forgive him, Lulu, and get on with your lives."

"I don't seem to be able to."

"You're a Catholic, aren't you?"

"I was brought up one."

"Aren't you able to commit sins and then confess them and be forgiven?"

"That analogy won't work, Caroline."

"Why not?"

"Because I'm not God. God seems to be a lot more forgiving than I am."

"Haven't you ever done anything you've been sorry about?"

"Sure, lots of times. I'm sorry I walked out of the restaurant tonight. But Neil isn't sorry. He thinks he was right."

"I think he was, too."

"You don't understand, Caroline. We were too close to betray each other. I was closer to those guys than I ever was to my family. I would've trusted them with my life."

"You know something, Lulu? You're never going to meet a man who's perfect. It just doesn't happen."

"I know that."

"I'd say Neil comes pretty close to being perfect."

"I know that, too."

"So if you want something lasting with a man, maybe you're going to have to lower your standards."

"I know."

"The two of you have already wasted enough time."

"I know."

"So if you know everything I'm telling you, what are you going to do about it?"

"I don't know."

"Damn it, Lulu, you're impossible!"

"I have to think about it."

"Just don't take forever."

LULU WAS JUST WALKING out of the door to lunch on Friday when Caroline pulled up to the curb in her Subaru. Lulu walked over, waited for Caroline to unlock the door, then got inside.

"What's up?"

"I came by to take you to lunch."

Lulu shut the door and waited for Caroline to yell at her to fasten the seat belt. When she didn't, when she just pulled out from the curb, Lulu noticed that she wasn't wearing one, either.

"What's the occasion?"

Caroline turned with a quick smile. "I found an apartment, a job, and I'll be back in school the first of the year."

"All in one morning? I'm impressed."

"Harvard said there'd be no problem about my getting into their graduate program. Not since I got my undergraduate degree there and it's not one of their more crowded programs. And I found an apartment nearby, in Cambridge, and a job in a bookstore. It doesn't pay much, but it'll be something to do."

"I'd be bored to death in a bookstore," said Lulu.

"Don't you read?"

"Not if I can help it."

"I won't be bored," said Caroline. "I love books. The apartment's one bedroom, furnished. The woman always rents to students, usually guys, but I talked her into letting me have it. I told her I was handy around the house, and she finally believed me when I fixed a light switch for her.''

"This sounds pretty final. Have you talked to Kevin at all?"

"I called him. Said I'd be stopping by for some of my clothes. You know what he said to me?"

"I can't wait to hear," said Lulu.

"He said his housekeeper would help me pack."

"Oh, yes, I've heard about the redoubtable Mrs. Esposito."

"Kevin told you about her?"

"It seems she makes the best lasagna in the world."

Caroline started to laugh.

"What's so funny?"

"Kevin and his lasagna. I'll be happy if I never have to see lasagna again as long as I live."

"I was hoping we could go for some Italian."

"Oh, we can," said Caroline, "just don't order lasagna if you know what's good for you."

"You coming out with us tonight?" asked Lulu.

"I wouldn't miss it."

"Oh, good. I was afraid, because of you and Kevin, you wouldn't want to come. Which means we'd end up with three houses with no doors."

"Where's it going to be? Is Bunker Hill still on?"

"As far as I know. I just hope there's not going to be another battle there."

"Don't worry, Kevin and I will act civilized. We won't embarrass you."

"I was thinking more of me and Neil."

"Have you talked to him?"

"No."

"Have you done any thinking?"

"Lots."

"Have you come to any conclusions?"

"Not really."

"Don't be a fool, Lulu—go for it. You're going to be missing out on a lot if you don't."

"If being with a man is so great, why did you leave Kevin?"

"He needs to do some serious growing up, Lulu. If he could manage that, then who knows?"

"I'm kind of sorry you're moving to Cambridge, just when we were getting to know each other."

"It's not that far. You can come out, spend the night, and we'll pick up some undergraduates."

Lulu laughed. "I might take you up on that. I always wondered what it would be like to date a Harvard man."

"Neil's a Harvard man."

"Oh, yes—but that was years ago."

"Well, it's not all it's cracked up to be."

"Really?"

"Really."

"You mean they're like anyone else."

"Essentially."

"Then why did you marry one?"

"Well, when you're a Harvard woman, that's about all you meet."

Lulu thought about Harvard men in general and one Harvard man in particular. She had given a lot of thought to her and Neil; in fact she'd thought of little else. One way or another, she was going to make up her mind tonight.

Chapter Ten

Andy called her just before five, telling her, "I've got a problem here, Lulu, and I'm not going to be able to get out of here in time to pick you up."

"That's okay. I'll see you at Flanagan's."

"I may not even make it there."

"Oh, Andy, you're not going with us tonight?"

"I didn't say that. I'll just be a little late, that's all. Why don't we meet you there?"

"Is Mary coming?"

"She wants to. Where's it going to be, Bunker Hill?"

"Right."

"How about if we meet you there at eight?"

"Okay. I think I'll go to Flanagan's early, get something to eat. It could take us all night to put three up."

"Why don't you call Neil and have him pick you up?"

"I can get there on my own."

"I'm sure he'd be glad to drive you."

"Andy, I'm quite capable of taking a bus to Flanagan's. I'll see you later, okay?"

NEIL TOOK OFF EARLY and met Kevin at the lumberyard. They both pulled into the parking lot at the same time and parked next to each other. Kevin was in a larger truck this time.

"Where'd you get the truck?" Neil asked him.

"I borrowed it from a friend. I didn't figure my brother's would hold enough stuff for three of them."

"So how's it going?"

"Everything should be ready. They'll even load the truck for us."

"I mean personally. How's it going without Caroline?"

"Who?" asked Kevin, a look of mock confusion on his face.

"Andy's in love, I live in hope of finally getting somewhere with Lulu, and you two break up. Can't we get this synchronized?"

"I gave you guys ten years. It's not my fault you two are so slow. So what's happening with you and Lulu?"

"Nothing's exactly happening, but I'm pretty sure she's in love with me."

"Oh, yeah, she's in love with you," said Kevin. "The stubborn brat has always been in love with you."

"Has she told you that?" asked Neil.

"That's not Lulu's style. Lulu thinks that admitting to love is a sign of weakness. If you love someone, it's as much as saying you need the person, and Lulu's never figured she needed anyone in her life. Give her time. She'll come around."

"I could say the same to you. I figure you and Caroline will get back together."

"Who needs her?" said Kevin. "I have something much better, I have Mrs. Esposito."

LULU GOT TO FLANAGAN'S early and sat at the bar. She didn't like sitting at a table by herself. At the bar she could talk to Patrick instead of having to stare at a wall.

"You're a little early, aren't you?" asked Patrick, pouring her a beer and setting it in front of her. "Your buddies aren't here yet."

"I wanted an early dinner before they arrive. Let me have one of your roast beef platters, Pat."

The news was on the TV with the sound turned down. It was the local news and nothing much of interest could have happened that day because all they were doing was interviewing some people on the courthouse steps.

Someone sat down on the stool next to her but she didn't look around. The bar was starting to fill up with men, and she didn't want to appear as though she were looking for company.

"Hi," someone said, and she turned to give whoever it was a discouraging look, but it was the long-haired guy who had been watching her the week before. By now he seemed like an old acquaintance.

"How're you doin'?" she said to him.

"Keepin' warm. How about yourself?"

She caught it then, the accent. Another Irishman if she wasn't mistaken. And in Flanagan's she wasn't likely to be mistaken.

"New in the country?" she asked him.

"Not so new," he said, and something about the way he said it reminded her of Mary. They both seemed to speak the same way.

"I'll bet you're from Dublin," she told him.

He smiled at her, looking pleased. "And how would you be knowing that?"

"I could tell by your accent."

"And I thought all the Irish sounded the same to you Americans."

"You sound like a friend of mine who's also from Dublin."

"You wouldn't be speaking of that dark-haired lass you were in here with last week, now would you?"

"Yes. You remember."

"I'd not likely forget seeing three such beautiful women all in one night."

"Well, the third one, the blond, will be here soon."

"She looked familiar, the dark-haired one. I think I might have known her brother in Dublin."

"Would that be Danny or Sean or Michael?"

"You know her brothers?"

"No, but she told me about them."

"It would be Danny, the youngest. We were in school together. I'd like to see her again. She's grown into quite the beauty."

"You stay away from her with that Irish charm of yours," said Lulu. "She's going with a friend of mine."

"The one with the red hair?"

"That's right."

"Good Irish lad?"

"The best," said Lulu.

"Well, if you see her, tell her James O'Hanlon sends his regards."

"I'll be seeing her tonight."

"She'll be in, then?"

"No, we're meeting them later."

Patrick set the platter down in front of her and poured her another beer. "Talking to this Irish riffraff, are you?" he said to Lulu.

"This riffraff will have another beer," said James. "Watch my beer for me, will you?" he said to Lulu, getting off the bar stool and heading for the men's room.

Right after he returned, Caroline walked in, and Lulu introduced them. Caroline took the stool on the other side of James and ordered an Irish coffee.

"I'm so excited about tonight," said Caroline, talking across to Lulu.

"I don't feel quite as excited as last week," said Lulu.

"I feel like we're making history tonight."

"History, is it?" asked James. "And what would you be doing tonight, the two of you, dressed all in black?"

"It's a secret," Caroline told him.

"That's as much as saying you're up to no good."

"Up to good is more like it," said Lulu.

"You're talking in puzzles," said James.

"I'll give you a hint," said Lulu. "If you read in the papers about something happening on Bunker Hill tonight, you'll know that was us."

"Isn't that where you fought the Brits?"

"That's all I'm saying," said Lulu. "You can figure it out when you read it."

Then Kevin and Neil arrived, and in the excitement of waiting to see what fireworks would transpire between Caroline and Kevin, James disappeared, and Lulu didn't get to introduce him to the guys. That was probably just as well since she didn't think Kevin would take well to seeing Caroline sitting with a strange man so soon. Particularly one with the looks and charms of James.

As it happened, no fireworks transpired as the two of them ignored each other. With Lulu eating, it got so that Neil was carrying the conversation single-handedly, so they finally decided to leave for Bunker Hill.

As soon as Caroline started the car, she said to Lulu, "You want to come home with me tonight, see my new apartment?"

"I don't think so, Caroline."

"There's twin beds in the bedroom, we wouldn't have to share."

"I didn't mind sharing a bed with you."

"You can bring that cat of yours if you want to."

Lulu smiled. "Mohammed hates riding in cars. Anyway, I was kind of hoping to talk to Neil afterward."

"Does that mean what it sounds like?"

"I don't know what it sounds like," said Lulu.

"It sounds as though you've finally resolved your thinking."

"I've decided I'm screwing up his life."

"It took you this long to figure that out?"

"I'm going to tell him that it's no good, it's never going to be any good, and to get on with his life."

"Damn it, Lulu, you're the most self-destructive woman I've ever met."

"I can live without a man."

"You can live without a million dollars, too, but wouldn't it be nice to have?"

"Look, this wasn't my fault, Caroline. I didn't ask him to walk back into my life. I was going along very well without him. I would never have been the one to look him up after all this time."

"Tell me you aren't dying to make love to him."

"What's that got to do with it?"

"Just tell me."

"If relationships were built on just sex, there wouldn't be a problem."

"Do you have to see everything in black-and-white?"

"I can't help it, that's just the way I am."

"Well, I think you're crazy. I'd go after him in a shot if I didn't still love Kevin."

"You try it, and I'll kill you," said Lulu.

Caroline chuckled. "That's what I thought."

ANDY AND MARY HAD GOT there just before them, and now they were all unloading the truck in silence.

Kevin pulled Lulu aside. "I don't like what's happening to Andy," he said to her.

"Nothing's happening to Andy," said Lulu.

"Look at her, little Miss Ireland, charming the pants off of him. He doesn't know what he's getting into."

"Why don't you try straightening up your own life, Kevin, and leave Andy alone?"

"Is that supposed to be a dig, Lulu? Well, my life's just fine. It's Andy I'm worried about."

"Andy can take care of himself."

"Did you see that watch he bought her? Almost five hundred bucks, a Heuer, one of those diving watches. Bought it for her in black so he could tell her it was cheap, that he got it off the street. Lights up in the dark."

"I'm sure it wasn't her idea. I'm sure she didn't ask him to buy her a watch."

"A diving watch. Just what she needs. Like she's going to jump in some loch with it on."

"Lochs are in Scotland."

"Whatever. What do they call lakes in Ireland?"

"Lakes."

Still grumbling, Kevin went over to Neil to help carry one of the structures.

Lulu looked over and saw Andy with his arm around Mary. She thought it was sweet. She was happy Andy had found himself a woman. And, of course, it also took some of the pressure off her. She'd been aware for years that Andy was in love with her, just as he had been aware she didn't reciprocate his feelings. Now they'd be able to be friends with none of that between them. She was happy for Mary, too. Andy would take very good care of her.

They set up the three floors several yards apart. Next week they'd set up three more in the same spot, and it would be like a little village. Tourists coming to see the historic site instead would see a new little bit of history being made tonight.

They unfolded the walls and set them on top of the floors, then broke up into couples and nailed the walls to the floors. Lulu was working with Caroline.

"What was that all about with Kevin?" Caroline asked her.

"Oh, he's just complaining because Andy bought Mary a watch."

"He figures just when he's becoming a bachelor, all of his friends are hooking up with someone. He probably pictured lots of nights out with the boys."

"He doesn't like Mary."

"He's just jealous," said Caroline. "He'd like a sweet, accommodating woman like that."

"I don't think so," said Lulu. "I think Kevin likes strong women. He married you, didn't he?"

"I was rather sweet and accommodating in college."

"I don't believe it," said Lulu.

"Well, around boys I was. But after we got married I got tired of that act in a hurry."

They finished first and went over to get the roof, which they carried back. They managed to get it in place, and then Neil came over and held it while they nailed it in to the sides.

"Got new doors for you tonight, Lulu," said Neil. "I got real ones, with peepholes in them."

"I noticed," said Lulu.

"Why do they need peepholes?" asked Caroline.

Lulu started to laugh. "This guy who moved into Mary's house was complaining about the lack of one."

"Next they'll be wanting window boxes and a patio," said Caroline."

"What do you bet we come over in the morning," said Lulu, "and they're all filled up?"

"I wouldn't be surprised," said Caroline. "I saw some guys peering out of the bushes at us before. Probably waiting for us to leave so they can move in."

"The least they could do is come out and give us a hand," said Neil.

Lulu turned in the direction of the bushes and was about to yell out, "Hey, guys, come on out," when several flashlights were turned on all at once, shining right in her eyes. "What the hell," she yelled, then shaded her eyes. Approaching the Rooftop Gang were at least a dozen uniformed cops, flashlights in one hand, guns drawn in the other.

"I don't believe this," said Lulu. "My God, you'd think it was a major drug raid."

"Don't start giving them a hard time," Neil warned her, but Lulu was already stepping forward.

She walked within a few feet of the cops. She wasn't afraid of them. Half the men in her family were cops.

"Hey, what's the story here?" she yelled at them. "What happened to Live Free or Die?"

"That's New Hampshire," yelled back one of the cops, sounding amused.

"I don't care, I still believe in it," said Lulu.

They seemed to be surrounded by cops now, more coming out from behind the bushes. An entire armed raid on the Rooftop Gang? It was like some fantasy of hers as a kid.

"What are the charges?" Lulu wanted to know. Neil came up beside her and was shushing her, but she stepped in front of him. She was in charge here, she'd take the rap.

And then the long-haired guy from Flanagan's, James, stepped into the light and pointed to Mary. "That's her," he said to the cops. "That's Mairead Mulroony."

Lulu felt a sense of disbelief, a sense that this was as crazy as her nightmares about the devil wanting her soul. "What's he talking about?" she said to one of the cops. "That's my friend, Mary Moore. She's visiting me from Dublin."

"Sorry," said the cop, "but she's wanted for terrorist activities, and we have to take her in custody."

Lulu looked over at Mary and saw the woman make a break for it, dodging around one of the cops and running in the direction of the street. Andy started after her, but one of the cops grabbed him, and several others took off after Mary.

Lulu ran up to James and started to pound him on the chest with her fists. "Why are you doing this? This isn't funny!"

"Thank you for the information," said James.

"What information?"

"Thank you for telling me where she'd be."

"We've got her," yelled one of the cops from the street, and the flashlights turned away and the cops and James departed.

"Stop them!" Lulu said to no one in particular.

Neil came up beside her and put his arm around her.

She shrugged it off, too upset to speak. She had betrayed Mary. She had done the worst thing she could think of. She had betrayed a friend's trust.

She took off across the grass at a run, wanting to lose herself, wanting to wake up from this nightmare. Her heart was thudding, and the blood was pounding in her head as she ran, not even watching where she was going.

She could hear someone behind her, gaining on her, and she increased her speed until she was running all out and couldn't run any faster. And then she heard a *swoosh*, and someone tackled her, and she landed hard on the damp ground.

She tried to get up, but a body pinned her to the ground. "You can't run away, Lulu," said Neil.

"Leave me alone!"

"I can't do that."

"I mean it, Neil!"

"Andy's going to need you."

Lulu thought about Andy. She had done it to him as much as to Mary. Andy was never going to forgive her. "I betrayed her, Neil. Who is James, some Northern Ireland cop? I as much as told him where we'd be. He said he knew Mary's brother."

"You didn't know what you were doing."

"That's no excuse."

"You didn't mean to harm her, Lulu."

"I should've known better. I knew she was illegal, I shouldn't have said anything." But because he had been cute and charming, because she wanted to sound mysterious to him, she had betrayed a friend.

"Come on, Lulu, we have some houses to finish putting up."

"You think I care about that now?"

"Lulu, there's nothing we can do about Mary until morning. We'll go see her, get a lawyer, whatever you want. But I doubt it'll do any good because they'll probably move to extradite her."

"He's got the wrong person. Mary couldn't be a terrorist."

"Then why did she run?"

"Because she's afraid. Because she's in the country illegally and she was surrounded by cops. I would've run, too."

"No, you wouldn't. We were doing something illegal, but you didn't run."

Lulu felt something wet on her face, and she realized she was crying. She lifted her hand to make sure. It wasn't possible; she never cried.

Neil got up and reached down a hand to pull her to her feet.

"Leave me alone," said Lulu.

"Come on, wipe off your face, and we'll go back."

"I'm not crying!"

"You don't have to be ashamed. You're only human, Lulu."

She wiped her face with the sleeve of her jacket. Not for anything would she let Kevin or Andy see her cry. Even Neil couldn't prove it, it was too dark for him to really see. He was just guessing.

She stood up by herself and then felt an overwhelming urge to be held. Nothing sexual, just a little comfort. She found herself pressing her face against his chest. His arms went around her.

"It'll be all right," said Neil.

"No. It will never be all right."

"Lulu, I've never known you to be anything but brave and honest and true with your friends. You were a good friend to Mary, and she must know it."

"I haven't been very brave and honest and true with you."

"That's another matter entirely and one we'll take up later. Right now is hardly the time for me to be telling you 'I told you so.'"

"Don't you dare!"

"I wouldn't think of it. Now come on—I think Andy is going to be needing a little of this comfort." He took her hand and led her straight back to the others.

Lulu went straight to Andy and hugged him. "Will you forgive me, Andy?"

"I don't believe it, Lulu. They must have the wrong person."

"I think so, too. They've made a bad mistake, and they're not getting away with it."

"I feel like I should go after them."

"I think we better wait until morning," said Neil. "We can make a few calls tonight, find out where she is, get in touch with a lawyer. They're not going to let anyone see her tonight, though. Actually, I think we're lucky we weren't arrested, too."

"I've got to tell you, I wasn't surprised," said Kevin.

"Shut up, Kevin!" Lulu told him.

"Well, she did move in with him awfully fast."

"We fell in love," said Andy.

Kevin said, "I don't doubt you did, Andy, but I have a feeling Mary didn't fall in love that fast. I think she recognized a good thing and took advantage of it."

"You didn't even know her," said Lulu. "Mary wasn't the type."

"Are we going to stand around her debating it all night, or are we going to finish the house?" asked Caroline. "Let's get this done and then go to Flanagan's and make some phone calls."

They worked silently, but when they were finished, three little houses stood on Bunker Hill.

LULU, CAROLINE AND ANDY were sitting at the table, and Kevin and Neil were making phone calls at the public phones outside the men's room.

Andy seemed in shock. Lulu couldn't remember ever seeing him so pale and remote, so uncaring about what was going on around him. He seemed to be in another world, or maybe just deep inside himself.

Caroline saw the traitor first. Lulu saw the stricken look on Caroline's face, turned around and saw James coming up to their table. She couldn't believe his gall.

Lulu sprang to her feet. "Get out of here," she threatened him, "before I tell every Irishman in the place just what you are."

"I'm sorry," he said to her.

"Not as sorry as you're going to be in a minute!"

"I'm sorry I took advantage of you like that. Under different circumstances, I would've liked to get to know you."

"I'm warning you, you better leave, you filthy traitor!"

"Lulu," said Andy, getting up, "I'd like to talk to him."

"You're the boyfriend?" asked James.

Andy nodded. "What did she do that was so terrible you had to bring half the police in Boston down on her? If she's in the country illegally, then I'll marry her tomorrow and make her a citizen."

James looked to Lulu, as though for permission to speak. With a nod in his direction, she sat back down. But she made very sure he wasn't offered a seat.

He leaned on the back of the chair. "She set a bomb that killed six schoolchildren. And we've implicated her in several other bombings. She's the leader of a radical IRA faction, some of whom we believe are also in Boston."

"She did no such thing!" said Lulu.

"Do you have proof of this?" asked Andy.

"More than we need."

"You might have made a mistake."

"Not with this one," said James.

"She met with some men while she was here," said Andy.

"Andy, you don't have to talk to him," said Lulu.

"Could you describe them?" asked James.

Andy shook his head. "Just old Irishmen, the kind you see in any neighborhood around here. They could be sitting at the next table. She led me to believe they were homeless, but they didn't look homeless."

"Anything else?"

"I don't know," said Andy. "She was always out, always going for walks. Likely she was meeting people."

"Likely," said James.

"Where's she being held?" asked Andy.

"At the Federal Building. I'll arrange for you to see her in the morning if you'd like."

"No," said Andy. "That won't be necessary."

"Well, I'd like to see her," said Lulu.

"That also can be arranged," said James.

"I don't want any favors from you," said Lulu.

James shrugged and walked off.

When he left, Lulu turned to Andy. "You betrayed her, Andy. How could you do that?"

"No, Lulu. Neither of us betrayed her. She betrayed us. She knew you cared about her. She knew I really loved her. She used us, Lulu."

"I don't believe that!"

"She wasn't what you thought. Or what I thought. I think I knew that right away, but I wouldn't let myself believe it. I wanted her to be sweet and helpless even though..."

"Even though what?" asked Lulu.

"Nothing. It's personal. I don't want to talk about it."

"I can't believe Kevin was right for once in his life," said Caroline.

"I can't believe I was wrong," said Lulu. "In fact I refuse to believe it. I'm going to reserve judgment until I've gotten a chance to talk to Mary."

When Neil and Kevin returned to the table, Lulu stood up. "Take me home, please, Neil," she said to him.

"We'll talk to you guys in the morning," said Neil. "Kevin will fill you in on what we found out."

Lulu followed him out of Flanagan's. "There's only one problem," he said to her when they were out on the street. "Neither one of us drove."

"I don't care. We can find a taxi."

Neil walked to the corner and flagged one down, and when they got in the back seat, he started to give the driver Lulu's address.

"I want to go home with you," she told him.

"Are you sure?"

"I've never been so sure of anything in my life."

They rode in silence to his house, but when they got out of the taxi, he said, "Lulu, I don't know whether this is a good idea. I think you're in shock now, and you might regret it in the morning."

"I'm not asking you to make love to me, Neil. I just don't want to be alone. I'd just like you to hold me, if you don't mind."

"How could I possibly mind?"

Once in the house, he sent her upstairs. She got out of her clothes, then found an old flannel shirt of his to sleep in. She was sitting up in bed when he came into the room carrying a tray with two mugs of hot chocolate and a plate of cookies.

He set the tray on her lap, then disappeared into the bathroom for a minute. When he came out, he was wearing pajamas. She almost laughed at the sight of him in striped pajamas, but he was too dear to laugh at.

He slid into bed beside her, careful not to bump the tray. "You know I love you, Lulu."

"I know."

"You know I also don't think you were at fault tonight."

"I don't believe she is a terrorist."

"If she isn't, then no harm will come of it. They'll probably let her go with an apology."

"Do you know what she's supposed to have done?"

"That British officer stopped and told us after he spoke to you. We'd already learned some of it from the police."

"And you believed him?"

"I think it's possible."

"She must really hate me. I befriend her, and then I betray her."

"No, you didn't betray her. You've got to have intent in order to betray someone, and you intended no harm. It's not the same as what I did to you, Lulu. I knew what I was doing, you didn't."

"But you had my best interests at heart."

"Not really. I had my interests at heart."

"You're not making this easy for me to forgive you."

"I'm not asking you to forgive me. I'm just asking you to love me and to know I'd never betray you again. Unless you ran away from me, of course, and then I'd tell your mother."

Lulu started to smile. "You'd *tell* on me?"

"Damn straight!"

"My *mother*?"

"Just bear that in mind if you ever think of leaving me."

Lulu wondered if that day would ever come.

THEY'D FINISHED THE HOT CHOCOLATE and Neil had turned the light out. She lay with her back to him under the covers, his arms wrapped around her. It was comforting, to be sure, but not as comforting as she had hoped, so when one of his hands began to stray, she didn't stop it. She did, however, tease him. "I thought this was supposed to be for comfort tonight, Neil."

"Don't you find this comforting?"

"Oh, yes—very comforting."

"Then what are you complaining about?"

"Who's complaining?" Certainly not her. Not when she'd finally found out exactly where she belonged.

Chapter Eleven

Neil drove Lulu to the Federal Building in the morning. He asked her if she wanted him along when she visited Mary, but she said no, she wanted to see her alone.

Mary was led into the small room handcuffed, and the guard stayed by the door while they talked. It looked to Lulu as if they were treating Mary like some dangerous criminal. Surely if she were concealing a bomb on her person they would have found it.

She looked for signs of anger in Mary, some clue to how she was feeling about Lulu's betrayal, but the woman looked mostly indifferent.

"Hello, Mary," said Lulu.

"Hello, Lulu."

"We're going to get you out of this. We've got you a lawyer."

Mary laughed, a harsh sound that seemed to bounce off the walls of the room. "This isn't something for the Rooftop Gang, Lulu."

"We want to help you."

"Ah, Lulu, go play at your little games of being urban revolutionaries, with your silly little houses for the homeless. What do you really know of rebellion?"

"I know you're not capable of bombing innocent schoolchildren."

"Innocent schoolchildren? Let me tell you something, Lulu Lenahan, my friend—there's no such thing as innocence anymore."

"Are you saying you did it?"

"I'm not admitting to a thing. I'm just trying to educate you, that's all. My father was killed by the Provos, as were my three brothers and all of my uncles. And in five years time, maybe less, those innocent schoolchildren would have been killing some other member of my family. It's a darlin' war, Lulu. Darlin'."

"Will they extradite you?"

"They'll try," said Mary. "And I'll claim political prisoner status and fight extradition. I may be here for years, Lulu. Will you come to visit? Will you bring me candy and books to read?"

"You haven't even asked about Andy."

"I'm sure the boyo's heart is broken. He was a safe house for me, Lulu, you can understand that."

"I betrayed you, Mary. I told James where we'd be last night. He said he was a friend of one of your brothers."

"Don't be losing any sleep over it."

"Will you forgive me?"

"There's nothing to forgive. You can't betray if there's no trust to begin with. And I think I fancy myself more as a martyr than I did hanging out on the streets of Boston. You can tell whoever's interested that I'm going on a hunger strike."

"Please don't do that, Mary."

"Get out of here, you stupid cow. Go live your complacent lives in your free country and leave us alone to do what we do best. We're used to being forgotten. We've never known any different."

Mary turned to the guard and said she wanted to go back to her cell. Lulu tried to think of something to say to her, some last message to give her hope, but none came to mind.

She ran through the building and pushed the door open to the outside. She stood in the doorway for a moment, gulping air, and saw Neil waiting for her on the steps. She ran into his arms and hugged him close. This was reality, not what she heard inside the Federal Building.

This was her world.

THEY WERE SIDE BY SIDE in Neil's bed, sharing the Sunday papers. She was reading the sports section, he was reading the front page, when he handed it to her and pointed to a picture of Mary.

"I don't want to read it," said Lulu, glancing at the picture for a moment. She didn't want to be reminded of Mary right now when she was feeling good about the whole world. She didn't want to be reminded that there was more than just her and Neil and what they had together.

"That could've been you, Lulu, if you'd grown up in Northern Ireland. God knows we used to play war games often enough. It would have been very easy to cross over the line into the real thing." He could easily picture her leading a gang of a different kind, in a different country. He thought she was every bit as strong and brave as this Mairead Mulroony who seemed to be a heroine in her part of the world.

"What does it say?"

"That she's on a hunger strike."

Unbidden, a picture of Mary, grown skeletal and pale, flashed across her mind. "Well I'm not, and I'd like some breakfast."

"You know where the kitchen is."

"You're rich, Neil, why don't you have a maid?"

"You really want someone walking in on us?"

"No."

"So we'll go downstairs and fix it together."

"Let me just finish this section first."

A few minutes later he shoved another section of the paper under her nose. "Read this." He thought it might cheer her up, get her thoughts off Mary.

"I don't want to read about that woman."

"This is about us."

"Us? You and me?"

He chuckled. "No. Not yet. We've hardly had a chance to announce anything officially yet. It's about the Rooftop Gang."

She took hold of the paper and began to read.

ROOFTOP GANG STRIKES AGAIN

Once again, the Rooftop Gang has struck Boston. Sometime Friday night, three small houses were erected on Bunker Hill. By Saturday morning they were occupied by several homeless men who said they were glad to have a roof over their heads. One of the men, who didn't want to be identified, told us. "It makes me feel like a human being again."

"This is wonderful," she said. "It looks like we're going to get some good publicity. But why don't they have a picture of the houses?"

"They'll probably get around to that."

"This is the best thing we've ever done, Neil. The very best."

"Next to falling in love."

"I meant the gang."

"I'm talking about us."

"Don't try putting words in my mouth."

"I don't have to. You told me at least six times during the night. Maybe seven."

"It seems like I've loved you forever," said Lulu.

"It seems that way to me, too. So am I going to have to wait another twenty years before you marry me?"

"Oh, no, not nearly that long," said Lulu. "I can't wait to move into this house."

"We could go by your place today and bring over whatever you need."

"Could we really?"

"I don't see why not," said Neil.

"Mohammed isn't going to like your cats."

"There's room enough for all of them."

"Come here," she said, throwing the paper on the floor. "Give me a hug."

"I'll give you more than that," said Neil.

As he took her in his arms, he pictured her in the house with him all the time, filling it up with love and laughter. And maybe the other bedrooms would become filled with children, their own little Rooftop Gang. Only they'd have to keep a close watch on them, not let them get away with the things they got away with as kids.

Lulu closed her eyes and gave herself over to his kiss. She couldn't wait to move in with him. She pictured them upstairs shooting pool, playing the games, she, of course, beating Neil at all of them. She pictured having all their friends over for parties. And then she began to picture something even more interesting. She pictured filling up this huge house with some of the homeless women who came into the shelter. She pictured little houses out in the backyard. They'd set an example for everyone else in the city, and soon there wouldn't be anymore homeless.

She thought she'd wait until after she moved in to spring that idea on him. And then, very, very gradually.

THE FOLLOWING FRIDAY, Caroline called Lulu. "Listen," she said, "would you mind if I brought someone along to-night?"

"Caroline, it's supposed to be secret."

"She won't tell, I promise."

"You're bringing a woman? I thought maybe you had met some nice young Harvard guy."

"The thing is, Lulu, she's very much like you. She came into the bookstore, bought every book we had on martial arts, and we got into a conversation. You know who her heroes are?"

"Bruce Lee and the boys?"

"No. The Rooftop Gang."

"And so you told her you were a member."

"No, but I will if I get your approval."

"So how is she like me?"

"She just is, take my word for it. What I was thinking is, I think maybe Andy would like her."

"I see."

"What do you think? Maybe it would take his mind off Mary."

"I think that's a wonderful idea, Caroline, and I should have thought of it myself."

"Well, if he likes you—and I know he does—I think maybe he'll like Susie."

"Okay, bring her along. But only if she'll swear to secrecy."

"Guess what?"

"What?"

"Kevin called me up and asked me out."

"Kevin asked you for a date?"

"Can you believe it?"

"Are you going?"

"You know what he had the nerve to ask me? If I'd like to have dinner at his house."

"*His* house?"

"Right. I gave him an unequivocal no."

"Oh, Caroline, at least he's trying."

"No, he's not. He just wants to show off that housekeeper of his. I insisted that he take me out to a real restaurant."

"Is he going to?"

"Tomorrow night."

"Oh, I'm so glad. Maybe you two—"

"Don't rush things. Tigers do not change their spots overnight."

"Stripes."

"Whatever."

"Well, I think this is great. And at least Andy won't have to feel out of it tonight."

"Tonight at Bunker Hill!"

"And Up the Irish!"

"KEVIN?"

"Yeah, Neil. You all set for tonight?"

"Sure am. I just wanted to ask your opinion on something."

"Shoot."

"There's this young architect we've got working for us, Nancy Flynn. She's real sweet, kind of quiet, very pretty. No boyfriend at the moment."

"Forget it, Neil. I'm still married, you know."

"Give me a little credit, Kevin—I figure you're the last guy I'd have to fix up."

"Then what're you talking about?"

"Well, she's kind of an activist, you know? Always involved in something. I just thought maybe I could bring her along tonight—"

"I thought you and Lulu finally got together?"

"If you'd let me finish a sentence... I thought maybe Andy would like her. In a lot of ways she reminds me of Mary."

"I didn't like Mary."

"Yes, but Andy did."

"Well, look, if you think you can trust her, bring her along. I know Andy's feeling really down, maybe it would help."

"Yeah, and he wouldn't feel so left out."

"It's okay with me."

"Great. I'll sound her out."

IT WAS A COLD NIGHT and overcast. Lulu scanned the sky as she turned the corner to Flanagan's. They'd be lucky if it didn't snow on them tonight. And how were they going to build houses when the snow on the ground got to be a foot deep?

She opened the door to the bar and stepped inside. She was early, having come directly from work. She looked around, not expecting to see anyone yet, but Andy was already down at the end of the bar.

When she got over to him she said, "Please let's not discuss the weather. I'm already frozen."

Andy grinned at her, then turned to a rather spectacular-looking blonde who was seated on the stool beside him. "Lulu, I'd like you to meet Shaw."

"Shaw?"

"Yes, she's one of our programmers. I hope you don't mind, but I let her in on our secret."

Shaw reached her arm across Andy, and Lulu shook her hand.

"I love what you guys are doing," said Shaw.

"Well, thank you," said Lulu, wondering what was going to happen when Caroline showed up with Susie.

Shaw smiled fondly at Andy. "I always knew there was an exciting, hidden side to the boss. I just didn't know what it was."

It was all Lulu could do not to burst out laughing. She had been so worried about Andy, but he seemed to be surviving Mary's betrayal without any help from his friends.

When Caroline came into the bar a few minutes later, trailed by a small, dark woman who seemed to strut rather than walk, Lulu got up to meet them halfway and warn Caroline that her matchmaking hadn't been required.

Caroline introduced her to Susie, who promptly said, "You guys are my heroes. Listen, I've got some good ideas about where to put up this housing—"

"Wait until everyone's here," said Lulu, interrupting her, then she said to Caroline, "You notice the woman with Andy?"

Caroline peered past her. "You mean the blonde?"

Lulu nodded.

"Andy brought her along?"

"Yes, isn't that great?"

Caroline started to smile. "Well, good for Andy."

They headed back to Andy, and introductions were being made when Lulu saw Neil and Kevin walk in with yet another woman. She saw Caroline noticing, too, her eyes widening. Either Kevin had had the bad taste to bring along a date, or... No, there was no way Neil would do something like that. Still, she was glad to see his eyes light up at the sight of her.

Just to make sure the latest woman knew who was with whom, however, Lulu gave Neil a big hug as soon as he got up to them, a hug that was returned in kind.

"Who's the woman?" she whispered in his ear.

"Who're the other two women?" he whispered back.

"Andy brought one, and Caroline brought the other for Andy. It seems to have been a mistake."

"Well, I brought this one for Andy."

"Oh, well," said Lulu. "I guess the more hands we have, the more houses we can put up."

Their group was now so large it was putting a strain on the crowd at the bar, so they went to the back and pushed two tables together.

After drinks were ordered and everyone had settled down, Lulu looked around the table. The Rooftop Gang was growing, but maybe that wasn't such a bad idea. If the point of their venture was to house the homeless, then the more people who helped out, the closer they'd be able to get to that goal. It might not be a bad idea to bring in even more people and really organize. They could even divide Boston up into sections and have small groups in charge of each section, with the original Rooftop Gang overseeing it all. With her in charge, of course. She felt Neil's arm go around her, and she leaned into it. Well, maybe she and Neil could share the leadership. They had done that as children, and it had worked out pretty well.

She saw Caroline and Kevin trying to ignore each other, but doing it so obviously that it made her smile. She saw Andy reaching for Shaw's hand as though laying claim to it. She saw Susie and Nancy looking a little bewildered. She turned and saw Neil grinning at her.

"To those of you who are new here," said Lulu, "welcome. I think we ought to tell you a little bit about the Rooftop Gang...."

Harlequin American Romance

COMING NEXT MONTH

#301 CHARMED CIRCLE by Robin Francis

One relaxing month by the sea was all Zoe Piper ever expected from her four-week stay at Gull Cottage, the luxurious East Hampton mansion, but it turned out to be a month that would change her life forever. And then there was Ethan Quinn, the skeptical Scorpio with the dreamer's eyes.... The first book of the GULL COTTAGE trilogy.

#302 THE MORNING AFTER by Dallas Schulze

The morning after Lacey's thirtieth-birthday bash, her head pounded, her eyes ached—and she awoke in a Vegas hotel room. When a man groaned beside her in the bed, she thought she knew the worst. But it was yet to come. She was married—to a man she had met at her party. Last night's revelry must have affected her groom's brain—because Cameron wouldn't admit they'd made a mistake.

#303 THE FOREVER CHOICE by Patricia Cox

Christine Donovan had run away from Detective Paul Cameron, the only man who had captured her heart. Now she was face-to-face with him again as they tried to find out who was embezzling money from her aunt's perfume company. They were both determined to play it cool, but what they hadn't counted on was a love destined to be, and a criminal in the family....

#304 TURNING TABLES by Judith Arnold

Amelia's outrageous sister had done it again. But to get herself out of jail this time she hired a lawyer determined to take her case to the Supreme Court. Before the incident became fodder for the tabloids, Amelia had to stop Patrick Levine. But Patrick had his own plan—and a passionate desire to see how straitlaced Amelia would react when pushed too far.

You'll flip . . . your pages won't!
Read paperbacks *hands-free* with

Book Mate • I

The perfect "mate" for all your romance paperbacks

**Traveling • Vacationing • At Work • In Bed • Studying
• Cooking • Eating**

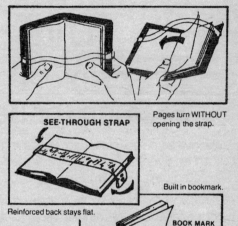

Perfect size for all standard paperbacks, this wonderful invention makes reading a pure pleasure! Ingenious design holds paperback books OPEN and FLAT so even wind can't ruffle pages — leaves your hands free to do other things. Reinforced, wipe-clean vinyl-covered holder flexes to let you turn pages without undoing the strap . . . supports paperbacks so well, they have the strength of hardcovers!

Pages turn WITHOUT opening the strap.

SEE-THROUGH STRAP

Reinforced back stays flat.

Built in bookmark.

BOOK MARK

BACK COVER HOLDING STRIP

10" x 7¼", opened.
Snaps closed for easy carrying, too.

Harlequin American Romance

Gull Cottage

The sun, the surf, the sand...

One relaxing month by the sea was all Zoe, Diana and Gracie ever expected from their four-week stay at Gull Cottage, the luxurious East Hampton mansion. They never thought that what they found at the beach would change their lives forever.

Join Zoe, Diana and Gracie for the summer of their lives. Don't miss the GULL COTTAGE trilogy in Harlequin American Romance: #301 CHARMED CIRCLE by Robin Francis (July 1989); #305 MOTHER KNOWS BEST by Barbara Bretton (August 1989); and #309 SAVING GRACE by Anne McAllister (September 1989).

GULL COTTAGE—because one month can be the start of forever...

Your favorite stories with a brand-new look!!

HARLEQUIN
American Romance®

Beginning next month, the four American Romance titles will feature a new, contemporary and sophisticated cover design. As always, each story will be a terrific romance with mature characters and a realistic plot that is uniquely North American in flavor and appeal.

Watch your bookshelves for a **bold** look!